Hands

Hounded at school by a particularly savage English teacher, Pistolet had turned against literature like an avenging god; he hated it far too much to leave it alone.

Madison found him at the terminal in his cubicle and sat down with a thump in the spare chair. 'Hang on a sec,' said Pistolet, cancelling out of the program he was working on. 'The system's *so* slow. It's all right to give customers these dinosaurs, but do they have to torture their own developers?' He turned and looked at Madison. 'Jesus, what happened? Are you in deep shit?'

'Minnie wants me back here.'

'But you would never last here. Madison, my friend the exile; like Hemingway, only in England.'

'You know that. I know that. But they think I'll be pleased; they think they're doing me a *favour*. Come back to the raft, Huck honey, we love you.'

'Can't you say you don't want to be loved?'

'Of course not. If I say that they'll say he isn't *worth* loving. Then they *will* fire me.'

Andrew Rosenheim was born in Chicago in 1955. His first novel, *The Tormenting of Lafayette Jackson*, was published in 1987. His writing has appeared in the *TLS*, the *Independent*, the *New York Times Book Review* and many other publications. He now lives near Oxford.

ANDREW ROSENHEIM

Hands On

To Martin

With love from

Easter 1993

xxx
xxx
xxx

Mandarin

A Mandarin Paperback
HANDS ON

First published in Great Britain 1993
by Mandarin Paperbacks
an imprint of Reed Consumer Books Limited
Michelin House, 81 Fulham Road, London SW3 6RB
and Auckland, Melbourne, Singapore and Toronto

Copyright © 1993 Andrew Rosenheim

A CIP catalogue record for this title
is available from the British Library
ISBN 0 7493 1361 7

Typeset by
Hewer Text Composition Services, Edinburgh
Printed and bound in Great Britain
by Cox & Wyman Ltd, Reading, Berks

In memory
of Norman Maclean
and W.K. Wimsatt, Jr.

The author would like to thank
Elizabeth Leeming, Jacintha Mack Smith,
Galen Strawson and Kim Scott Walwyn
for their criticism and encouragement.
And Elizabeth Clough for her asperity.

Part One

1

'Happy New Year.' It was Pistolet across the trans-Atlantic phone, sounding jaunty.

It was early April, so Madison sensed a hidden agenda. 'Aren't you a little late?' he asked warily.

'Less than you think. It's the Year of the Rat – the Chinese New Year. I thought it politic to let Minnie Lu know I knew this fact. Needless to say, she seemed unmoved by my sensitivity.'

'Why were you talking to Minnie Lu?'

'I wasn't. I never talk to Minnie Lu; she talks to me. In any case, it was you she was keen to talk about.'

Madison's adrenalin surged like a racehorse fresh out of the gates. 'Why me?'

'Why not? She wants to see you. Next week, Wednesday at ten. You'll fly Tuesday, I imagine. Expect a FAX later today.'

'But I'm not due to visit for two months,' Madison protested. 'Besides, I thought you were coming *here*.'

'I still am. But Minnie's never shared my thirst for travel: she wants to eyeball you on her own turf.'

'What on earth for?'

'Beats me, bud. Listen, I've got to go; they've taken to auditing the phone bills. See you Wednesday.' And over three thousand miles away, on the eighth floor of corporate headquarters, Pistolet hung up.

What did Minnie Lu want? Madison thought of the

minefields of the corporate landscape; where next to march, how to tread softly. There was little to object to in his present incarnation, for did he not have the best of both worlds? He enjoyed the benefits of corporate affluence without having to endure the hardships of life at the headquarters of Ling Enterprises, his employer, where *anomie* was a daily companion. Why else leave Harvard and the prestige of an ill-paid post? The money; yes, the money was better (his salary had doubled), but the real lure had been the chance to do his own work, uninterrupted, no lectures to give or papers to grade, no undergraduate whines to endure.

When the offer came, he was already employed as a part-time consultant for the company, working out of term. Give up teaching, Ling Enterprises had declared; life is not the Linguistics Department of Harvard U. Move to the vanguard of new technology and make things happen; don't just theorise. He thought of his theories, or rather his one novel idea – how he'd moved from models of parsing into the virgin conceptual territory of how to make language. One article, in the journal *Computational Creation*, with its single model of a creative machine; somehow this had attracted Ling's attention, leading first to his consultancy, then the offer of a full-time job. Your work, the lulling corporate voice had intimated, is potentially seminal; we'll give you the time and facilities to make it a reality. You, Assistant Professor Madison, are going to teach a computing machine to write.

Only his father had been displeased. 'Leave Harvard for good?' he'd shouted over the phone when Madison explained he would not be returning to academe. This from the failed undergraduate, class of '44, expelled for poor academic performance and 'anti-social' behaviour. *Pro*-social really; he'd got a Radcliffe girl pregnant.

He had been even angrier when his son explained he'd be based in England, native country of his mother

4

(the elder Madison's ex-wife) and constant object of his father's abuse. 'Why *there*?' his father had demanded. Why indeed? It had seemed odd to Madison at first, the company's insistence that his work be done abroad. 'Orders from on-high,' came Personnel's reply to his queries about this; 'company policy says hush-hush research flourishes best abroad.'

Torn by his love of New England, his relationship with his then girlfriend Sally (herself a Ling employee, met during his consultancy work), Madison had hesitated. How can you turn this down? the company countered. You may be the only man in the world who can make this breakthrough now. Dither, wait five years, and the kudos will shower like gold-dust on someone else. Unnerved by the prospect of glory within his grasp but carelessly thrown away, Madison had accepted the offer. Three weeks later he had flown to England, and settled himself into Ling's Oxford outpost.

Feeling vulnerable, now, after Pistolet's warning, Madison gave up any attempt at work and went out. Wellington, the editor, was already at lunch, and Dorothy, his secretary, was on holiday. He walked to the market, where consumerist Britain had at last discovered food. In the market could be found fresh bread and pâté, good cheese, crisp vegetables. Spring was best: early peaches from Italy, melons from Israel and Spain; later would come English strawberries and punnets of raspberries. He passed a flower-stall, chock-full of iris. His girlfriend Catherine's father thought fondness for flowers an unfailing indicator of homosexual tendencies, but then he had also described a Sri Lankan neighbour as 'a bit smokey', and spoke, like a *fin de siècle* burgher, of psychoanalysis as 'a Jewish science'.

Madison stopped at W.H. Smith, chain-store purveyor of information in an Information Age. Here he browsed through *Byte*, bypassed the *International Herald Tribune*, and moved furtively down-market to *Time*. Among his less appealing Oxford acquaintances was one Samson, would-be biographer of his father; Samson had passed on certain rumours, so Madison was not entirely surprised, upon reading the 'Milestones' column, to find:

> *Married*: For the fourth time, Frederick Morton Madison, 62, hard-drinking Hemingway of the poetry world; to Monica Thompson, 37, former model and aspiring actress; in Tuscany.

'Hemingway of the poetry world' – how that would grate on the old man. The 'aspiring actress' part did not augur well for the marriage; Madison could not envisage many outlets for Monica's ambitions in the Tuscan countryside. There was plenty of money for travel, however; money enough for anything since the success of his father's one and only novel.

He put down the magazine and walked slowly back towards the office. Minnie Lu loomed large in his thoughts, and anxiety moved in on a moderately threatening wave. If, by virtue of his Yankee upbringing, Madison was not of the back-slapping hail-fellow-well-met kind, he was also by no means a misanthrope. Not for him Pistolet's evident enjoyment of the role of *provocateur* and pain-in-the-ass. Madison had grown accustomed to a place on the fringes, as an unnoticed member of the side, half in the game, half out, and he liked his life to be in that balanced state, wishing neither to move closer to the action nor to be without any part in the play.

Not that he wanted to be a Jamesian hero, a figure of *sensibility*. On the contrary, he rather fancied a life led by brisk command, short and powerful imperative. *Go for it*, perhaps, especially when he thought about his work. *Seize the day*? Sometimes, though, he didn't know just what day it was . . .

His office was, in his American boss Cromwell's words, a dinky development office, such an improbable building for a large centralised company like Ling that an academic acquaintance had once – drunk at a college dinner – accused Madison of working for the CIA. It sat in a small street just off the one-way system that circled unintelligently around the university and town centre; a four-storey block so thoroughly unprepossessing that the occasional marketing types who visited from Ling U.K. or Ling Europe were frankly appalled. The façade Ling elsewhere presented to the world was a high-tech constant of slickness, speed, and space; here, the walls needed paint, the floors were dirty. Not the obvious place for a world-shattering breakthrough, but then had Chomsky needed chrome chairs and plush carpets? Of course not.

When Madison entered his office he discovered that Wellington was back. Wellington occupied the small warren-like room that lay between Madison's own office and the reception area which held Dorothy's desk and the office's working library. He combined a high level of genius with extreme personal dishevelment, and this accorded nicely with Madison's conception of what an erudite grammarian-cum-lexicographer should be. For a mixture of academic and publishing reasons, the city was full of such creatures, most of them working freelance. The men were usually hirsute, in tattered brown cloth trousers and black buckled sandals with black socks; the women had long, unwashed hair and unshaven legs. Poorly paid, their unworldliness made them sitting ducks for exploitative employers, though for the most part they were content to work ceaselessly, remorselessly on words. Madison had lied to Cromwell about local wage-levels so as to pay them more.

As Madison walked in, the phone promptly rang and Wellington turned a page of the *OED* Supplement, impervious. Exasperated, Madison marched through to his own desk to pick up the phone. By which time it had stopped ringing. He found a FAX on his desk from Minnie Lu. 'Please be in my office Wednesday at 10 a.m. to provide up-to-date account of progress. If otherwise engaged, cancel other engagement.'

'Duncan!' he shouted, and Wellington eventually lumbered into the room. He wore the same jacket he had worn all week; more disturbingly, he wore the same olive shirt. With her usual tact, Dorothy had complained of the odd smell left in the office after Wellington spent time there.

'Hello,' said Wellington with his head down. He rarely looked his employer in the face, indeed had failed to do so even when Madison first offered him the job. There had been several other contenders, none of Wellington's unsurpassed weirdness, and none with his grammatical skills. 'So where do we stand?' Madison asked him.

'We have made some excellent progress,' said Wellington, and Madison almost groaned. This was his own standard reply on trips to headquarters. 'Does it make sense?' he said. 'Can it pass as Shakespeare?'

'Only to an untutored mind,' said Wellington, and Madison wondered if he was referring to him.

'Are you working on the sonnets?'

'I still say they form the perfect constrained domain, but I don't seem able to discover what's missing.'

'Try genius,' said Madison. 'What you've made is not bad pastiche, but it's certainly not Shakespeare. It will be some time before we can teach a machine *that*.'

'I suppose so. In any case, I'm going to move on to the weaker dramas. I thought *Pericles* might do. It's a minor play; some of it is almost certainly not by Shakespeare – the first two acts are thought by many to be the work of a man named Wilkins, though they *may* have been written by Shakespeare and got mangled in the transcription. They're markedly inferior to the next three acts, which read like very good Shakespeare indeed.'

Madison raised his head; if he didn't stop Wellington now he'd have to hear the equivalent of a critical article. 'Very interesting,' he interjected. 'But what's it do for us?'

'I thought we could have a go at rewriting parts of the first two acts. As Shakespeare would have done them.'

Madison shook his head. 'I don't think so. You'll only run into the same problems you've had with the sonnets – an unduplicatable quality of writing. No, what I propose is output along the lines of what already exists – the first two acts are inferior to Shakespeare, you say, but surely they're competent late Elizabethan prose.'

'Jacobean, you mean. *Pericles* was one of the later plays.'

'Jacobethan, actually,' said Madison gleefully, knowing Wellington hated to be one-upped in erudite exchange. 'But all right, have a go, though that's not all I want you working on.'

'Meaning?'

'Business letters.'

'Not again.' Wellington spoke of business as if it were a venereal disease.

'I'm afraid so. Only this time it would be nice to be more successful. I'll be away next week,' he added, to explain his new sense of urgency, though he did not mention his impending interview with Minnie Lu. There was no point in panicking Wellington. 'I know it's a bore,' he concluded, 'but I think we should do what we can to cover our tracks. If you have any success with *Pericles*, we can try and transfer it to some kind of writing my superiors will understand. Then they might leave us alone.' He looked at the stack of papers on his desk awaiting his attention. Wellington took the hint and went back to his room.

How much danger was he in, then? Madison asked himself as he sat down at his desk. Times were getting tough for Ling Enterprises, and were made still tougher by the contrasting fortunes of Ling's competitors. Elsewhere, earnings multiplied, salaries soared, and the Dow Jones Industrial Average peaked: Ling's growth had slowed and its stock nose-dived. Perhaps Madison should jump ship, before the iceberg was struck and the *S.S. Ling* went under.

Yet where else could he work on text-generation? The industry still dismissed it. No, he had unwittingly found the perfect niche, at least if he survived his encounter with Minnie Lu. Looking back, he knew that even at Harvard he had already been tired of parsing, the subject of his dissertation (*Deterministic Parsers and Phrase Structure Grammars: A New Theory*) and his first published work. Instead of analysing text by machine, how much more exciting to *create* it by machine.

Yet when he was honest with himself – not often – Madison would concede that it was only after that angry phone conversation with his father that his present work had become an obsession with him, rather than the subject of one highly speculative article. Visiting New York, his father had telephoned on the day Madison left Harvard and joined Ling as a full-time employee.

'If you don't want to teach,' his father had boomed, 'at least you could do something real.'

'*Real*? What I'm going to do isn't real?' This seemed a bit rich, coming from a poet.

'No, it's not. It's just machines, for Christ's sakes; teaching them to do things we used to do for ourselves. But stupid, pedestrian things – counting and sorting and picking our fiscal noses for us. The one thing I know for sure is that no goddamned machine can write as well as I do.'

What had irritated Madison most about this conversation? His father's insulting his vocation, or the arrogant assertion of superiority over any 'goddamned machine'? All Madison could say for certain was that his father had doubled his determination to make a computer write.

Yet his father might have had a point, for despite some recent hullabaloo about 'thinking machines', nothing yet existed to prove a computer could write like a human. There was some software development of templates for form letters, and in Oxford Madison had soon discovered it was possible to pre-program many kinds of business letters – a process abetted by their similarity: 'Where is the money?', 'Here is the money', 'We haven't *got* the money'. But this was just tricks, clever tricks. It had nothing to do with what Madison was interested in: genuine Artificial Intelligence.

So in his first year in England he had moved past pre-programmed assemblage of text, and set forth for the uncharted waters of natural language text-generation – or, to laymen, getting a machine to write. His first task was to isolate a domain, to choose a particular 'kind of writing' – examples of which could be fed into the computer's knowledge base, where it could draw on them for the content, style, tone etc. of its own compositions. He had begun again with business letters – but had rapidly floundered: for all their banality and mindless repetition, they still constituted much too wide a domain for his generator to draw on. And, of course (though not to be admitted back on the eighth floor), they were deeply, fatally boring.

Thus his second year in Oxford had seen a search for more suitable domains, while he hired Wellington to build a lexicon with sufficient grammatical information to serve as the base for generation. Madison wanted structured writing that could be read just like that of a writer of consequence. He had begun with letters, but not business ones; using *The Day of the Locust*, *The Loved One*, even a couple from Richardson's *Clarissa*. Nothing doing. Then he had moved to subjects; golf, close to Madison's heart, and cattle-ranching, rather further away. Wellington had popped up with his suggestion for an ersatz Shakespeare,

11

but the sonnets he'd failed to produce did not bode well for *Pericles*. And that, thought Madison with a sudden bump, was where things lay. No wonder Minnie Lu was making noises, the company beginning to stir like a proverbial giant, aware that the gnat at its knee (in this case Madison) wasn't nipping and annoying as it should. Madison still did not have a domain, and without that he could only be quiet.

2

As he drove up the steep gravel drive there was no sign of Catherine's car in the crescent sweep in front of his rented house. He found his keys buried in his briefcase and slowly opened the oak door. In the hall he found a note. 'Darling, Papa is coming to London. Back Monday night but will ring tomorrow. XXXX Catherine P.S. George is in the run and will need walking.' Her riding boots were under the table; at weekends – though not this one, apparently – she taught at a nearby riding school, and worked as a PA in London during the week.

His post consisted almost entirely of bills, so he left it and walked through to the kitchen and out of the back door. From the lawn he could see George in his fenced run, agitated now that he'd heard the car. Behind the run was the small orchard that ran down to the stream marking his property's western border. In the distance he could see with unusual clarity the Downs stretching out towards the West Country; in autumn and winter, mist or cloud shut off the view, giving the place a tight, hemmed-in feeling.

He walked across the soft grass and unlatched the door of the crude run. George came out and did a wild dance on the lawn, running back to the kitchen door, then returning to jump high on to Madison's chest. Madison gently set the dog's forelegs down and patted his large golden head.

He had rented this house the year before; he lived there alone, but it had been leased at least partly with Catherine in mind. She disguised from her Home Counties parents her weekend stays there; it was never clear whether her titular chastity was in deference to her parents' Tory morality or her own respect for convention; Madison had never been willing to press the point and find out. There were many things that weren't worth pressing with Catherine; she was not inclined to explain her preferences.

He looked at what his rent money had bought him and saw a large, brick, 1930s-built house which might at a pinch be described as neo-Georgian. It was big – *6 bed, 3 recep, 3 bath* – but it was the *three acres* and the *small existing orchard and stream* that had been the key attractions for Madison.

He should walk the dog, he knew, but he was too tired. He let George into the kitchen and poured a shot from a bottle of single malt. The kitchen was large and bare, like most of his house, awaiting the oak cabinets and Aga stove Catherine had in mind. Madison made do with a one-oven electric stove and a tiny refrigerator.

He went out into the hall, which at least had prints on the wall, then up the staircase. Sipping his whisky, he took off his clothes, then got under the duvet and lay looking sleepily out of the window.

Soon the view of the birch copse gave way to a disembodied perspective of maples. He was in his old mahogany bed covered by his great-aunt's patchwork quilt, looking out at the stand of hardwoods that led to his uncle's

13

house. Now the door creaked open and a female walk announced itself – crisp but light. In his dream, it was Catherine. She came around to his side of the bed and drew back the duvet. He reached down to stroke her hair – but the hair was gold now, and the face belonged to his ex-girlfriend, Sally Zehring. She kissed him coldly on the lips, then moved away, only to return with a sudden thump on the bed. She began, strangely, to lick him gently on his cheeks, while Madison reached out and stroked her large mane of hair.

'Oh for God's sakes,' said Madison out loud. He pushed the dog off the bed, then got out of it himself. It was half six. He dressed and went downstairs, fed George from a tin, then ate two crackers he washed down with water. He took an old shooting-jacket from the hall and let himself and George out of the back door.

He walked around the house to the front, where he found Catherine, weeding. 'I was going to leave earlier,' she said, as they went in and embraced in the hall. 'I have to be in London in two hours.'

Half an hour later Madison lay back under a single sheet, watching as Catherine got dressed again. She was of medium height, with auburn hair that she wore swept back in a bun. She was brushing it now, with a silver hairbrush that Madison's granddaughter-less grandmother had left him. Catherine had a large, square face, and very pretty clear skin; her figure was well-built, almost luscious.

They got along for the most part, rarely quarrelling, never openly fighting. 'I'm not very nice,' Catherine had said on their first afternoon together, and it was true – she wasn't. They had met at the Hampshire house of a distant friend of Madison's mother and had been left alone to talk after Sunday lunch in the sitting-room. Since Madison, miserable and lonely now that Sally Zehring was

14

seeing someone else back in the States, didn't think himself very nice either, Catherine's admission was a more alluring advertisement than might have been expected. She was on her own too, getting over a rather tedious romance with a British army officer.

What Catherine saw in him, Madison wasn't certain. Perhaps she was taken by his mix of presentability and sudden irreverent humour. Socially, he supposed, he was acceptable, even to her insufferably snobbish father. Madison was the right kind of American – New England, Ivy League, product of the right schools. His father's fame probably did him no harm either, and of course he had a reasonable amount of money. Though not *that* much; if money was what mattered to Catherine, she could have done far better among her county friends.

And she gave him? Companionship, after twelve solitary months since his arrival in the UK. Sex, much needed after an almost entirely chaste year. That Catherine's personality was so well-defined was another attraction for Madison, who felt his own character to be amorphous and ill-shaped. An air of professionalism surrounded her: she was potently organised, from her careful breakfast of coffee, orange juice and toast, to the fourth (and last) use of her toothbrush before bed. In bed itself, this demeanour translated into a brisk sexuality that occasionally strayed into bossiness. 'Lie on your back,' she might say, before mounting him with a dominant polish. 'Harder, please,' she would whisper through clenched teeth in more engaged moments of passion. The schoolmarmish aspects of her performance were not erotic, but her attention to detail was.

Now, she finished brushing her hair and looked down at Madison. He told her about his forthcoming trip.

'I hope you told them you're jolly well not going.'

'I have to go, I'm afraid.'

Catherine snorted. 'Nonsense. You mustn't be so easily

15

bullied. All the Chinese are like that. I know; Daddy was in Hong Kong for years.'

'This wasn't a racial decision.'

'You know you're very employable – there are loads of companies that would love to have you.'

'Loads?' he said, thinking of the highly rarefied field he seemed to have created for himself. 'Yes, I can get another job, but not doing what I want to do. That's the problem. I need more time – at least six months, if not a year.'

Catherine opened her handbag, looked inside, nodded at the contents and snapped it shut. 'I've never understood why, if the Ling people don't really mind about your project, you do. It's only a job, darling.'

As he began to explain ('It would be a tremendous breakthrough, just think of a machine taking over our writing chores'), he saw her eyes move restlessly around the room, as if she were looking for some commonplace that had somehow got misplaced. This was her characteristic reaction when he began to talk about his work; he stopped talking, feeling suddenly quite hopeless.

'Oh,' she said, slipping into her shoes, 'I meant to tell you. There's a letter for you I took to London by mistake. It's from your father. I would have brought it along but I forgot in the rush.'

'I wonder what he wants.'

Catherine shrugged. 'I was half-inclined to throw it away. Considering what a brute he's been.'

Madison felt a surge of irritation at this protectiveness. 'It's *my* letter. Don't even dream of throwing it out.'

Catherine turned to the standing mirror, adjusted her collar, inspected herself, nodded, then came over to his side of the bed. 'I must rush,' she said, leaning down to kiss him on the cheek. 'I *should* have thrown it away, you know, and never mentioned it. Mentioning your father always does upset you so.'

3

He slept badly that night, dreaming tense, neurotic dreams in which first anonymous women, then Catherine, then finally Sally Zehring floated in and out of a stage-like set while he, from the wings, futilely tried to direct them.

The curtains borrowed from Catherine's mother until the fulfilment of her daughter's decorative ambitions did not cover all the windows, allowing the morning light at this time of year to pour in well before six o'clock, waking Madison even before the community of blackbirds and starlings began their cacophonies of chat. He breakfasted, read the paper quickly, and went out to work in the orchard. He sprayed the cherries, pruned dead branches that he'd missed the previous autumn, and put more potash around the base of the trees.

After lunch he went into his study, sat in the old green pile armchair, and thought – which was what he did most of the time. Explaining this to Catherine, chronic doer that she was, he had not been understood. 'Call it thinking, contemplation, whatever you like, but just sitting there never got anything done.'

He drove to Beckford Golf Club. He beat a four-ball to the first tee, then played the first nine deliberately. Of course his handicap had grown a bit since his fanatical high-school days in Vermont, so that when he came to the turn only four over, he felt pleased with himself, having managed to submerge all thoughts about his work. This was what golf had always done for him since the lonely, painful days after his father left home. Then, he had

17

taken up the game with a vengeance, playing daily after school, then throughout the summer, shirking his duties at his uncle's dairy, sometimes playing as many as fifty-four holes in a long summer day.

Madison had tried golf for his text-generation project, using Rabbit Angstrom, protagonist of the Updike Rabbit novels, in trials. Yet he had forgotten the dense, opulent worldliness of Updike's prose; the generator had returned:

> To the eighteenth, which unfolded
> like a Japanese fan, inviting admiration
> for its workmanship, the detail
> of its varnish trim.

So far so good, Madison had concluded. Updike might not rent the generator for his next novel, but at least the program was writing prose. But then:

> An inconclusive drive off the heel of
> a thin three-iron. The dimpled Titleist
> soared comet-like then dipped, rolling
> through a crust of rough until it lodged,
> half-buried in a rabbit scraping.
> Lapin despaired; leveret swung; hare coursed;
> PUTT and quit rabbiting on

The generator crashed. Closer inspection had revealed a fatal failure to disambiguate; the knowledge base, designed to impart worldly information to the system's theoretical framework, had confused Rabbit the character with rabbit the mammal, and both of them with 'rabbit *v.i.* to talk at length and in a rambling fashion'. Madison had given Updike up as a bad job.

Hooking into some pines on his drive at the fourteenth, he carefully chipped out, then hit his approach six feet from the pin and sank the putt for his par. As he collected his ball he

18

thought how his father would have played the hole – thrown caution to the wind, thrashed wildly out of the rough in a desperate attempt for a miraculous recovery.

What a hothead, thought Madison, then promptly hit his tee-shot to the par three 15th some twenty-five yards over the green. The ball lay half-covered in deep grass; he took a sand wedge and popped it smartly up into the air. It just missed the flag, bounced twice more, then rolled into a bunker. From which he exploded aggressively – too aggressively, the ball rolling quickly off the green onto the fringe on the other side. Two putts and he was now suddenly six over, and he nearly threw his ball into the woods. He bogeyed all of the last three holes and slumped home in a bad mood with an 81.

4

On Monday he drove into work late, opening his windows to let the breeze dry his hair, still wet from the bath. Parking near the railway station, he walked the two hundred yards to his office, aware as always of the good fortune that had for the past two years put him there, giving him the happy illusion that he – not Minnie Lu, not Virgil Peabody, head of Research and Development at Ling – was master of his fate.

He spent the morning on admin. and went through the post, both the electronic variety on his terminal and the stuff that came through the front door. Most of the on-screen messages were trivial, personal announcements from Ling Britain's headquarters announcing cars for sale and farewell parties for departing secretaries. There were several phone messages, including three from Samson. The printed stuff was mostly nugatory: fliers from Information Technology consultants peddling seminars, paycheck stubs for Dorothy and Wellington, vacation request forms. He found several unpaid bills in the stack, two of them final notices. He was looking at these as Dorothy came back to work.

'Come in, Dorothy, please.' He reminded himself there was nothing to be gained from getting angry, for it had been clear from the day he drove her down to Ling Britain in London to sign her employment contract that he and Dorothy were not suited. She had told him about her last boss. 'He wanted to be *friendly*,' she said scornfully, as if Madison's predecessor had pinched her bottom. 'Not professional at all,' she added, and Madison had sensed he was doomed; he was running a development office, not the marketing operation Dorothy would have preferred. She was at home in the world of sales, the land of shined shoes and done-up ties; she wanted Madison to dress better and behave more seriously, mistaking his comic turns for lack of dedication to his work. She also had a vast sense of social inferiority, which Madison's safe position outside the imprisoning bars of England's class structure only seemed to intensify. 'Very grand, I'm sure,' she would sniff if he so much as mentioned what he had done or where he had gone over the weekend.

Now she was dressed smartly in a green dress and bone necklace that highlighted the last of her Spain-acquired winter tan. She had also had her hair done. 'You're dressed up today,' Madison remarked.

'I'm getting married,' she said, as if this explained everything.

'Today?'

She looked angrily at him. 'Of course not today. In three months' time. I suppose you'll want me to give in my notice.'

'Why?' he asked, though indeed he would like nothing better.

She shrugged. 'I thought you only wanted single girls around.'

What did this mean? Did Dorothy think he fancied *her*? Best not pursue it. 'Who's the lucky fellow?' he asked lightly.

'His name is Gordon,' she said, and he nodded. A nice English boy for a, well, an English girl. She added, 'He's Mexican.'

Madison must have looked surprised, for she went on hastily, 'He's not very dark. And he's from a very old Guacamole family.'

He looked forward to meeting this man. 'Well, congratulations,' he said as heartily as he could. 'And no,' he lied, 'I don't want your notice.'

He went through Wellington's final sonnet drafts, left on his desk for inspection. He was not encouraged, for the poems were completely unreadable. Just occasionally a strange line emerged that made a certain kind of sense – 'My tongue has danced a sconce upon your lips'; 'Your eyes are something like the amber moon' – but basically the generator was simply spewing gibberish. There was not even embryonic promise to its output. Maybe *Pericles* would be better.

He went out to lunch at Kaminski's – actually Kaminski's Bar and Grill, but known to admirer and detractor alike simply for the eponymous owner. He could usually be found at the bar, a sweeping curve of oak that served as meeting place for his many friends, and where the odd bemused tourist, waiting for his table, was treated to snatches of conversations that dwelt solely on cricket and sex.

This eclectic mix seemed to work: the restaurant did almost a thousand meals a day. Other Oxford restaurants came and went, but Kaminski's success endured, created by a savvy combination of inexpensive American-style food (much of it grilled over mesquite on a quite un-English grill in the middle of the restaurant) and by the pretty waitresses

21

who, keen on sun-beds, flashed unseasonably orange legs to cheer the greyest customer on a February day.

Kaminski was at the bar drinking a beer when Madison arrived. He was built roughly along the lines of a large black bear, but first impressions of potential menace were soon dispelled by his relentless affability – he acted less like a grizzly than one of those spoiled exhibits at Yellowstone Park that doze happily in the sun and pose for snapshots with both paws around the tourists' shoulders. The suit he wore now was expensive and, characteristically, crumpled; his hair was tousled, his glasses slightly askew.

'Beer at lunch? Steady on,' said Madison.

'I'm working today, for a change. I need the drink. Debby's cross with me; she found out about the redhead. That was bad enough, but when I came in this morning I find out the redhead's quit without notice and Deborah's suddenly taken three days holiday. Once things get moving today I'll be waiting tables myself.'

Deborah was as steady a girlfriend as Kaminski seemed likely to have. Madison had always found one sexual relationship at a time ample; he was never sure how to advise Kaminski, so rarely tried. Catherine had more than once told Madison that he would 'go to the dogs' by spending time with Kaminski, little realising that in the early days of their friendship (and before he knew Catherine) Madison and Kaminski *had* in fact gone to the dogs – watching greyhounds sprint around a track at White City in the company of Deborah and her friend Louise, Madison's one conquest during his first year in England.

Someone spoke from behind Madison's shoulder. 'I thought I might find you here.'

A voice that had come to plague him, even in his dreams. Sinister, low, Northern, menacing. It belonged to Arthur Paul Samson, who stood out sprucely in the raffish ambience of the restaurant's bar. He wore a blue blazer and striped tie, though the dapper effect was marred by his Wellington-like insistence on sandals and socks.

Next to Madison, Kaminski visibly shuddered. 'You'll excuse me,' he said, 'there are waitresses I must attend to.' Samson quickly moved his slight frame onto the stool. 'Let me buy you a drink,' he offered, saved by Madison's almost full glass from having to deliver. Madison looked hopefully among the bar's regulars for someone else to talk to. No one.

'I see your papa's got married again,' said Samson. 'Go to the wedding?'

'Certainly not. I've told you a million times before, we're not really in touch.' He thought of the letter Catherine would be bringing down from London.

'Presumably it's just cover anyway. Lots of homosexuals get married these days. It's back in fashion.'

When Samson had first bearded Madison, visibly excited as an aspiring biographer to meet his subject's son, he had been deferential, though even then persistent in his inquiries. Each rebuff seemed only to renew his keenness. It had not taken long for him to begin to impart his own theories about the older Madison, which changed monthly, ranging from the inane (hadn't his father beaten his mother, and the young Madison simply 'blocked' the memory?) to the absurd (his father married younger women in order to sleep with the daughter he had never had).

Most recently, Samson had decided Madison's father was homosexual – 'Whether he knows it or not,' Samson had added insightfully. The evidence was less than overwhelming: the elder Madison had lost his father when he was three, and thereafter he and his two older brothers were raised by their mother and grandmother, a kind of matriarchy Samson thought most peculiar. 'Did they dress him as a girl when he was very young?' Samson had asked. 'Wrong writer,' Madison had replied.

Now Samson said eagerly, 'You realise your father is arguably the Grand Old Man of poetry, now that Graves is dead.'

'Was he queer too?'

'Not to the best of my knowledge. Though he affected much the same *machismo* demeanour. A boxer and all that.'

'All pugilists are gay?'

'Poet pugilists tend to be. Even in Hazlitt you get a faint sense of it.'

'You mean, "Reader, have you ever seen a fight?"'

'Precisely. Any interest in lunch? There are several questions I'd like to ask you.'

Madison's appetite suddenly failed him. 'I'm afraid not. I'm supposed to meet someone here.'

'Then I'll keep you company until your friend arrives.'

'Don't bother.'

'My pleasure,' said Samson, unbuckling his schoolboy's satchel. 'I have some notes here,' he said, withdrawing a sheaf of handwritten pages. 'Let's see, how old were you when your father left your mother? Was it fourteen or fifteen? And how did you react to your father's departure? Were you at all upset?'

'Excuse me,' said Madison, 'I'll be back in a moment.' He got up and left the restaurant. Continued hunger seemed an infinitely more agreeable companion than Samson. Outside, the pavement was blocked by masses of Italian schoolchildren. Each spring ever greater numbers of Continental adolescents came to Oxford, ostensibly to learn English, in practice to crowd the streets, eat hamburgers and cheap ice-cream, buy t-shirts for their friends at home.

He took the canal path back to his office, walking slowly along by the green water, watching the ducks. There were the usual drunks, now lying asleep on the grass in the sun. He came up onto his street and walked to his office, where the afternoon post brought an announcement of the quarter's results from Sammy Ling:

To All Company Employees:

I am messaging you more than a week ahead of our official

24

results because I could not wait to share the good news with all of you.

Results this past quarter will be, if interpreted correctly, most encouraging. Revenues increased to a record $216 million. Bookings have increased by a record 8%. Sales of our new low-end offerings are especially encouraging.

In the current tough business climate, it's especially thrilling to be able to pre-reference such encouraging progress. You have shown in the last year a new maturity, necessary to survive in and also impact this increasingly competitive environment. I am proud of your realism. I am proud of your sacrifices. Good going! I know that next year's results will be even more indicative of this company's upward trend.

Samuel Ling

All balls, of course: what about *earnings*? Virgil Peabody himself had said they would be in the red, unless – unless what? Sell a building? That's what Pistolet had predicted, naming a large skyscraper near Battery Park in New York City as the likely victim. And ominously, according to Pistolet, orders for the company's large, profitable systems were down; low-end machines (the ubiquitous PCs) had almost non-existent profit margins.

Yet what else but optimistic drivel could Sammy spout? Times are tough, keep your head down, jump ship before the ship jumps you? New employees or especially dumb ones might actually take encouragement from his words. Veteran members of the workforce could easily disinter the reality behind his fictions: 'maturity', 'realism', 'sacrifices' – these were infallible signs that results would be bad, the company was struggling.

At six thirty, avoiding the evening rush hour, Madison drove home, and over drinks and the Channel 4 news he sat side by side on the sofa with Catherine and gave her an account of his day. 'Ugh,' she said, when he mentioned Kaminski, so he quickly moved onto the ubiquitous Samson.

'Your father as a queer?' she asked when he finished recounting Samson's latest interpretations. 'He's bad enough without that.'

'It's the contemporary theory of biography. Creativity lies rooted in unresolved conflicts; the most powerful conflicts are sexual; ergo, truly creative people like my father suffer from sexual conflicts. In this day and age, that means sexual ambivalence – nobody seems to find impotence sufficiently frightening any more to make it a chief cause of sexual anxiety. And whatever my father does only serves to confirm this argument to Samson. If he marries more than once, he's a compulsive womaniser running away from his homosexuality; if he stays married to the same woman, he's doing the same thing. And if you don't get married, well, case proven.'

'Poor bugger hasn't got a chance,' said Catherine.

'A nice choice of words. No, he hasn't; that is, if he wants to listen to dumb pricks like Samson. Fortunately for my father, this kind of criticism washes right off his back. He's only interested in what the big hitters have to say.'

'I wish you wouldn't use that word.'

'Which? Hitters?'

'No. The other one.'

He thought furiously. 'Oh,' he said in sudden enlightenment. 'You mean "pricks".'

'Yes,' she said emphatically. 'Such an ugly word. It's the kind of word your father must have used. Otherwise, I can't see where you picked it up.'

There was not a lot to say to this: his vocabulary had been formed by a fairly normal range of acquaintance, in Vermont as a kid, at prep school, at Harvard. 'Speaking of my father, did you manage to remember his letter?'

'It's in the hall. I'll get it for you later.'

It was much later when he got round to reading it.

First they had dinner, cold roast beef and boiled potatoes, thick runner beans, chilled summer pudding and
ice-cream. It was good but stolid; not for Catherine the
spicy food – Mexican, Chinese, Greek – he used to gorge
on in the company of Sally Zehring. He had grown up on
simple New England food (his mother had elevated her
lack of culinary skill into a virtue) and nothing could be
as dull as Yankee pot-roast, hot dogs and baked beans. At
least here there was wine with the meal, what Catherine
called 'some cheap Wop stuff' – in fact a Barolo he was
happy to drink most of.

After dinner Catherine went to take curtain measure-
ments in the drawing-room and he returned to his study
to work some more, still restlessly searching for a domain.
The criteria were clear. The domain – the range of writing
– must be well-defined. It should have certain formal constraints. A business letter, for example, required formal
salutation, farewell, address, etc.; a first-person novel
used that pronoun exclusively in recounting narrative.
The choice of vocabulary could range widely – indeed
it should not be too limited – but it also needed to be
well-defined and recognisably part of common written
English. No *Clockwork Orange* glossaries or Mitford-like
patois. The overwhelming majority of words should exist
in the generalised lexicon.

He could define these criteria again and again (as in fact
he had done during the last year) and still be no closer
to finding a domain that worked. He had a fine general
lexicon, built by Wellington a year before, but without a
context to feed into the computer's knowledge base, any
writing the machine managed to produce would be hope-
lessly confused as to meaning, tone and register. *The quick
brown fox jumps over the lazy dog*, for example, might be
either a simple statement of fact or someone testing out
a typewriter. 'Hit me again' could be a blackjack player's
request or the plea of a masochist.

27

So what could he do? He looked idly at his book-case. God knows he knew the literature, backwards and forwards. He picked up several Artificial Intelligence compendiums, scanning the bibliographies, hoping for inspiration. 'The Computer as Poet: Lyrics from a PDP-11.' He remembered reading the article and, worse still, the poems. They had been a hodgepodge of lines, images lifted arbitrarily out of nothing, representing nothing: nonsense masquerading as free verse. The domain was too open-ended; in Madison's other experiments, using particular subjects or various kinds of letter, the domain had been too restrictive.

He got up in frustration and walked idly around the ground floor, watching Catherine stand on a chair with pins in her mouth and a tape-measure in her hand. He looked at her abstractedly for a moment until she glanced at him over her shoulder and broke his concentration. He walked out into the hall, and saw in the white and blue pottery bowl by the door the envelope addressed to him by his father. He took the letter and went back to his study to read it.

It was an aerogramme with an Italian stamp. He opened it carefully with a brass letter-opener; he could get more for it from a dealer, he thought cynically, if he took pains. He found the all-too familiar scrawl no trouble at all to read.

Dear Bobby,
I'm sending this to the last address your mother provided and trust it will catch up with you. I wanted to tell you, in case you haven't discovered it elsewhere, that I'm a married man yet again.

Elsewhere? How modest for a man who tracked his appearances in *Time*'s 'Milestones' the way a farmer counts his cows.

This time I mean to make it last. Monica is a swell gal – I know you'd like her. We're settled here for the duration. Let me know if you make your way here.

Your fond Papa

'A swell gal' – honest to God, the longer his father lived away from America the more corny his lingo became. *A hell of a guy, gee whillikers, holy smokes, for crying out loud* – the phrases tumbled out like the patter of a depressed advertising man in a 50's Cheever story. And this from a poet of such verbal mastery in his youth that he stood comparison with the early Auden.

So what was going on? 'Monica is a swell gal.' He remembered his own tuition from his father, the careful schooling that began when he was nine, or was it ten? It was not involuntary, not done to the exclusion of other activities with his friends. He played football on the Green each autumn afternoon, skated and skied all winter, played baseball daily from late spring until Labor Day. No, it was simply that as some boys learn an instrument, others collect minerals or learn to swim at the Y, so Madison and his father sat down once a week with a long white pad of lined paper and a stack of sharpened pencils (always pencils, never pens).

They had begun with couplets, looking at Pope ('Don't ever listen to any jerk who tells you he wasn't a poet'). The young Madison wrote without any sense of its being odd, an all-American boy writing poems; he supposed that everybody's father wrote poems, as well as shot animals, boxed and wrestled, fought in the war – all the Hemingwayesque activities Frederick Madison was known for. It was after his father suddenly left home that Madison began to be aware of how unusual a man his father was. It was only then, too, that he began to read his father's poems; gradually the voice of the poems grew stronger than the memory of the live speaking voice.

It was such an inimitable voice: powerful, American, rich and dense – it had been there from the first lyrics that burst upon the scene, all the way through his latest collection, darker in its brooding, more abstract, intense. It embodied a fine-strung tension between lush lyricism and the sharp-sighted colloquial. Always it possessed a unique and sonorous roll, an intimacy that seemed both spawned by and part of its uncanny sense of rhythm. The voice, like the Hemingway *persona*, projected a massive authorial confidence, as if the language were the writer's kingdom, his domain.

Domain? Yes; funny, the way the words had led back to his own search. But why not? It was already so often parodied, this voice, yet somehow inimitable. So far.

Why not? Did he, the younger Madison, know it well? Of course; much of it by heart. Could he catch the cadence, the lift and sing that only his father could provide? Better than anyone else. So why not? And if ever there was one voice he was perfectly prepared to consign to oblivion – 'a machine could do better than' – it was the thick, incantatory drum of his own old man's bass chords. *Eureka*, I have found my domain.

Part Two

1

Madison walked slowly down an aisle named Software Alley towards the cubicle assigned him during his visit. He was back among the prestigious congregation – the intense carrels of Research and Development, where the pressure mounted as the machines refused to sell and only the programs they ran made money. Software; so soft, the *lumpen* hardware boys seemed to say, nothing *tangible* – no boards, or chips or keys, no current. Only a tyranny of code, erasable, not hard-wired, infuriatingly nebulous. Yet really, when you came down to it, all that mattered. Otherwise, what was the point of the hardware, these boards and chips, this farrago of physical stuff?

He passed the cubicles of senior software engineers, which were wider by perhaps ten inches than those of junior software engineers. Almost all the cubicles showed common evidence – newspaper clippings, cartoons, drawings – of their inhabitants' determination to individualise their work-space. Leisure activities were prominent: pictures of ski-trails, rosters from an egghead's baseball association statistical league, even the accreditation papers of an official toastmaster. Madison turned a corner and nearly ran into the lanky figure of Pistolet.

'Madison,' Pistolet declared languidly, extending his hand. He wore clothes of fastidious casualness – a Harris tweed jacket with elbow patches, striped Brooks Brothers tie, blue Oxford shirt. He was tall, almost gaunt, and a quivering aristocratic slice of nose stuck out from his angular face like an ice-cutter's prow. His hair was a flop of straightish blond fringe; eyes of grey steel. The effect was of supercilious intelligence. 'Back in the arms of the Republic. When do you see Minnie Lu?'

'Ten o'clock.' When Pistolet raised an eyebrow he added, 'I know. I may be gone for good by lunchtime.'

'They say the process is painless.'

'Sure, like acupuncture.'

'She's a Bishop now, you know.'

'Oh Christ, when did that happen?'

'Just yesterday.'

'Oh well, hot air rises. Listen, can I use your phone?'

'No way,' said Pistolet emphatically. 'Last time you were here you must have called England twenty times. Cromwell almost killed me when he saw the bill. Use his phone.'

'Where is Cromwell? I should see him first.'

'He's on the tenth floor now. West Nave – near Edel's old place.'

'Cromwell's on ten? What's he doing up there?'

It was Pistolet's turn to shrug. 'Ling needs a floor between Cromwell's temper and the people who work for him. You're lucky – you have an ocean between you.'

'I better go find him. If Minnie's going to do me in, I'd like to know in advance.'

'Don't count on Cromwell telling you. Come by after you see Minnie. I'm back in A.I. Alley now. Number thirteen.'

'They're using numbers now? Where the hell is number thirteen?'

Pistolet shook his head. 'For an Anglophile *poseur* you talk awful rough. Actually, I live not far from here.' And stretching up on his long legs he leaned over the partition of a cubicle, bringing a thumb in a downward sweep to indicate that the cubicle directly opposite them was his.

'You made it sound like it was in Iowa.'

'Or Taipei.'

'I thought we weren't supposed to make jokes like that,' said Madison.

'You can't. I can; I'm half-Chinese.' And Pistolet went into his cubicle and closed the door.

Actually, thought Madison as he walked towards the elevator, the closest Jeffrey Forbes Pistolet came to Asian blood was his mother's volunteer work in the genteel quarters of the Milton Massachusetts China Trading Museum. In the ethnic music of the corporation Pistolet danced a WASP gavotte. A mix of social *hauteur* and technical brilliance. Even at boarding school he had been a marvellous coder, the quickest writer of BASIC when BASIC had been best. Only Simpson the drooler had come close, and now Simpson drooled anonymously in an IBM office in Cleveland.

He thought of Minnie Lu's recent promotion, and of the senior positions at Ling Enterprises: Archbishop, Bishop, Dean, Deacon and Vicar. The ecclesiastical sound of this internal hierarchy had puzzled the rest of the computer industry for years. Some thought it a misguided attempt to allay American suspicion of a China (wo)man; others viewed it as a ham-handed ploy to sell computers in the Evangelical South.

In fact it had been lifted wholesale from the Anglican Church. From England itself, where a youthful Sharon Ling had taken refuge in 1942, escaping from Singapore just ten days before the Japanese captured it, arriving in Southampton with her ageing father (an engineer and close acquaintance of Chiang Kai-Shek) after a tortuous progress: through the Middle East, around the Cape of Good Hope, via Gibraltar, on a motley succession of sea-craft – one destroyer, a Norwegian fishing boat, a refitted passenger liner, even, briefly, a small submarine.

'We go to America,' young Miss Ling on landing

declared to a preoccupied Home Office official, but the German U-Boats managed to keep her and her father on the island for six months more. In the bizarre fashion of the War years, they were quartered in a vicarage on the outskirts of Winchester. As the resident parson soon discovered, both Lings were already Christian, of the simple Baptist variety moulded by American missionaries. In return for their bed and board, young Miss Ling was happy to help her host sweep the aisles and dust the pews of the small church, to pass out hymnals before services, even take round the collection plate on Sundays – to the considerable bemusement of the dwindling congregation. Yet if Sharon Ling's presence baffled the natives, there was much more that proved astonishing to her. The grandeur of the neighbouring cathedral, for example, the comparative pomp of the Anglican service, the complexity and formality of its organisation – these were to her all entirely new features of religious life.

She took them undiluted to her heart. When at last she and her papa sailed for America in 1943, she went not only as a convert to the Church of England but as a firm believer in its deeply corporate structure. After two degrees taken at MIT, and the death of her father, she founded a specialised electronics company in the town of Madison, Massachusetts, with the aid of her small paternal legacy; and it was to this company that she brought her heart, soul, and love of the Anglican creed. The four buildings that housed it, built at various times during the ten years of the company's dramatic expansion, were identical, each twelve storeys high, and diamond-shaped. Collectively they were known as 'The Cathedral'. They were interconnected, and formed a four-leaf clover shape. Erected on swamp on the outskirts of Madison – in fact the town was named after one of Madison's ancestors – these buildings were a regional Pentagon in their immensity; they sat heavily near the connecting highway linking town and interstate, appropriating a special exit for themselves. At night they loomed eerily, two Naves topped by a long glowing *LING* that hung like a luminescent nightcap over the mainly darkened floors below. Architecturally they were utterly without distinction, prodigious examples of how much money can be spent on something truly ugly. They could have been designed by Albert Speer.

Madison walked through aisles of COBOL coders; COBOL, that mainstream parlance of the Ling world, the basis of so much of its software. These coders had the status of bricklayers among their fellow software engineers; needed, of course, but not to be socialised with. Even the height of their cubicles was lower, and Madison could hear conversations float up over the soft plywood partitions. A private conversation was inconceivable; for one noteworthy week a database designer named McClatchy had unwittingly attracted an audience of secretaries, who listened unobserved in the corridor as he spent his lunch hour on the phone to his wife, lamenting his propensity for premature ejaculation.

Madison came to the elevators between the Naves and ascended to the tenth floor in the company of a pretty marketing executive. He could tell she was in marketing by her dress – black suit, white blouse, crisp bow-tie, moderate heels. She wore a light scent, only just detectable in the Lysol-soaked elevator air. She seemed to case him with equal speed: as he entered she made a rapid survey of his attire and frowned, as if he were hard to place. When the doors closed she sneaked a second look, inspecting his trousers (neatly pressed) and his inferior shoes (high-quality leather but unpolished and beginning to crack). She smirked, having clearly concluded that he was simply an oaf from R & D. Her eyes returned to the papers she held in her hand.

And that was the relationship between Marketing and Research & Development summarised in an eight-second elevator ride. The people in Marketing wore suits; their floors crackled with the sound of crisp collars and what the Victorians called clean linen. R & D was rather more unsavoury, its members leaning towards jeans and sweaters, beards and t-shirts. There was less ventilation on the R & D floor, and greater need of it. Like Pistolet, Madison tried to pretend he was unaffiliated: he was part of R & D yet wore a jacket and tie.

The characteristic intimacy of the tenth floor meant no one seemed to know the location of Cromwell's office. At last, in an open cubicle in a far corner, Madison stumbled onto Judith, Cromwell's ageing secretary, remarkable for being perhaps the only person at Ling over fifty years old, apart from the company's founder, the Empress herself. Cromwell's name was posted on the door of a window office, but Cromwell was not inside.

'Hello, Judith. I was looking for Gus.'

She failed to recognise Madison. 'Mr Cromwell should be back in a minute. He's in the Spires seeing Virgil Peabody.'

'Fine, I'll wait for him. I'm just going to use his phone for a minute.' And he walked into Cromwell's office and closed the door before Judith could object. Doubtless he was in violation of several company regulations.

The call took forever to go through. 9, then 011, then 44, then 865, then the last six digits. He looked out of the window towards the New Hampshire border only a few miles north. The forest stretched in an uninterrupted expanse of black: only a keen eye could articulate an individual tree or the faint light tinge that signalled the first buds. It looked as dense and impenetrable as it must have done three centuries before, but it was as fake as the front of a Western movie's Main Street – beneath the horizon were villages and towns, factories and roads, sprawling malls and traditional spires, whole communities more attuned to the vagaries of consumer fashion than to memories of the pilgrims' wilderness.

No one answered at his office, which was not a good sign, since it was early afternoon there. He put the phone down as Cromwell came in, bristling in a suit of navy blue. He was shorter than Madison, but had square shoulders and a crisp ginger moustache that combined to make him seem formidably larger. He was always, in Pistolet's words, about one-half degree short of explosion.

'Back one day and already you're using my phone. What's wrong with your own phone?'

'I haven't got one,' said Madison defensively. 'The cubicle I've been assigned is *sans* chair and *sans* phone.'

'Don't give me that French faggot talk. Aren't you ever satisfied? Use somebody else's phone down there.'

'I was calling the office. Anyway, I'm allowed to call home every two days, even if it is trans-Atlantic.'

'What, so you can talk to your fucking dog?' Cromwell sighed and threw a manilla folder on his desk. 'For somebody out in left field you sure know how to go by the book when it suits you. I never pull that crap on my boss.'

'That's because you have a less understanding superior.'

'Oh fuck you,' said Cromwell, more in fatigue than irritation. 'What's up?'

'You tell me. When did you move up here?'

Cromwell sat down in the visitor's chair, across his own desk from Madison. 'Last month,' he said.

'So you're in Marketing now. Who's going to take over the A.I. group?'

'You'll find out soon enough. For now it's still mine.'

'Yeah, but if you're up here wearing suits and talking about commercial surveys, how can you control the egg-heads downstairs?'

'Since when did I ever control them? Since when did

your pal Pistolet listen to me? Since when did I ever control *you*?'

'I wish I'd known you'd moved.'

'What's it to you? Two floors won't make a whole lot of difference to someone three thousand miles away.'

'So why am I here? Was it your idea?'

Cromwell said nothing. 'I wasn't due for a visit for another two months,' Madison complained. 'Minnie Lu wants to see me in five minutes. Why am I in the doghouse?'

'Who said you were?' Cromwell asked, and stood up and opened the door. 'You can't keep Minnie Lu waiting. Come back later and I'll buy you lunch.'

'Out?'

'Are you kidding? I've only got thirty minutes to eat. But you get a choice. East Nave cafeteria or West Nave.'

'When Minnie Lu gets through with me I may not be hungry. What time do we eat?'

'Come back at eleven thirty.'

'Eleven thirty?'

'This is America, where the Free lunch early. Welcome home.'

2

Some of Madison's trepidation as he went to see Minnie Lu resulted from the fear that whatever she had to say to him might prove only partly comprehensible. To the first-generation Asian-American employees at Ling, the English language posed problems not dissimilar to those Madison had faced the first time he used chopsticks, proving slippery, intractable, seemingly incapable of providing the service for which it was intended.

Some of these employees never came to grips with their adopted country's mother tongue, retaining an impenetrable syntax reminiscent of Charlie Chan. Others were more successful, speaking in clinical tones devoid of accent or rhythmic variation; still others drifted between the two extremes. Minnie Lu, for example, usually spoke in the caricature sing-song of someone fresh off the boat (though she had landed many years before), only to break out during her frequent displays of displeasure into a movie-bred Brooklynese.

It was not difficult to incur her displeasure. She was opinionated, decisive, capricious, powerful: a frightening array of traits. She was not Madison's boss, but she had the power to extend her long, slim fingers down among the employees and poke about – like a hedge-cutter destroying half a dozen rabbits' warrens. Should a lower manager, say at Vicar or Deacon level, have the temerity to protest, she would telephone the Empress herself, lay out the relative merits of the case, and await judgment. It was usually impossible to question Minnie Lu's impartiality, since her presentation was conducted in fluent Cantonese.

Yet her advance in the company could not be attributed to her race; other Chinese-speaking employees played tennis with Sammy, the Empress's son, or parachuted with Leo, a cousin and the black sheep of the Empress's tribe, but did not necessarily prosper. More than by Asian connection, Minnie Lu was served by her long tenure at the Cathedral; in fact she had been an employee when there was no Cathedral – the North Nave had only been erected some fifteen years before. She was famously loyal to the Empress.

Now, seeing Madison hovering outside her office, Minnie Lu waved him in curtly and they both sat down at a conference table. Her office was perhaps three times the size of Gus Cromwell's window office, five times that of a junior engineer. It was nonetheless smaller than Madison's own office in England, a fact he thought it best to keep to himself.

'I think we make mistake with you,' she began crisply, unfazed by the admission of error. Madison said nothing. He had not expected this.

'Sending you to England,' said Minnie Lu. 'How long it's been? At least two years. It was not really fair. You are too talented to waste in such obscurity.'

This seemed to demand a reply. 'Thank you. But I like to think I'm contributing to the company in England.'

'Of course,' she said dismissively, less impressed than he expected by this ritual avowal of allegiance.

'And I think I'll have some interesting things to show in the next six months.' He felt confident he was at last on the edge of a breakthrough, if – a big 'if' – he was given the time. He might have found his domain too late.

'Maybe,' said Minnie Lu, then added sharply, 'but interesting is not enough. This is not a university, you know. We are not in business of competing with MIT. Or Harvard,' she added pointedly, then paused. Her face softened. 'It's time we had you here. It's only fair for your future.

'You know,' she continued, 'you have value. So I say, why we send you to Siberia?' She giggled. 'Maybe England not that cold, but you know what I mean. You work hard there. Gus Clomwell, he say so all the time. So I think you should have a chance to come here, be a real part of us.'

'I see,' said Madison slowly. Buy time, collect thoughts, step carefully. 'And what would I do here?'

'Big job. Very big job. Parsing,' she announced, as if he would never have heard of it. 'Under Gus,' she said, 'but I tell you confidentially, not for long. Maybe someone else who is under me.'

He was at a loss for arguments. Parsing: the mainstream

of linguistic work in the natural language field. Parsing: even in its sophisticated incarnations, the same dreary grammatical analysis that (once) every schoolboy learned. Yes, parsing, where he had first begun to show promise as an undergraduate, where he had first prospered as a scholar in his own right. It was said of linguists that when they grew tired of parsing they were tired of life. Yet compared to the promise he saw in making text, parsing now seemed utterly stale, like asking a critic turned poet to go back once more to the secondary world of close readings, the sheer deadness of writing about another man's work. It represented life at one remove, as if a ship's drowsy number two, energized by the drowning of his captain, was suddenly returned to a subordinate tedium when a new skipper was helicoptered in. Having found his domain, Madison was loathe to let it go. After years of detached abstraction, he found himself, happy if apprehensive, suddenly at the helm. His life now, for better or worse, was strictly hands on.

'I'm very flattered,' he said slowly, 'but I do still have a lot to do over there. I wouldn't want to damage my own project by moving too hastily.'

'Oh, I would not expect a move by you for some time.' Relief welled up, then soured when she added, 'Maybe two, three months. But unless you have real results by then, we will want you to come back. You talk to Gus. He is very pleased at prospect of your return. Then come see me again before you leave for England. Or Siberia,' she said, with a harsh laugh. She stood up to show the meeting was over.

He left her office needing to talk to someone. Pistolet was the obvious choice. Perhaps his oldest friend, if not his best. Pistolet: his friend, despite a certain smart-ass brutality Madison didn't need right now, and a tiring penchant for dated hipster lingo – 'daddy-O' had once passed his lips to the astonishment of a senior marketing executive.

When drunk, which was often, this mild hipsterism grew inflated, becoming more alliterative, wildly tangential. His misquotations were notorious – and deliberate, Madison had long before concluded. Hounded at school by a particularly savage English teacher, Pistolet had turned against literature like an avenging god; he hated it far too much to leave it alone.

Madison found him at the terminal in his cubicle and sat down with a thump in the spare chair. 'Hang on a sec,' said Pistolet, cancelling out of the program he was working on. 'The system's *so* slow. It's all right to give customers these dinosaurs, but do they have to torture their own developers?' He turned and looked at Madison. 'Jesus, what happened? Are you in deep shit?'

'Minnie wants me back here.'

'But you would never last here. Madison, my friend the exile; like Hemingway, only in England.'

'You know that. I know that. But they think I'll be pleased; they think they're doing me a *favour*. Come back to the raft, Huck honey, we love you.'

'Can't you say you don't want to be loved?'

'Of course not. If I say that they'll say he isn't *worth* loving. Then they *will* fire me.' Madison shook his head. 'No more pure research for this boy.'

'The Times They Are A Changing.'

'The pricks. After all they've done to fund it. And now they want me back on parsing work.' He thought wearily of the tensions of the Artificial Intelligence group in the Cathedral. He had been spared them in his British 'Siberia', seen as a gifted exile. He didn't think he could stand day-to-day A.I. combat in the corridors of Ling; he suddenly remembered a former member of the Natural Language group chasing Pistolet down the hall, waving fifty pages of technical specification in his hand, shouting 'Fuck your case grammar, fuck your case grammar'.

As if on cue, two men in security-guard uniforms came

running down the aisle, one of them shouting incoherently into a walkie-talkie. An unusual sight: security was usually confined to the ground floor. There it manned the entrances to the building, alternately vigilant and indifferent as seven thousand ID cards were flashed before its uniformed eyes each morning. When something happened actually requiring their putative skills (escorting a fired employee from the building, searching for the very rare intruder), security sprang to life and showed an aggressive gung-honess.

The two men's keenness now was infectious; several people from A.I. Alley emerged from cubicles and followed them down the aisle. After a few minutes one of them returned, and Madison saw with a start that it was Sally Zehring. 'What is she doing here?' he demanded.

'Relax, it's not a conspiracy to upset you, Madison.'

'I thought she was off-site at MIT.'

'She came back last month. I guess Sammy Ling wanted her close at hand.'

'I can't believe that's serious. She can't possibly like the guy.'

Pistolet started to speak, but stopped. 'Back in a minute,' he said suddenly, and went down to Sally's cubicle. Madison watched him with a sudden terrible sense of mental agitation. Pistolet soon returned, smiling broadly. 'Sally says it's a false alarm. For a minute I thought we had a jumper.'

'What?'

'You know.' He made a whistling sound like a bomb dropped from a B-52 in a documentary, ending in the low registers by saying, 'SPLAT.' He paused briefly then continued, 'We had one six weeks ago. Someone in graphics named Dirleck.'

'Dirleck? I know Dirleck. His wife teaches at Harvard. I sent him a poster he wanted of Oxford – a photo of the dreaming spires.'

45

'I know. I've got it at home. I decided he'd want me to have it.'

'What happened to him?'

'He was included in the last lay-off; they gave him two weeks notice and he jumped that day. Funny that, I bet management was pissed he didn't wait and work the fourteen days. If you want to use a phone his cubicle is free now. One could mind the plants, as you Anglophiles would say. There's no reason they have to die, too.'

'Jesus.' Madison looked up at the ceiling tiles. 'I don't think I could stand it here.'

'Maybe you could. The Prince of Parsing Returns. We'll welcome you with open arms. Even Sally.'

Madison shook his head. 'No way.'

'Well, it was a pleasure working with you.' And Pistolet turned back to his screen. Madison watched for a while as Pistolet worked on a LISP routine, then left this parenthetical world to go and see Cromwell.

3

'So, McDonald's or wholesome food?' asked Cromwell.

'McDonald's? I thought you said we couldn't go out.'

'I can't, but there's a McDonald's in East Nave now. Opened last month.'

'You're joking. How did the company persuade them to do that?'

'It wasn't very hard. There are seven thousand people working in the four Naves. That's a big enough market for a franchise.'

'I'd have thought most employees ate salad and yogurt.'

'That's just R & D. There are plenty of Irish peasants like me who want nothing better than a Big Mac and fries. Come on, I'm buying.' When Madison looked reluctant, Cromwell said, 'Don't be so snooty. Your friend Pistolet eats there all the time.'

'So?'

'So he's from a toney family, too. Though what kind of name is Pistolet? He sounds like a Canuck, not a Yankee.'

'It's French; his father's from New Orleans. His mother's a Forbes.'

'His mother's a what?' asked Cromwell.

'A Forbes. Of the Boston Forbeses. "The Lowells speak only to Cabots and the Cabots speak only to God." Well, the Forbes find even talking to God a little vulgar.'

'How do you know all that?'

'We went to the same school.'

'Oh yeah, you two went to school with Sammy Ling.'

Madison stiffened. 'I prefer to think he went to school with us.'

'One of those boarding schools, I suppose. Christ, I'm surrounded by the upper class.'

'I'm not upper class. I'm a common man. With a common touch.'

'I thought this town was named after your great-great-great-grandfather. And even I've heard of your father.'

'Look what it's done for me. I still have to eat lunch in McDonald's with an Irishman.' He added fairly hastily, 'Just kidding.'

'You know,' said Cromwell, returning to his original theme, 'your friend Pistolet is not some kind of lovable screw-off. He's just a screw-off, pure and simple.'

'But a very talented one.'

Cromwell sighed. 'I guess so, but sometimes I wonder whether it's worth putting up with. And I'm not the only one.'

True. To Minnie Lu, Pistolet was a *bête noire*; he seemed to revel in rubbing her up the wrong way. His periodic banishment from the A.I. group to the drudgery of assembler code usually came after one of his run-ins with her, and this inculcated a deep unease in Pistolet's peers, who worried that association with this maverick might mar their chances of advancement. Only Sally Zehring, through loyalty, and Madison, through longevity and a partly shared facility for impudence, were really friends of Pistolet.

There were no arches in this McDonald's, although the people taking orders wore the conventional uniform. Cromwell and Madison took their trays and found a table in the back of the cafeteria room, which was immensely long but low-ceilinged, painted in varying institutional colours, with a speckled white linoleum floor and the smell – a mix of disinfectant and too much white bread – of all cafeterias everywhere.

There was also an executive dining-room at Ling, but it served bad food and was wineless. For a company in a capitalist culture, Ling imposed a curious dreariness in its trappings, an egalitarianism that levelled down. The company was intended to comprise a classless society, cannily created by the Empress to rule out internal social schism. She had long before sensed that to hire cadres of snot-nosed Harvard brahmins would be disastrous: they would have sniffed at their fellow employees, and might well have challenged her own autocracy, seeing her as a very remarkable inventor, but what else would you expect from the Chinese? No, it was far better to surround herself with less sophisticated but diligent and grateful members of the upwardly mobile working-class. The odd Yankee, even an Ivy League grandee like Pistolet (or Madison, deny it though he would), could survive, but only by keeping his head down – and by working in R & D, since that suggested you were a thinker, a weirdo, no threat when it came to corporate politics.

'So how'd you get on with Minnie Lu?' asked Cromwell before biting into his Big Mac.

'Terrific. I think I'm in love.'

'Take it easy. Nothing's cut and dried; you should know that by now in this place. No one's telling you to come back right away.'

'Minnie Lu said two months.'

Cromwell looked surprised. 'She did? Oh golly, I'm sorry, Robert. I thought I'd bought you at least the third year. She promised me that. At least, I thought she did.'

'That's not what she told me. Why the rush anyway?'

Cromwell finished a French fry before replying. 'Things have been better here. I think she feels a certain urgency that maybe she didn't feel when I spoke to her.'

'When was that?'

'Only last week,' Cromwell admitted. 'But results are due in two weeks; she's probably heard they're going to be bad. Everybody knows they're certainly not going to be good.'

'So what else is new?'

'It's a little more desperate than usual. Frankly, hardware sales are shot. I wouldn't want to say it too loud because this *is* a hardware company. But you have to be realistic. In three years, maybe as many as five, everybody's going to have more power in a desktop computer than they'll know what to do with. Four, five megabytes of RAM, as much storage as you need – I mean, gigabytes if they want them, whether on optical discs or even outsized Winchesters – full multi-tasking, the speed of the 80386 chip – what more does anyone want?'

Madison suddenly realised he had been too long in the computer industry, for he had understood every word Cromwell had said. He said, 'You sound just like one of our ads.'

'Aren't they terrific? Anyway, what will the hardware I'm talking about cost – two grand? Maybe three? Maybe five hundred dollars if the Japanese are allowed in. Whatever it costs, the margins will be trivial, next to nothing. So what's going to make us money?'

'Software.'

'Precisely, and not just any old software. What are we going to do, claim our spreadsheets are better than Lotus? Say we make better PC language than MicroSoft? We were once the leading text-processing company in the world; I bet next to IBM and Wang we still have more word-processing terminals installed than anyone else. But our edge is gone. And it's getting worse. In large installations we're getting undercut; in the stand-alone market we just haven't been a player. And that's what we have to change.'

'How? You can't just launch our standard package as a low-end program and expect customers to fall over themselves. Expectations are much higher now; every executive thinks he knows what's what, thanks to his little boy's PC at home.'

'We're going to have to build a really super package, with every bell and whistle we can find. All the value-added material: spellers, style alerts – these are prerequisites now. But we also need something entirely different, something really innovative. Something intelligent.'

'Don't use that word, please.' Madison had a haunting feeling he knew what was coming.

'They'll put a Natural Language front-end on the thing.'

'So you can type "Edit the last uninteresting memo I wrote" without using a menu, and the machine will know what to do? Whoopee.'

'I agree it's no big deal. What *can* we use to make this really sing? To catch the customer's eye, win us publicity, get us back into position as a leader?'

'And?'

'And the answer is *Write Right*, a new program using the latest in Artificial Intelligence techniques that helps you write a document and tells you what you've done wrong when you write.'

Madison chewed on the ice from his coke. 'Very interesting,' he said blandly.

'I'm sure Minnie Lu would want you to show a little more enthusiasm.'

'Thanks but no thanks. I'd rather just stick to document generation.'

'I'm sure you would. But let's face it, Robert, you've had two years and haven't really gotten anywhere. We all admire the research, and certainly you're on the cutting edge of the text-generation field. But the cutting edge just isn't cutting it.'

'And *Write Right* is? Sounds to me like it's two years off and of questionable value in any case.'

Cromwell shook his head. 'I don't think you really believe what you're saying. To do it well will take a team with a real leader, an expert at Natural Language Processing.'

Natural Language – in such unnatural times, words fallen out of nature into a world neither man's nor Mother Earth's, but the habitat of machines. Machines, marketing, merchandise, *machismo*, mercenary, monolith – what Sally Zehring had called the 'dangerous M' words.

Cromwell was saying, 'Someone with some genius for linguistics. PhD level of course, an expert in parsing, and the generative side – that's what they call it, isn't it? And he needs LISP at a nuts-and-bolts level; he's got to understand the code, even if he's not writing it himself.'

'Why do you keep saying *he*?' Madison asked with irritation, trying to steer the conversation away from its obvious end. 'People Resource wouldn't approve of your sexism. I imagine there are many women qualified for this post you're talking about. What about Sally

Zehring? She has a PhD in linguistics; she's an expert on the generative side.'

Cromwell shook his head. 'She may be doing other things soon. No, the consensus seems to be that only one person really fits the bill. He's a little flakey, maybe, used to be an academic after all, but uniquely qualified.'

'Are you talking about me again?' said Pistolet, putting a tray on the table and sitting down with them.

'Saved by the gun,' said Madison. 'Or should I say, the pistol?'

Two other men also sat down. One was an old A.I. hand named Jimmy Greenfield; notoriously morose and prickly, he got along well with none of his colleagues, and fared especially badly with Pistolet. The other man was a stranger to Madison; Pistolet introduced him, saying, 'This is Edward Morgenstern. He joined the group in December. He used to be in database design for DEC, poor bastard.' Madison stared at perhaps the thinnest human being he had ever encountered, dressed in classic R & D outfit of faded sweater and jeans.

Morgenstern wrapped pencil-like fingers around Madison's hand and said eagerly, 'I've read your book.'

'Ah,' Madison was non-committal. How the past would intrude.

'Yes, it was what first got me interested in parsing. I probably wouldn't be here today if I hadn't read it.'

'Should we consider that a cause for thanks or regret?' mused Pistolet. 'I wonder. You may think you speak in Natural Language, tongue of angels, the universal grammar that will set us free. But you linguists speak the lingo of the lost. Here Code is King. And don't you forget it.'

'We'll talk some more later,' Cromwell said ominously to Madison, and got up to leave. 'There's a one o'clock in Conference Room Three, East Nave, tenth floor. I would appreciate your being there.'

'Where else would I be? You've scheduled me.'

'Precisely,' said Cromwell, and left.

'What was that about?' asked Pistolet.

'My invitation from Minnie Lu to join you guys in the manifest pleasures of Cathedral life.'

'Oh,' said Morgenstern perkily, 'like an offer you cannot refuse. The Tong is hard to turn down, I gather.' Madison noticed that he had two large orders of French fries on his place, along with a Big Mac, a milk-shake, and a hot apple pie. Where did the calories go? he wondered, looking at the man's ectomorphic frame.

'Don't be racialist,' Pistolet told Morgenstern in a bad imitation of an English accent.

'I'm not racialist; I'm Jewish. We're the white man's Chinamen.'

'What?' said Madison.

'Sure,' said Morgenstern confidently. 'Actually, the Chinese-Americans are this generation's Jews. Thirty years ago the Westinghouse Science Prizes for budding high-school geniuses used to go in numbers way out of proportion to people named Goldberg. Or Morgenstern, for that matter. Nowadays there's the same imbalance, only the winners have names like Wong, or Chan, or Lee.' He took an enormous bite from his Big Mac.

'So what?' asked an unimpressed Greenfield.

'It's a repeat of what happened to earlier immigrants. The Asian-Americans are like the Jews of the 1930s – not the *echt Deutsch* kind from *Our Crowd*, but the Eastern Europeans who came over with nothing. They worked hard, made their kids go to school, ran little shops nobody else could be bothered to run – sound familiar? But now instead of Manny Nathan's boy winning the scholarship to MIT, it's Carey Lu's. Both groups, Asians and Jews, embody industry, thrift, a faith in the family, a belief in education. Both groups have all these American virtues – *and everybody else hates them.*'

53

'No they don't,' said Madison. 'I don't, anyway.'

'You probably do,' said Pistolet. 'You just try very hard not to show it.'

'The way this guy Sammy Ling runs things,' Morgenstern remarked, 'I can't really blame you.' They all laughed – even Greenfield – and Morgenstern looked puzzled.

'Tell me,' Madison said to him, 'have you actually seen Sammy Ling yet?'

'No. I meant to go to the shareholders' meeting, but I had a bug to fix in the C compiler.'

'If you saw him you might be surprised.'

'Why? Is he a big guy? There are some tall Asians, you know.'

'Yes,' said Madison, 'he's a big guy all right. But that's not all.'

'What is it, then? Is he handicapped?'

Pistolet answered him. 'You could say that. In the eyes of some of his relatives he probably is. In fact, some of them probably wish the Empress had put Sammy out on a mountain-top to die. Just like Octopus, or whatever his name was. You see, Sammy looks just like you and me. *He's a white boy*. And to the Chinese that can be a bit of a drawback. You may think *we're* racist, but believe me, we've got nothing on them.'

'Is Sammy's father white?'

'Yep,' said Pistolet. 'And so's the mother. Sammy Ling's not only white, he's *adopted*.'

'Jesus! But why adopt a white kid?'

Pistolet shrugged. 'Beats me. Maybe they ran out of Asians that year. Why don't you ask the Empress?'

'Yeah,' said Greenfield sourly. 'I dare you.'

'We'll give you a dollar,' said Madison.

'I surrender,' said Morgenstern, 'but I still don't get it.'

Pistolet stood up to leave. 'I'm sure the Empress would be very concerned that you don't understand.'

4

Madison went upstairs alone. He'd always imagined he admired the Chinese-Americans, respected the industry with which they clambered up the greasy pole of American life. Greenfield said that linked them to the Jews. But the Jews were no longer mysterious while the Chinese still were. Perhaps another generation's worth of MIT education, pens in white shirt pockets and black tie-shoes, would wipe out their exotic aura, but at present there were echoes, in even the youngest of Ivy-Leaguers among these Asian-Americans, of junks with ragged sails in Hong Kong harbour, streets filled with cage-held snakes and dogs awaiting their places on restaurant menus. This *was* racist, but the echoes persisted nonetheless.

So why, since the Empress had never married, had she adopted young Sammy? To have an heir, presumably, but why a *white* heir? As the Empress had in recent years taken a smaller role in the day-to-day operations of the company, so Sammy had assumed greater responsibility, until now, in his mid-thirties, he was the chief executive officer – or in Ling parlance, Archbishop. Yet as a white man at the top of an Asian–American company, Sammy Ling sat like a Gibraltar transplanted to the Great Plains, like a carbuncle on the face of Brooke Shields. Sammy could speak Chinese, after a prep-school fashion; he could play mah-jong with the best; but his big balding head, his six-foot frame and his bulging nose meant nobody, anywhere, was ever fooled into thinking he was Chinese.

Which made it odd that there lingered at Ling not only

a whiff of ginger-and-soy-sauce-stained chopsticks, but also a sense of cabals and closed doors, of Masonic-like ritual linking the Asian employees. A strong feeling of exclusion ran amongst the *non*-Asian employees that not even Sammy Ling's pink cheeks, and an official policy of egalitarianism, could suppress.

Early for the meeting, Madison paced around the corridors of the tenth floor. He was on edge, for he usually worked in almost unbroken isolation, seeing very few people, and seeing them alone when he did. Yet at Ling everyone seemed to do nothing but attend meetings. Sometimes after a week at headquarters Madison would come away wondering how any products got made – how, indeed, the company survived.

Pistolet was beckoning him from the elevators. 'Why are you waiting down there? The meeting's in East Nave.'

'That *is* East Nave.'

'Suit yourself,' said Pistolet. 'But Cromwell and everyone else is over here.'

Madison sighed and followed Pistolet to a conference room in East Nave. It was a small room with a large table and many people crowded around it. The meeting was just starting as they arrived.

'Nice of you to join us,' said Cromwell sharply, then adopted a chairman-like tone. 'All right, let's get started.'

Madison examined his assembled colleagues, recognising most of them. There was Pistolet, Greenfield, Morganstern, Sally Zehring and himself from Natural Language Processing group. At one end of the table sat three men who worked on Speech Recognition and managed to be silent most of the time. Then there were half a dozen Expert Systems people basking in the new cachet of knowledge-based systems. Finally, there were two Cognitive Modellers, both fierce, attractive women with raven hair and swarthy skin; MIT PhDs both, they scared most people.

'I have an announcement to make that affects everyone here,' Cromwell announced dramatically.

'Re-org,' Pistolet sang out in two long syllables. Cromwell blushed and struggled to control himself. 'As of this Friday,' he said formally, 'you will be working under a different reporting structure. All of the groups you represent are going to be part of one group which will be called Intelligent Systems.'

'Semi-intelligent systems,' said Pistolet, and Madison knew right away that his friend had gone too far.

'Shut up!' Cromwell suddenly shouted, and the room went entirely silent. He blushed even deeper. 'I mean, would you please let me finish?'

He continued, 'This new group will not be led by me. Lisa Adams will be its Vicar and from Friday you will report to her. Please sign the necessary paperwork by Monday morning at the latest: you'll probably receive it tomorrow.'

Madison looked at Pistolet. 'Who is Lisa Adams?' he whispered.

'The Blue Rinse Lady,' Pistolet answered back. His propensity for coining nicknames sometimes seemed inexhaustible; on each trip to the Cathedral Madison felt like a Bletchley decoder during the War, trying to catch up with his colleague after three months' sick-leave.

Cromwell said, 'Lisa will be joining us in about five minutes to talk about the company's plans for the group. Before she gets here, do any of you have questions?'

'Yes,' said one of the Expert Systems people. 'Why yet another reorganisation and why in this form?'

'You must be new here,' Pistolet remarked, 'if you expect reasons for re-orgs.'

Cromwell ignored him now. 'There is a feeling upstairs that our efforts in Artificial Intelligence are not paying off. There have been no products, and many projects are seen as excessively open-ended.' He looked at Madison pointedly, Madison decided, feeling suddenly paranoid. 'They're losing patience upstairs, so it was thought advantageous to merge all the A.I.-related groups and develop a unified strategy.'

'Nobody else is any further along with products,' the questioner said. 'It's not as if we're losing the race.'

Cromwell shook his head. 'Who's to tell? IBM may come out with something tomorrow that's terrific.'

'So might we.'

'What?' Pistolet interjected. 'Madison's document generation project? It will write a letter stating the opposite of what you intended in just under twenty minutes.'

'Shut up,' said Madison, punching Pistolet only semiplayfully on the shoulder. 'I am approaching a breakthrough point.'

'Here's Lisa now,' said Cromwell, and Madison quickly saw why Pistolet had called her the Blue Rinse Lady. It was not because of her age – far from it – or ostensible gentility, but because across her large nest of curly blonde hair ran a band of grey that also contained a distinct, though subtle, bluish tinge. It was not just this Punkish allusion Madison found unusual: average in height, Lisa Adams had a clear, stunning face and zinging eyes that made her seem very much larger than life. She wore a bright red silk shirt, open at the neck, and black leather trousers that made her look leggy and, to Madison, very sexy indeed. As she reached the far end of the table Madison decided that she looked like a New York literary agent of precocious success and sublimated Lesbian tendency. His father had once had just such an agent.

This impression suffered when she opened her mouth. 'Go die,' she said harshly, leaning on both hands and clenching the end of the table; Madison did a small double-take before he realised she was Australian and merely saying hello. 'Let me get right to the point. As Gus may have told you, there's a feeling in senior management that our A.I. efforts haven't jelled yet. Because it's thought to be such a key area, I've been called in to set up a coherent strategy for our A.I. development.'

Marketing had never been known for its modesty; still, Madison was a little amazed by this casual assertion of self-importance. Gus Cromwell looked decidedly grim, and Madison suddenly felt certain that the change in his superior's responsibilities could not be considered a promotion.

'It's a bit early,' said Lisa Adams, 'for me to have any strong opinions yet. When I reach them, though, don't worry – you'll hear them. For instance, why is everything you guys do written in LISP? I'd have thought C would be more useful.'

'Not really,' said Madison.

Lisa looked at him blankly. 'Are you a LISP fanatic?' she asked.

'Since childhood,' Pistolet interjected. He pointed a long finger at Madison. 'This man "lisped in numbers fore the numbers came".'

'Come on,' said Cromwell. 'Listen up, you two.'

'Sorry,' said Pistolet without conviction. 'I was thinking of his father.'

'Shut up,' said Madison, and he meant it.

Lisa Adams looked right through Pistolet and kept talking. 'What I'd first like to do is see a demonstration of what all of you have developed. I've talked with Gus and he's suggested Thursday morning. At the same time I want to meet you individually, then start to develop a strategy. That's when we can all meet together again, lock the doors and go at it.' Lest anyone think she meant to reconvene for orgiastic purposes, she added, 'Really hammer out a strategy. Okay?'

No one said anything, and the meeting adjourned. When Madison signed the list for individual appointments with her, he felt Lisa's eyes coolly appraising him. He noticed that all the times were for the following week and explained that by then, blessedly, he would be back in England.

'England? You don't sound like a Pom.'

'I'm not.'

'So what are you doing over there?'

'Many vital and important things.'

She was not certain how to take this, and asked his name. When he told her, she nodded. 'I know you. You're the man of the moment. We've got to talk. How about tomorrow morning?'

'Sure. What time?'

'How about eight fifteen?'

He tried not to blanch too obviously. 'I've got a breakfast meeting, actually,' he lied smoothly. 'How about later on? Say ten?'

'Ten fifteen,' she said, consulting a diary. Madison felt the unprofessional lack of one. 'I can give you fifteen minutes.'

Since it was she who wanted to see *him*, fifteen minutes struck Madison as ample. 'Where do you live?'

'Near Nashua,' she said, then laughed. 'Oh, you mean here. Down from Gus Cromwell. This floor.'

'See you tomorrow.'

In the hall he saw Cromwell and Pistolet talking, presumably about the demo Lisa Adams had commanded, so he moved quickly away towards the elevators. It was vital not to become involved in any other meetings: there was only so much he could take on the first day of his visit. He decided to go and see International on the fourth floor, where he was usually a welcome visitor since he worked overseas.

Waiting for the elevator, Madison was suddenly confronted by a terrible sight. Olney, Macaulay and Smith: a trio of senior managers from Personnel – or People

60

Resource as it was called at Ling. Professional nice guys – decent, clubbable, straightforward men, Dartmouth graduates all, bachelor degrees in affability. 'Bring your sticks next time,' they'd say, learning that Madison played golf. 'Is there a Mrs Madison?' they would inquire on the way to arranging barbecues at the Ling Country Club.

They were also the company hit-men. When an employee was fired, some managers (such as Minnie Lu) seemed to relish supervising each step of the severing process, but most found it entirely repugnant. It was then that People Resource – and Olney, Macaulay and Smith in particular – were called in. Gone the personable masks, away with the back-slapping bonhomie; joined by an officious representative of security, Olney (or Macaulay, or Smith) would stand guard and watch as the employee cleaned out his or her cubicle. It was harsh, authoritarian – and intelligent, since five minutes alone at a terminal were enough for a disgruntled ex-employee to cripple an entire system for months.

People Resource would also argue that it functioned as the company's version of the Environmental Protection Agency, available to help with 'human' difficulties, chiefly psychological. The three men approaching Madison themselves claimed to have prevented several homicides (one, interestingly enough, a boss wanting to kill a subordinate), many suicides, a dozen or so nervous breakdowns. Their Samaritanism was subject to the constraints of corporate economy: if the likelihood of an employee regaining full working status was slim, less time was spent on him.

An elevator opened and Madison shot into it; he was about to sigh with relief when a hand protruded between the closing doors, and the terrible trio walked in, beefy, big, and smiling.

They never forgot a face or name: Madison was no exception. 'So how's jolly old England?' one of them asked. Was the questioner Olney, Macaulay, or Smith?

Did they themselves know?

'Fine, fine,' said Madison, jabbing at buttons – anything to stop the elevator and let him get away.

'Over here to get in out of the rain?' another one said, and slapped Madison roughly on the back. The doors opened and Madison rushed out, waving a farewell vaguely behind him. He was not on the fourth floor, however, but on the sixth; he could see the company library down the hall. Forget International for now, he decided, and went to hide in the reading room. There, only a few engineers were studying arcane periodicals, and Madison looked fruitlessly for the librarian. A pretty woman from Indiana, she was shy and unknowledgeable about computers. He had persuaded her to subscribe to the *Times Literary Supplement* to ensure he had something to read on his rare visits, but she had drawn the line at *Esquire*. Now he picked up the *TLS* and the latest *InfoWorld* and went to sit in a far corner, hidden from the door.

He looked at *InfoWorld* and its reviews of the latest microcomputer software. A product caught his eye: A.I. Speller. Here was a program, the advertisement said, that used intelligence to 'help your documents read right'. He read on with amused fascination. Intelligence my ass, he thought. This was a simple spelling verifier, running concurrently as the user typed a document, with its dictionary compressed and thrown into RAM. Old stuff in a new package.

He looked at his watch. It was barely three o'clock: too early to go back to the hotel, though he could certainly use a drink – it was eight o'clock in the evening at home. He suddenly remembered that Pistolet knew how to cope with boredom in the Cathedral. Madison got up from his seat and went to the rear of the library and its room of stacks. There were only three rows of them, but the room holding them rose two floors in height, with a spiral staircase rising to a steel balcony that ran right round the room. This had been a rare moment of expansiveness for the architect; even in the executive Spires there were no rooms two floors high.

Technical journals covered the wall on one side, and Madison walked around the catwalk balcony to look at them. He was not sure which one he was searching for: it was a choice between *Computational History* and the *Journal of Electronics and Telecommunications*, both dating from the 50's and bound annually in thick red vinyl boards. 'Nobody reads them,' Pistolet had confidently asserted when explaining his choice of hiding-place. 'Nobody reads anything at Ling except their own memoranda.'

Madison began delicately pulling out early volumes of *Computational History*, first looking down to see if he was being watched from below. He was not; turning to the journals, he hit pay-dirt on the fifth volume he extracted. Wedged in the back of the shelf was a tin First Aid kit with a rusting Red Cross seal across its front. Opening it carefully, Madison discovered a paperback copy of *Lucky Jim* and a pint of Scotch. There was always something in the way of a sweetener: one year a joint, once a half-bottle of Château Margaux. Since he thought it unlikely he would be asked to kiss Minnie Lu, at least not this afternoon, Madison risked whisky fumes on his breath and took a long pull. He returned the bottle to its place in the tin, and carried *Lucky Jim* down to a carrel on the floor below with a *déjà vu*-inspired frisson of fear: Pistolet had once been caught reading that very copy of the novel by Minnie Lu when he was supposed to be meeting two hardware engineers.

Madison lost all track of time in the mixed world of Jim Dixon and memories of his own early days at Ling. Ah Sally, how odd it had been to see her again; having decided she was out of his life, he'd assumed she would not be around to remind him of the time when she was so much a part of it. Why had he assumed that? 'What does that signify, Robert?' as Sally would say, her voice growing gravelly after two bourbons, her laugh lower. Stop it. That was all in the past; nurse it, and it was guaranteed to hurt.

At the end of a chapter he noted with surprise that it was half past five. Quietly he returned the novel to its hiding-place, then went upstairs to the eighth floor and the cubicle he had been assigned for the week. There was no one about, a sure sign that morale was low at Ling: when it was high, developers never watched the clock, but flagging revenues, rumoured lay-offs, anticipated pay-cuts meant the attention of a software engineer turned all too rapidly to home and family.

Madison collected his briefcase from his cubicle and made his way out of the building. It was a warm day for April, and as he came through the revolving doors and past a security guard, there was little change in temperature. Later in summer it would feel like leaving a fridge for a frying-pan.

Moving through the parking lot, he examined the curious collection of cars around him: a major Yuppie component of Datsuns and Golfs – R & D types pretending they were still in Cambridge; the pseudo-redneck airs of the hardware engineers, represented by Dodge pick-ups and an occasional jeep; the opulent sliminess of Marketing, shiny in tan Mercurys, even the occasional foreshortened Cadillac. What was perhaps surprising was the number of old cars, slightly dented, rust-prone, in need of a wash. Perhaps the result of the new insecurity at Ling: why spend money on a new car when you might not have the mortgage in hand the following month?

Yet it was not *what* you parked at Ling, but *where* you parked that mattered. Bishops had special places reserved near the Cathedral; Deans and Deacons filled the spaces slightly further away. Winners of monthly 'Ling Merit' awards were allowed to park for one week relatively close to the buildings. Otherwise it was dog-eat-dog in the daily battle for proximity parking: the lot stretched for a mile and a half over asphalt-covered Massachusetts marsh. During the company's fat years, to arrive after eight thirty in the morning meant having to park in the furthest reaches of the parking lot, a long cold hike in the dead of winter. Since the lay-offs of two years before, the worst walk was three-quarters of a mile.

Madison found his rented car with less trouble than usual, and drove to the hotel. He checked in, and the young girl at reception giggled at his surname and its eponymous link with the town. 'You have family here?' she said jocularly, and he smiled. There was no one left that he knew of; his ancestors had moved north to Vermont at the turn of the century, after taking an inordinate share of the wealth created by the nineteenth-century commercial explosion in textiles.

His room was spacious and utterly impersonal, but at least it was convenient and not uncomfortable. Since it was owned by Ling Enterprises, it was also not expensive. Madison poured himself a whisky from his duty-free bottle and looked out of his third-floor window. An uninspiring view over the horseshoe parking lot in front of the hotel; in the background, improbably, sat a large white pine church with a handsome bell-tower. Closer inspection revealed it to be the headquarters of a savings and loan association.

He lay down on the bed and dialled the U.K.; it took a long time for the connection to go through. He let it ring for almost five minutes to no avail, entranced by the rhythmic double pulse and the image he had of the phone in the upstairs bedroom of his house. Catherine wasn't there. He wondered if the dog was on his bed, awakened by the phone.

Giving up, he tried his mother in Vermont, but got

no answer there either. He would try again later, but now he went down to the lobby, which was full of the overspill from the hotel's downstairs bar. Most of them were Ling employees – he could tell by the name tags they had forgotten to discard when they left the Cathedral, or simply by their sales rep costumes and loud, jokey behaviour. Madison felt he was among representatives of the American Dream: salesmen, marketers, gung-ho boys who wore suits, chomped steaks and drank Scotch, but also jogged, and knew their California wines.

Madison ordered a bourbon and took a seat by the windows which looked out over the river. It was just now turning dark. When he had finished his drink, he walked towards the elevators, and passing the dark, cavernous bar, thought for a moment he saw Sammy Ling – then decided he hadn't. Relieved, he stopped at the news-stand and bought the *New Yorker*; but returning to the elevators, he passed a tall man in aviator glasses and realised with a start that it was Sammy Ling's bodyguard. They had met two years before, when Madison was about to leave for England. The bodyguard had been assigned to 'brief' Madison on the dangers of international travel – this after a couple of hijackings had put otherwise grown-up Americans into a paralysis. Almost inevitably, it had turned out that the bodyguard's sole excursion 'abroad' had been a weekend in Mexico.

In his room Madison ordered a small steak and salad and half a bottle of California Cabernet. He ate slowly, turning the pages of the *New Yorker*. Afterwards he dialled his mother again, and let the phone ring twelve times before hanging up. I tried, he told himself. He would wait now until the next day: unless something had greatly changed, after eight o'clock in the evening she would be virtually incapable of speech. Jet-lag and a new sense of depression served suddenly to fatigue him, and he fell asleep.

He dreamt that he had children, three sons, to whom he was recounting tales of his father. His boys found these accounts incredible. They were unimpressed that their grandfather had been Ivy League Middleweight Boxing champion as a sophomore at Harvard, had watched the Normandy landings first-hand as a correspondent, was a great shot, a fine fisherman; as the recital progressed, they began yawning. Madison, overwhelmed by the futility of his narrative attempts, awoke – to find himself son-less, the television and lights on, and seized by a tremendous thirst. His watch said it was three o'clock in the morning. He went to the bathroom and drank straight from the tap, then turned off the television and lights and fell back to sleep.

This time he dreamt that his father had died, and he stood in the small Vermont town where he had been born and brought up, feeling an immense sadness and a haunting sense of guilt. He stood in front of his aunt Peg's store. She, who had helped raise him, was standing there helpless at his grief. She went back into the store and he felt utterly alone. Somewhere a voice intoned two lines from one of his father's poems:

> Blue is not your dying
> in an old country store . . .

This time when he woke it was light outside, though it was very early, not even six o'clock. He felt drained by his dream and only half-believed at first that his father was not dead. He had not seen him in over four years, or talked to him in over two. News of his marriage must have triggered the dreams. Did he, Robert Madison, want his father dead, as a Freudian would say about the dream? – for it was *his* dream, his creation. He had thought his aversion to his father was behind him now. 'Do something real'; their last conversation had been the night before Madison left for England. So scornful of England his father was; understandably, perhaps, since his ex-wife – Madison's mother – was British. The other target of his contempt had been more provocative; the old man wouldn't leave it alone. 'A.I.,' he'd boomed over the phone, 'what the hell is that? An Anglican version of *oi vey*?' Worse was to come two months later when Pistolet sent him a copy of the *New Yorker* with his father's now famous satiric poem about computers splashed across two pages. What was it called? 'The Irishman from IBM.' That was it.

He showered and dressed quickly to escape the room and the residue of his dreams, then ate a large breakfast of waffles and sausage in the hotel dining-room. He shared his table with a Ling sales rep from Grosse Point, Michigan, who talked gloomily about the company's pending quarterly results. Profits would be virtually ectomorphic – like Morganstern.

It was not yet eight o'clock when Madison arrived at the Cathedral, but already the ground-floor cafeteria was full of doughnut-eaters. He collected a coffee in a large styrofoam cup and went out to the elevators. He thought of taking the express lifts, which skipped the first seven floors and began their stops at the eighth. At least, they did so in theory; in practice they were inclined to rebel, and zoom straight to the Spires. There they opened onto a large central lobby with stunning abstract Expressionist oils on the walls, furnished with expensive designer couches in what Pistolet called turd-coloured calf.

In the Spires were the offices of the company's senior executives: the Empress, Sammy Ling, many Bishops. Visits were by invitation only, which naturally made uninvited trips a favourite diversion of Pistolet's. He liked to take the elevators up and wander around, snitching the odd ashtray from the Italian marble coffee tables, telling the worried-looking secretaries that he was very important.

Taking the local lift, Madison listened to the talk of his fellow passengers: raquetball, the odds on Sammy Ling getting married, and somebody's car trouble – in that order. Madison got out on the eighth floor and walked to his temporary cubicle. Pistolet was there, writing him a note.

'Lunch out today, my man,' said Pistolet cheerily.

'Where? I am not going to McDonald's.'

'Wherever you like. Sally Zehring wants real food, so let's hit it, dude.'

'It's too early to talk like that. Anyway, I don't want to have lunch with her.'

'Oh come on, man, the girl's mad about you. Do the right thing. Just sit back and think of England.'

'Forget it. Life's bad enough without that. I've got Lisa Adams later this morning.'

'You know the routine?'

'No. Tell me.'

'It's simple, really,' said Pistolet, elongating the last word in a mock-Australian drawl. 'The Blue Rinse Lady has a Theory of Personality. It says that the world is full of, and I quote, "Wankers, Shakers, Plodders and Fakers". What's a wanker, by the way?'

'Pud-puller,' said Madison. 'Jerk-off.'

'I thought it was something attractive like that. Anyway, the Blue Rinse Lady claims to have derived this theory from astrology, in which she also devoutly believes. She is not a stupid lady, but after you've heard this theoretical crap twice you realise that, far from being a brilliant blueprint of the world, it's just a pretentious way of labelling the hundreds of people she doesn't like, and the two or three people she does.'

'Just what I need.'

'Don't worry, it gets worse. The Welsh Lunatic is looking for you.'

'No!'

'I kid you not; he was on the floor a little while ago. I told him you were in a meeting in International. I should have said you were stuffing your face at company expense in the hotel. I love breakfast.'

'And breakfast loves you. Where does the Welsh Lunatic live now?'

'He's got the big corner down from Cromwell on the tenth floor. Be polite: he's a Dean now and rumour has it he'll be a Bishop one of these days.'

'I will bow and scrape when I see him.' Madison grew serious for a moment. 'Isn't there some way I can avoid him?'

Pistolet shook his head. 'It's not really you he wants. I got work to do. See you at lunch.'

Madison nodded and sat down, feeling depressed. He opened his briefcase and looked at his notes. What notes? A Visa bill, long overdue; a golf card filled out in fading pencil. His new blueprint for document-creation lay strictly in his head.

'So how are you?' boomed the dreaded voice of Lewis Llewellyn Thomas.

Madison stood up self-consciously and Thomas pumped his hand. He was an unpleasant-looking man, short, with ferret eyes, a gaunt, pockmarked face and limp, greasy black hair. He had a sharp, canny mind, and a strong academic background in database design. There were only a few distant Celtic antecedents in his lineage, but Pistolet had seized on the abundance of l's in his many names to dub him the Welsh Lunatic. Both Pistolet and Madison knew the man's Christian names because Thomas had told him what they were; indeed, Thomas was usually happy to tell all to anyone: he would have told Beethoven about his weaker string quartets, informed Renoir that Andrew Wyeth had made his nudes superfluous. But the catholicity of his opinions did not dilute his one major interest, which, unfortunately for Madison, was poetry

70

– specifically, the poetry of Madison's father. As Sally had once remarked, 'The man's just ga-ga about your pa-pa.'

'Come on upstairs for a minute,' said Thomas. 'You don't seem very busy.'

There was no point in resisting; Madison would be forced to have a tête-à-tête at some point during the week. So he went resignedly up to Thomas's office, which had a stunning two-sided view east and north of the Cathedral. It gave Madison the slightest sense of vertigo, reinforced when Thomas conspiratorially closed the door behind them and motioned him to sit down. Sitting down at his desk, Thomas opened a lower drawer and extracted a purple folder from underneath a stack of papers. He faced Madison, lightly waving the folder with both hands, as if fanning himself. 'How is your work going?' he asked casually.

'Busy,' said Madison. This was a standard opening defence. He took a deep breath, ready to catalogue his achievements.

Thomas was not interested. 'Good,' he said curtly, 'glad to hear it.' With that out of the way, he turned to the real business in hand. Here a certain shyness crept into his manner. 'All well at home?'

At home? thought Madison. What home? His new house? He nodded dumbly.

'Parents well? Hear from your father?'

Ah, of course, that's what he was after. He nodded again. Thomas would have to work for this.

'He's well?' He paused. 'Is he writing much? They say he's at work on a long poem. Very long. A kind of *magnum opus*.'

'I couldn't say,' said Madison. For all he knew, the old prick had dried up completely. Serve the bastard right.

'I admired his last collection very much.' Thomas leaned his head back archly and recited a famous line from

The Love of Fairfield Station: '"The daily ritual that defers to the pain it provokes."' He looked at Madison and mistook embarrassment for enthusiasm. 'The title poem,' Thomas said appreciatively, 'simply stunning.' He continued quoting: '"Blue is not your dying/in an old country store."'

'What?' They were the same lines Madison had dreamt about the night before, and he could not contain his astonishment at the coincidence.

'You know, the title poem. What a talent,' said Thomas, looking down at the folder he continued to wave back and forth. Pursing his lips, he said softly, 'When you see your father next . . . '

'Yes?' prompted Madison.

'I'd like you to do two things.' Thomas was so used to giving orders that even this was not put as a request. Madison was damned if he would make even the smallest sign of assent.

'First, I'd like you to tell him how much his work means to one of his readers. I'd like to think I'm one of his better readers.' Thomas stared at Madison, who refused to nod. 'The other thing I'd like you to do is give him this.' He proffered the folder with both hands and Madison reluctantly accepted it.

'I'd like him to know that somewhere far away from him, another voice is at work. A kindred voice, I'd like to think, still unknown of course – but who knows, especially with a word from him, might not even the ficklest of publishers come forward? Tell him they are poems that require careful reading, much as his do, and with the same sensitivity, I hope, that his own work demands.' He finished this reverie by bowing his head. Looking up, he added quietly, 'Some of them may seem a little strange.'

A kindred spirit? Madison now remembered the opening lines of 'The Irishman from IBM':

Twenty-three years
makes the corporate kiss less chaste,
and wipes away the independent taste
that hovers on your lips like tears.

'I'll be happy to pass them on,' Madison said loudly,
standing up to go. 'But I wanted to ask you one favour.'

'Yes,' said Thomas slowly, a note of wariness entering
his voice.

'I've been working in England for two years. My
operations there are well established and, frankly, my
bosses here seem to think I've done good work. Gus
Cromwell does, anyway.'

'Good,' said Thomas without interest.

'There's just one thing. Minnie Lu called me into her
office yesterday morning and said she wanted me working
back here in the Cathedral by the end of Fall.'

'I heard something along those lines,' Thomas said with
a broad smile. 'To lead the *Write Right* project. It's a
wonderful move: congratulations. Let me know when you
move back for good so we can have another chat.'

Oh Christ, thought Madison, not him too. 'But you see,
it will throw my whole life upside-down.'

'Don't worry. The folks in People Resource have a
whole package to help you readjust. I'm told it works
really well.'

Which argument to pursue? The importance of document generation by machine – plead that, to this half-mad
amateur bard? Try a personal tack instead. 'I've just got
engaged to an English girl,' he lied.

'Congratulations. I'm sure she'll love it here. Bring her
to work in the Cathedral.'

'But you see,' Madison said, feeling he was talking to a
man with a white cane, 'we don't want to come back. We
want to stay over there.'

'Really?' asked Thomas with distaste, as if a tomcat had

73

decided to spray in the corner. 'I don't know what you expect me to do about it. You'll have to take it up with your own superiors. And Minnie Lu.'

'You've always seemed to take an interest.' Plaintive appeal; was he that desperate?

'Always happy to talk,' said Thomas, rising to indicate the interview was over. As Madison moved to the door Thomas said, 'Let me know as soon as you have any feedback.'

'What?'

'Feedback. From your father about my poems. Let me know as soon as you can.'

5

Lisa Adams's office was in the same Nave but there were fifteen minutes before he was due to see her, so he got a coffee at the end of the floor and went to sit in an empty conference room. Opening the folder, he saw that there were dozens of poems inside. They were mainly short poems, with an odd array of titles – 'On My Daughter's Birthday', 'Lady at Toilet', 'Air Sickness'. 'To a Turtle' caught his eye, and he read:

> O graceless oaf,
> whose green and loaf-
> shaped shell doth hold
> me in its bright and bold
> spell, do tell . . .

'Loaf-' – what kind of line-break was that? He could hear

his father's voice booming above him as he sat at the kitchen table, pages in hand: 'Who do you think you are, a half-wit like Robert Lowell?' Madison had been twelve years old then, and it was only weeks before his father left, all lessons in line-breaks gone forever.

There were several other poems stapled together with a covering title, 'Translations from the Esperanto', and one poem beginning

> Kreita lingvo, kiu multaj homoj
> alproprigis kiel unu etan pason

which Madison realised was *in* Esperanto. He could not bring himself to read more. He went to see the Blue Rinse Lady in a feisty frame of mind.

'Our A.I. efforts are not very productive,' she began promisingly.

'On the contrary, I think they're going very well.'

'Well, you're just about alone, pal,' she said curtly. 'We're no longer on the cusp, so I can't admire your patience. If we wait two or three years to bring out product, there may not be a company left to show it.'

'Artificial Intelligence may be a new technology, but believe me, there aren't any sudden breakthroughs in it. It's a hard slog.'

'It's not as though we've got anything to show for our slogging.'

'We will have,' said Madison. 'Expert Systems will have a shell out in six months.'

'What good is that?'

'Quite a lot. It allows someone who doesn't know anything about Expert Systems,' (like you, thought Madison, looking at her nodding at him) 'someone who doesn't know inference from reference, to create a knowledge base for his or her own business. It's perfect for insurance, or banking, or for our own diagnostics.' Expertise for the inexpert; the machine will set you free, free to stay stupid.

'Is there anything else?'

'Natural Language work. Jeffrey Pistolet will have an N.L. interface for information retrieval: you could use it on anything from the simplest database program to CD–ROM.' He decided not to say when. 'The Speech people – well, I know they're making progress but I can't predict the market there. Ask them. My work on automatic generation of documents is moving along nicely,' he added. Was it? No, not yet. Would it? There were so many schools of thought. So much of the small group of A.I. people involved in text-generation were head-cases, nuts really, loopy flakes. On the rare occasions he went to church, Madison made a prayer that he was not one of them. What had his father said? 'No machine will take over from me,' and more than once. We'll see, Pop.

'I suppose the chief reason to have a machine write for you is because you can't write yourself,' he continued, leaving the implications of the pronoun rudely vague – was 'you' here the American for 'one', or Lisa herself? He was doing rather well in seizing the initiative from this tough little Aussie. She was really quite pretty, he decided, thinking satisfied thoughts. The blue streak was rather interesting; in time he could almost grow to like it.

Suddenly Lisa jumped up and approached the blackboard – all the larger offices in the Cathedral were furnished with a markerboard and supplies of coloured felt pens. 'That's all very interesting,' she declared, 'now let me show you what's really going on.'

'Where?'

She looked at him coolly. 'Upstairs. With Virgil Peabody. And Sammy Ling. The Empress herself takes an interest. Minnie Lu, of course. And me.'

For the next fifteen minutes she drew whirling lines and square boxes and spoke with corporate gusto of her vision of A.I. At first this seemed simply to consist of the three units – Expert Systems, Natural Language Programs, and Speech Recognition – that Madison himself had just outlined to her. The difference came when she added something ominously entitled Future Developments. Under this she wrote in smaller letters, *Write Right*.

'Our goal here,' Lisa Adams declared, 'is nothing less than the automation of information creation, distribution, interchange and interpretation. That's what Sammy Ling himself has said.'

'Machine through machine to machine.'

'You got it, mate. Those were almost Sammy's exact words.'

The repeated invocation of the founder's son's name was a tactic that soon lost its force when overdone. When memos were sent out, especially by those at Vicar level and below, among the list of recipients there would suddenly pop up an improbably prominent name, such as Sammy Ling, or Virgil Peabody, the head of R & D. Typically, such memos addressed, say, the failure of employees to pay for their coffee; the more insignificant the memo, in fact, the more likely these names were to be found on its distribution list.

And when bobbing Sammy Ling's name in and out of her recital like an over-used yo-yo, Lisa Adams did not know how well Madison had once known Sammy, or how well his prep-school dislike had survived the metamorphosis of their relationship from classmates to employee and boss.

Sammy had transferred to Madison's school from one of lesser prestige, full of the sons of the newly rich – indeed, Sammy's old school's nickname had been St Goldblatt's. So the chips already stood out on young Sammy's wide shoulders, and they were only heightened on his first day at school when someone – Staley? Burgess? one of the dimmer athletes? – asked him what sport he hoped to play that Fall. 'Varsity football,' he'd declared. Back came the answer, 'You haven't got a Chinaman's chance in hell.'

Poor Sammy, odd vicarious offspring of a Chinese *entrepreneuse*, it could not have been easy for him to fit in. But others had, finding a hobby here, a friend there, while Sammy took pleasure only in football, the weight-room – and beating up the younger boys. Tellingly, Sammy had adapted to change by turning into the School Bully.

Apparently Lisa Adams was now asking him a question. 'I'm sorry,' Madison said, 'I'm not quite sure what you mean.' This was usually a safe way to have a question repeated, though capable of boomeranging when the query turned out to have been, 'What is your name?'

'I said, aren't there lots of products coming out of other companies that use A.I. techniques?'

'Really? I would have said very few. There are some Expert System shells and some large, pretty chunky Expert Systems *per se*. I don't know any good Natural Language front-ends. All the other parsers are still no faster or more accurate than ours.'

'What about spelling?'

He was baffled. 'Spelling?'

'Yes, like this.' And she shoved an *InfoWorld* towards him with the same advertisement for A.I. Speller that he had seen the day before. 'This sounds like A.I. to me,' she said accusingly.

'No, it's not.'

'It says it has an intelligent correction system. And Ryerson in Text Tools says we should have built something like this. In fact, he's built one himself – you'll see it at the demo tomorrow.'

'Who's Ryerson?'

'You'll meet him tomorrow. He may not have an A.I. background but I'm very impressed by his ideas.'

Madison sighed audibly. 'I have to tell you it's a case of the emperor's new clothes.' He was about to elucidate on this in fairly pompous style when Lisa Adams's phone rang in a peculiar, muted way. 'Excuse me,' she said tersely, 'that's the Spires.'

While she listened intently to the important person on the other end of the line, Madison thought about the preposterous claims of A.I. Speller. Spelling correction really *was* a case of the emperor's new clothes, for by far the greatest number of spelling mistakes people made were not in fact spelling errors, they were simply typos – and once a user had had the errors pointed out to him, he knew what to change and didn't need a program to tell him how. So why was so much time and research spent on spelling correction, on building phonetically-knowledgeable algorithms that could take the misspelled word 'nome' and suggest, as well as 'name', the word 'gnome'? Simply because it was *interesting*. Interesting, but futile. Spelling correction was the South Sea Bubble of the Artificial Intelligentsia.

'That's all I have to say,' announced Lisa Adams as she hung up the phone, making Madison wish she had said that before the phone rang. Keeping him waiting seemed a fairly juvenile way to demonstrate her authority. 'Anything you'd like to add?'

He shook his head. When he was leaving she got in her parting shot, 'We're all waiting for *Write Right*. I'm sure you won't let us down. See you at the demo tomorrow.'

Madison went downstairs to find Pistolet for lunch. Sally Zehring was in Pistolet's cubicle. She wore a blue skirt and a large bone-white sweater with loose sleeves she had rolled up to show off the early tan of her arms. This was slightly formal attire for her: in the past the uniform had been jeans and a Brooks Brothers shirt – usually blue, to match her eyes and contrast with her honey-blonde hair.

They said hello, for the first time in over a year, then stood subdued while Pistolet finished a routine. This could be very difficult; what was Madison to talk about to her? Pistolet would be useless as a buffer, indeed would delight in crassly embarrassing them both. Spying the thin figure of Morgenstern standing in A.I. Alley, Madison excused himself and went quickly to confront him. 'Are you busy right now?' he demanded.

Morgenstern looked startled. 'No. Why?'

'Come to lunch. Right now.' When he saw hesitation start to build in his victim's eyes, he added, 'On me. Come on.'

'Sure,' said Morgenstern, with the sound of a man who hadn't had a square meal in years. 'If you're buying.' He went to get his coat and joined them at the elevators.

They drove in Madison's rental car the two miles into town to Artie's Fish Shack. It was built like a diner, with counter-stools, and booths padded in red vinyl. The menu was written on chalk boards and there were six kinds of beer on tap. Madison ordered scallops, Sally and Morgenstern asked for fried clams (three orders, two of them for Morgenstern), and Pistolet casually ordered a broiled lobster. When they came, Madison's scallops were the size of half-dollars, fried to a crisp light brown. He squirted half a lemon over them in a generous stream and ate them slowly one by one, alternating their sea tang with bites of onion rings and an ice-cold Coors.

He managed to keep Pistolet off the topic of A.I. or his own status at Ling; Sally talked quite formally about a new algorithm. Half-listening, eating intently, Madison briefly forgot all about the threat of Minnie Lu.

'So,' said Morgenstern as he ate perhaps his fiftieth clam, 'are you easy to work for?'

'What?' said Madison, startled.

'He only has freelancers over in England,' Pistolet said. 'They're all complete loons but easy to manage. Isn't one of them named after a general – Eisenhower or Montgomery?'

'Wellington. He's not easy to manage. I tell him what to do, he nods politely, then he goes and does whatever he wants to do. He makes programmers look normal.'

'I'm sure you'll be a wonderful boss,' said Sally Zehring with a sarcasm that only Morgenstern would not detect. 'We're all looking forward to it.'

'I'm not sure I know what you're talking about,' said Madison, but of course he did.

'*Write Right*, of course,' said Morgenstern. 'I'd really like to talk to you about it. I've got some ideas of my own. I'm no longer certain the parser should be deterministic.'

'Really?' Madison said without enthusiasm.

'Yes, there's a lot of excitement about the project in the company.'

'From whom?'

Sally interjected, 'Sammy Ling for one.'

'That bozo,' Morgenstern said blithely. 'He almost ruined this company when he ran Finance, and look what happens – his mother promotes him. It's a wonder we're still in business.'

Sally went so suddenly quiet and blushed so deeply that even Morgenstern noticed. When she excused herself and went to the ladies' room, Morgenstern, mystified, asked, 'What did I say?'

'The worst thing you could say,' said Pistolet. 'Most people don't like to hear their fiancés called bozos, even if they are ones.'

'Meaning?'

'Look at her left hand when she comes back. From the size of it you could guess she's not engaged to your average software engineer.'

It was Madison's turn to act surprised. He was not the sort of person who noticed rings on people's hands – even

81

when the person concerned was an ex-girlfriend. 'She's gone that far?' he said. 'They're actually engaged? Why didn't you tell me?'

'I figured she would tell you herself. How did I know you'd spend half the week ducking her?'

'Oh my God,' said Morgenstern, 'there goes my future at Ling.'

'Relax,' said Pistolet. 'Sally won't say anything to Sammy Ling. I don't think she'll even hold it against you. To tell you the truth, she knows everybody thinks he's a jerk.'

'So how can she marry him?' asked Morgenstern.

Pistolet looked at him in amazement. 'What do you mean, how can she marry him? Because he'll be worth a billion dollars is how she can marry him. Shit, for a billion dollars *I'd* marry him.'

'So she's marrying him just for the money?'

'How can you say "just"? This isn't your average two-bit sleazebag promising the young bimbo a swimming pool if she hops in the hay. This is the big-time, jack, the plutocracy, the marital stratosphere. It's not as if she's going to ever have another shot at it. This is a once-in-a-lifetime opportunity. You can hardly blame the girl for being tempted.'

'Tempted?' Madison said. 'You said she's going to marry him.'

'Some days she gets cold feet. It's not Sammy that worries her so much, she says, but her future in-laws. Or in-law. She's not sure she can stand twenty years of mah-jong with the Empress. And the Empress isn't too wild about her either, at least racially, that is.' He turned to Morgenstern. 'They're even worse than you Jews about intermarriage. Sammy may be Caucasian, but to the Empress he's her boy, and that makes him honorary Chinese. And your presence,' he said wagging a finger at Madison, 'is not exactly what she needed to help accommodate herself to love with the young computer heir. You too have got a famous father, after all, even if it's put nothing in your pocket. That, and your fairly latent preppy charm, is proving disconcerting to the young lady. Here she comes. Don't let on you know, either of you – it's still supposed to be a secret.'

'Mr Discreet,' said Madison. For the rest of the lunch he stayed quiet, unexpectedly depressed by the news of Sally's engagement. He thought he'd learned not to be let down. Feelings are mad, bad, and dangerous to have.

They returned to work and he dropped the others off, then went to the far end of the lot to park. He walked to the Cathedral and took the elevators, which stopped inexplicably at the second-floor lobby. This held the reception area for visitors, and he saw from the elevator the large smoked-glass room that was the closest thing the Cathedral had to a museum. On joining the company, Madison had been given a tour that included a stop at this room. Inside, on velvet-lined stands of corporate purple, stood examples of early Ling hardware. There was the Invincible, a dumb terminal from the early 60's with surprisingly few keys. Next to it stood a smaller programmable calculator the size of a portable typewriter, built in 1971, and with less power than the smallest solar-powered calculator contained in the 80's. But it had grossed over $600 million for the company. There was also a word-processing terminal of the mid-70's, earning for itself a special plaque: the Ling Lingua, System 8800, 1975. These machines had put the company into the billion dollar league. They seemed so simple now, Madison thought, but then so did the Model T. It would probably be easier, now, to find a working Model T than a Ling Lingua 8800 in operation, such was the inherent obsolescence of the technology.

Upstairs, he went furtively to his cubicle to collect his briefcase and escape unnoticed. Pistolet caught up with him as he had almost made it back to the elevators.

'Don't tell me, you have an urgent meeting off-site. Back in your hotel, no doubt.'

'This place isn't big enough for the two of us, Jeffrey. I'm letting you have it all.'

'Have you forgotten tomorrow's demo for the Blue Rinse Lady? She's dumped it all onto me. I could use some input from the Prince of Parsing.'

'You'll do it brilliantly,' Madison said, and moved towards an open elevator.

Pistolet kept the elevator door from closing. 'Hey, is that any way to treat an old schoolmate?' His flippancy did not completely cover the slight tension in his voice.

'All right,' said Madison, capitulating. Pistolet had often helped him. 'But I can't help you now. I'll come in early tomorrow.'

'Please. Like seven thirty. The demo's at ten.'

'That woman.'

'I know. Even Doris Weber called her a douche-bag.' Doris was one of the Expert Systems group, and an ex-nun.

'Oh come on. She did not.'

'She did too. She may be an ex-nun but she grew up in Southy. Man, can she swear.'

6

When he got back to his room, the message light on his phone was flashing. Mother, he thought, but reception had a message from Sally Zehring: Please call. Why was she calling now, what was the point? Pistolet must have said he had caught Madison sneaking back to the hotel.

He went for a walk in the town, going out of the back of the hotel and across an elaborate footbridge above the river, which picked up speed as it narrowed a few hundred yards short of some small cascading falls. He went down an alley between two refurbished factory buildings, and out onto Main Street. The shops here were large and prosperous, housed in nineteenth-century red brick buildings that had been sand-blasted, their trim painted, their new plate-glass windows decorated with mock-antique lettering. Madison had been founded as a mill-town in the early 1800s. It had one or two entirely new buildings, such as the hotel in black glass and grey concrete, and in the town's residential areas there were a few Federalist houses still standing from almost two centuries before; but in the centre everything was built in Victorian brick, no building older than the oldest of the river's great long mills.

He passed a Richardsonian town hall, then realised from its plaque that it was designed by Richardson himself. Where the main street turned he saw the Madison Armory, and next to it the Madison Museum. He had been told the exhibits mentioned his father, as if to show that the clan's vitality and talent endured. Strange, that, since Madison's father had never lived in his namesake town. Madison himself had never set foot in the museum, and had no intention of breaking precedent; feeling singularly unaccomplished, he returned to the hotel as it grew dark.

He dialled Vermont and was reassured to hear only the faintest slurring to his mother's voice when she picked up the phone. 'Dahling,' she said with an accent that remained more English than American, even after forty years. 'When did you arrive?'

'Just yesterday.' He told himself it was only a small lie.

'Will you be coming up here this time?'

'I'm sorry. Next trip I will.'

'You said that last time.' She did not bother to wait for

a response. 'Aunt Peg will be so disappointed. I told her you were going to be in the country and I know how much she'd like to see you.'

He said nothing to this. After a moment he asked softly, 'Have you seen about father?'

'No,' she said sharply, and he was certain she was lying. Why did she still care? After all, since leaving Robert's mother, Frederick Madison had had two other wives, in addition to the recent Monica, the aspiring actress attachment.

'Okay,' he said calmly. 'How are the dogs?' A perennially safe topic. She raised pugs, showing them with varying degrees of success.

Curious how ensconced his mother had become in Vermont life, in the closeted family routine of his uncle and aunt and cousins. After all, she was not the Madison: she had grown up in Norfolk, England, daughter of an unsuccessful English solicitor and a transplanted Long Island debutante. Yet after his father walked out she had turned to her American in-laws for support, not to her own dour parents. Uncle Billy, rich and affable, had opened the collective arms of the Madison clan to her, finding her another, more affordable house on his very own town holding; picking up the odd bill not covered by his youngest brother's erratic alimony payments; seeing that Robert got enough education to be admitted into Philips Academy when the time came, then helping to pay for him at Harvard. In time, his mother had become so well assimilated that she had taken to using the same pompous 'we' that his uncle invoked when expressing familial Madison sentiments. She had even sniffed when a Dupont married a cousin, muttering something about the vulgarity of so much money.

He thought of his Uncle Billy, elder of the two brothers, now in his late sixties. He had played football for Harvard and, in a weak year, made second-team all-American as a tight-end. He was still fit, chopping wood at the farm, shingling the barn roof the summer before; only the slightest trace of paunch belied his taste for a gin and tonic, a growing sense that he could afford to take it easy. Always a busy man, but affable, calm, not a big talker.

Not, in fact, much of a family for rabbiting on; only his father had been a talker. Now, his mother finished her account of the dogs, and a silence lay heavy between them. She didn't ask about his life in England; she never did, preferring, it seemed, to keep her view of her ex-homeland unchanged. For her, that country was a mosaic of memories – of her courtship by his father in post-war London, of Lyons tea-shops, of a world where clerks wore bowler hats and doctors charged you in guineas. Her visits to Madison in England – there had been two during his two years there – were a mix of nostalgic pleasure ('That's where your grandfather bought me my first party dress') and pain ('Aren't *any* of the bus conductors white these days?'). He was not prepared to break the silence now with an update on his doings. They said polite goodbyes, Madison drank a small glass of whisky neat, thought briefly of phoning Sally Zehring, read a thin mystery while watching an HBO film and eating room service sandwiches, then fell asleep.

The next morning he found Pistolet in the large conference room on the ninth floor, inserting an extra memory-board into a desktop computer. He was wearing a fedora and singing:

> In Lamaland
> There's a one-man band
> and he'll toot
> His flute for you

He looked up and saw Madison. 'About time you got here.'

Madison looked at his watch and shook his head; it was

87

not yet seven-thirty. He had forgotten Pistolet's surprising if occasional aptitude for immersion in work.

'Bad news,' said Pistolet. 'The Blue Rinse Lady is insisting on having some cretin from Text Tools demo his stuff.'

'I know. She told me she planned to. He's called Ryerson and he's going to show us the future of spelling applications.'

'She wants to show us up. Bring us down to earth; remove our heads from the clouds; expose us to a short sharp shock of reality. Show us we're winkers.'

'Wankers.'

'That's right. But don't worry, I've fixed him.'

'Who's that?'

'Barleycorn or whatever he's called. The man from AA. That is, unless he brings his own computer along. You'll see.' And he said no more but set Madison to work on the tie-in of Pistolet's Natural Language interface with the group's Slow Parsing program. At ten o'clock they were just finished when Lisa Adams walked in with Ryerson from Text Tools, who had several pens in his shirt pocket. Others from the A.I. group came in, including Sally Zehring, who gave Madison an angry look.

The demonstration began with the Text Tools man loading a floppy into Pistolet's machine and showing his 'value-added' programs to beef up Ling's current word-processing offerings. He demonstrated a fast spelling verifier, an electronic thesaurus, and a good indexer. Lisa Adams crowed over them: 'And wait until you see the spelling corrector.'

Pistolet feigned great excitement. 'Oh yes,' he said like an overgrown schoolboy. 'Do show.'

'We've got a very good corrector,' said Ryerson, 'with phonetic knowledge intrinsic to its operation.'

Famous last words. 'Let me have a go,' said Pistolet, moving to the keyboard. 'You wouldn't want anyone thinking your demo was rigged.' Ryerson looked uneasy but could think of no reason to protest. It soon became clear that the 'intelligence' in the corrector had stepped out for a beer. Pistolet quickly typed the word 'neccessary' with an extra 'c'; quite properly, the verifier flagged it as an error. When he then asked for suggestions as to how the word should be spelled, the corrector supplied the following on screen:

> niece
> nicety
> nicotine
> brassière

'Brassière?' asked Lisa Adams.

'I'll forgive it that,' said Madison, 'but the rest is not very impressive. The right word is obviously "necessary". That's not even listed.'

'Be fair,' said Pistolet, 'give the man another chance. Let's try something else.' And he typed *To think the good employee must be either assertive or unctuous is fellacious*.

'I've deliberately misspelled the word "fallacious", as in "erroneous" or "illogical" or, pardon my crudity, completely fucking wrong. Let's see what the "intelligent" corrector suggests now.' He looked sharply at the hapless Ryerson, ran the verifier (which promptly flagged 'fellacious' as a misspelling), then hit another key for the suggested alternatives and waited. After a lengthy pause only one suggestion appeared:

> fellatio

'What does that mean?' asked a man from Speech Recognition.

'How unfortunate,' said Pistolet. 'I think the corrector

89

is having us on. Maybe it's *too* intelligent.'

'Well, at least it works lickety-split,' said Madison.

'A felicitous choice of words,' said Pistolet. He turned to the Blue Rinse Lady and politely asked, 'Can we move on to A.I. now?'

They began by showing Lisa Adams a Natural Language interface. When Pistolet typed *schedule a meeting*, it said *with whom*? Pistolet typed *with Julie next Thursday*, then proceeded to schedule several other meetings. When he returned and said *change the meeting with Julie*, the interface not only remembered who Julie was, it scheduled a meeting with her in the gaps made by the other meetings. Everyone around the table found this mildly impressive, except for Ryerson, who was still disgruntled by his spelling corrector fiasco. 'What about pronouns?' he demanded, and took the keyboard away from Pistolet. He typed in *ask Julie if the meeting with him was her idea or theirs*. The screen suddenly went blank and the system hung.

'Oh well,' said Pistolet with fake cheeriness, rebooting the machine. Matters were not improved when his parsing program took over four minutes to check the syntax of a single paragraph. The Blue Rinse Lady was not slow to show her displeasure. 'Pretty grotty, fellahs,' she announced. 'Is that the best you can do?'

'Now that you mention it,' said Pistolet, 'we have got one new project. But it's not meant to be a product; it's more a prototype for products.'

'Nothing you've shown me yet could be a product. What you really mean is that it's just more pure research.'

'Not if you believe in the stars.' Pistolet paused. He added solemnly, 'Some people laugh at astrology. I'm not one of them.'

'Neither am I,' said Lisa Adams, sounding positive in her negativeness for the first time.

'Really? Well then, have a go.' He motioned to the

keyboard and Lisa Adams sat down. Pistolet leaned over and hit a sequence of keys. On the screen a question appeared.

> What is your name?

Lisa Adams she typed.

> What is your age?

She looked at Pistolet, who said diplomatically, 'Type anything. Say you're eighteen, it doesn't matter.' She typed *18*.

> Are you tall, medium height, or short?
> Medium.

> Man or woman?
> Woman

> Light or dark colouring?
> Light

> Assertive by nature or passive?
> Assertive

> Sincere or restrained?

An odd question, thought Madison, then he realised he was witnessing the computerised implementation of Wankers, Shakers, Plodders and Fakers. *Sincere* she typed.

> Happiest when active or relaxed?
> Active

> Confident or uncertain?
> Confident

Suddenly the hard disc whirred and cranked. *Please wait*

the screen flashed in blinking letters of reverse video. Then it read:

> You are a Virgo, born in
> the early part of September.

No one said anything until Sally Zehring burst out, 'Well? When were you born?'

Lisa Adams stared at the screen and said slowly, 'September seventh.'

'Jesus!' Ryerson exclaimed.

'How does it do it?' someone asked.

Pistolet shrugged. 'Inferential reasoning, common to expert systems, was the first step. But the real knowledge base came from astrological principles.'

'Astrology?' asked the man from Speech Recognition. 'I thought you first gave your birth-date and then astrology told you the rest. Not the other way around.'

'Ah,' said Pistolet, arching his eyebrows in his best lecturing manner, 'reverse engineering at its best. We build up to the birth-date from the personality traits, rather than the other way round. Backwards chaining: a novel approach and a nice piece of work, if I say so myself.' He looked at Lisa Adams. 'Even if it is only pure research.'

She ignored this, saying, 'It's terrific, mate. We could sell thousands. Wait till I tell Sammy Ling about it.' She ran a hand through her blue streak. 'In fact, I'm going right up to the Spires to tell him now.'

'Hang on a minute,' said Pistolet, but it was too late; Lisa had swept up her briefcase and left in a rush, followed by a thoroughly depressed Ryerson.

Madison clapped Pistolet on the shoulder. 'Congratulations,' he said, but Pistolet winced.

'God,' he said, 'now I'm going to get hammered.'

'Why?' said the man from Speech Recognition. 'Lisa Adams loved it. I'm sure Sammy will, too.'

'You mean, you think it works? You moron.' He pointed to the monitor. 'That's a rigged one-off. The lady could have entered anything and she'd have got the same response.' He sat down in unfeigned pain. Puzzled, everyone but Madison and Sally moved away from him.

'Relax,' said Sally soothingly. 'Sam's in Pittsburgh until Friday.'

'So it's "Sam" now?' said Madison snidely.

She blushed under the full force of his gaze. 'Screw you,' she said. Pistolet looked up at her in surprise. She continued, 'And you too, Jeffrey. I thought that was very immature; dirty words to get a laugh. Why don't you two grow up?' And she walked out of the room.

Madison sat down next to Pistolet. 'Wow.'

'I told you she still carried a torch for you, Robert. God knows why: Sammy Ling spends more on shirts than you do on rent.'

'Tell me, how the hell did you rig that?'

'Who says it was rigged?'

'You just did. How did you manage it?'

'Someone named Felicia in Human Resources. Two dinners, a quick but satisfying tumble (she liked my BMW), and presto, I get five minutes alone with the Blue Rinse Lady's Personnel file. Date of birth; medical history (she has high blood pressure); company rating (not as high as she pretends); it's all in there. But don't tell a soul. I mean that.'

'Why, would you get fired?'

'Who cares about that? But Felicia might: those files are supposed to be sacrosanct. And I can't have her leaving; she's promised me that next time we can do it in my car. Just like high school.'

He left Pistolet and walked back to his cubicle. Sally was sitting there, looking cross. 'I'm sorry,' he said right away. 'I don't want to fight with you.'

'Then why have you been avoiding me?'

'I haven't.'

'Where were you yesterday? I left a message at the hotel for you to call me.'

Why did she deserve an explanation? Well, providing one would forestall a scene. 'My mother's not well. I was up there last night.'

'That's a long drive to Vermont.'

'I told you, she's not well. I may have to go up there again.' How easy to lie, how simple to slip into a pattern of casual deceit. Be honest with her. Why? What was the point? *She* had hurt *him*.

'How is your mother?'

'Much better.'

'I like her; I always have. She was always very nice to me.'

'I bet she was,' he began sourly, but said nothing more. He had compassion, he supposed, a trained kind of warmth for his mother, but nothing she said seemed to influence him any more. The titanic scale of her boozing: doubtless it had been sparked by his father's desertion, doubtless it was not her fault, yet it filled him with impatience all the same, made him resist all her demands. He was hard on her, and guilty about it. His uncle had remained her steady financial pillar; Madison had ceased to be a solid emotional prop as soon as he moved away. In a sense, he had never come back. As bad, in that way, as his father. Father had done it first.

Sally scratched one of her hands with the nails of the other. 'I want to see you, Robert.'

'Here I am.'

'Not here. Outside the Cathedral. Tonight.'

'I can't,' he said reflexively.

'Why not?'

He couldn't think of a reason fast enough; Sally stood up impatiently. 'I thought as much. I'll come by the hotel at seven. Be in your room.'

94

7

In the lab at International he found the usual medley: an Ethiopian relation of Haile Selassie who had graduated from MIT and could not safely return home, was looking intently at a screen full of Arabic characters; next to him a German stood shouting at a processor. '*Bitte!*' he yelled, and Madison wondered what he was so cross about. He looked at a colour monitor next to the computer and saw the word *Danke*. '*Danke!*' shouted the man, and momentarily the word *Bitte* appeared on the monitor's screen. Clearly, the Speech Recognition boys had been down for a visit.

He looked around for someone he could talk to, particularly hoping to avoid a lugubrious Pole he knew, who was expert in character sets. Fortunately there was no sign of the man. Then he spied Sal Lombardi at a table at the far end of the lab. Sal was short and bald and wore a white short-sleeved shirt with pens clipped to the breast pocket. Almost entirely Chinese, Sal owed his improbable surname to a great-grandfather from Naples who had visited Hong Kong in the 1890s and stayed.

'What are you doing down here?' Madison demanded, since Sal had always worked in the word-processing group.

'Robert, what a pleasure. Sit down.' He got up and fetched Madison a chair. Returning, he said with a sigh, 'It's a long story. But in a nutshell, I had a fight with Minnie Lu. Guess who lost.'

'Don't tell me; I may soon be lost myself.'

'An ultimatum was presented: leave Ling or switch

departments. Forgive my timidity, but I thought it safest to stay at Ling. So I moved here to International.'

'You could have had a good job somewhere else, Sal.'

'I'm not so sure about that. Two years ago, during the first lay-offs, other companies were happy to hire Ling employees. Now I think they're starting to feel there's something really wrong here, that we can't be all that valuable.'

'I wouldn't have predicted you'd fight with Minnie Lu.'

'Why? Because I'm Chinese? That simply made it worse. Especially because I don't speak the language very well. I learned it growing up, but holy smokes, Robert, I was born in America. Minnie used to shout at me in Cantonese and I had to ask her to repeat it in English. That made her even angrier. Once she even accused me of being an Uncle Ben.'

'Uncle Ben?'

'It's a Chinese Uncle Tom.'

'What made her angry in the first place?'

'I thought her views on document architecture were completely out of date. To her, ODA means Out-of-Date Architecture; but I tell you, we have to standardise or we're lost. She still thinks we can foist our own solutions on customers. What arrogance. And you know she can't take criticism. Times are difficult here; perhaps she's just showing the strain. She is never very predictable.'

'I'll say. She's suddenly decided she may want me back here.'

'Really? Are you interested?'

Madison shook his head.

'How long is it you've been there now?'

'About two years.'

'Ling won't give you the push. You're too valuable. Especially these days. They know how good you are and what a breakthrough it would be if you're successful.'

'Maybe, but getting a machine to write can't be done

overnight. The way Minnie was talking, they've run out of patience.'

Sal said nothing to this. 'You want a coffee? It's pretty decent here.' When Madison nodded, Sal stood up and went over to a machine in the corner. He returned with two full mugs.

'How did you manage this?' Madison exclaimed when he tasted it, for his mug was full of cappuccino.

'International has to have some perks. I told these guys down here, if you let them treat you like dogs, they will. I've tried to bring a little pride to these people, but it's hard going.' They both sipped contentedly.

'Tell me, do you really like it over there?' Echoes of Uncle Billie. The insularity of the States, the inability to imagine anyone living happily anywhere else. 'I liked Paris all right, but give me Waukegan any day.'

'I've got used to it, I guess. Until now, I could do my work without being bothered. No politics, no interference. I just wish I could keep it that way. I need a breakthrough.'

Sal shook his head. 'This wouldn't really be your cup of tea. You prefer things a little grander, don't you? This is all a little too democratic for your taste.'

'What do you mean?' said Madison, taken aback.

'No offence, Robert. It's probably how you were brought up. Rather patrician, weren't you? Maybe a little bit of a snob. I don't mean to be rude. I respect that, in a way. My son, I want him to feel like that. I'm trying to get him into boarding school now. Groton or Milton. They're good schools, aren't they?'

'Very good.'

'You went there?'

'No.' And he told Sal where he had gone to school.

'Is that better?'

'Much the same. Only bigger.'

'I see. Do you know anyone at Groton or at Milton?'

Madison thought for a moment. 'I know a teacher at Groton; I went to college with him. Why do you ask?'

'Would you be willing to write for my boy? He's very bright, but I don't think he'll get in.'

'If he's bright, he will.'

Sal shook his head. 'They don't like to take too many Asian boys, even if they are bright. And we have no connections at either school.'

'I don't really think my writing would help, Sal.'

Sal said nothing for a moment. 'Would you say that if I were white?'

'For God's sake, Sal, what makes you say that?'

'I'm sorry, Robert, forgive me. It's just sometimes I get very angry about this proper Bostonian business. But I don't mean to get angry with you.'

'Forget it,' said Madison, suddenly depressed. They sat in silence for a minute, then Madison finished his coffee, thanked Sal as cheerfully as he could, and left. When he passed the Ethiopian, he noticed his screen was now full of Hebrew characters.

He went upstairs into East Nave to bother Cromwell, and found Pistolet in an aisle, who said loudly, 'I need a smoke.' He led Madison towards a corner room.

'I thought you'd quit.'

'So did I. Sometimes even I'm wrong.'

Pistolet opened the door into the smoking-room. There were supposed to be no second-class citizens at Ling Enterprises, but the lot of smokers showed this not to be the case. It was as if smoking had replaced negritude, Roman Catholicism and Judaism as grounds for persecution. On each floor of the Cathedral there was one room allocated for the use of nicotine addicts, a sealed chamber left deliberately unfurnished except for a few Spartan plastic chairs, a formica-top table, and a couple of half-filled ashtrays.

No official policy forbade making these rooms less

repugnant, but an unspoken agreement among the addicts themselves – like convicts so ashamed of their crimes they agree not to try to escape – kept anyone from trying to brighten up the walls. Once Pistolet in an exuberant burst had put up a Salem cigarette poster that showed a Yuppie couple lolling on rocks by a river, casually inhaling, but within a week this cheery photograph had disappeared.

'So what do we do about Ryerson?' Pistolet asked, lighting up.

'The man from Text Tools?'

'Precisely,' said Pistolet. 'I need that little nerd hanging around asking questions like I need a hole in the head.'

'They were tough questions.'

'I know they were. With him around, someone might actually start asking me when I planned to have a product ready. We can't have that.' He took a deep drag. Suddenly his face lit up and he stabbed out his cigarette. 'I know what to do. I'll send a note, anonymously of course, to People Resource saying Ryerson's been harassing female colleagues. I'll copy Lisa Adams to make sure they contact her about it.'

'And what will she say?'

'Make sympathetic noises of a feminist tenor; what else can she do? They'll then confront Ryerson and reprimand him. He may even get suspended for a few days.'

'You mean, they'll believe anonymous accusations, even if Ryerson denies them?'

'Of course,' said Pistolet blithely. 'From their point of view, harassment lies in the eye of the perceiver.'

'What perceiver?'

'Who cares? They don't. You continue to miss the obvious point: as far as management's concerned, the accusation can't be wrong.'

'Why the hell not?'

'Because if People Resource don't act, it's going to be

some feminist employee, not horny Ryerson, that will sue the company's ass!'

'Jesus,' said Madison with true appreciation. 'Now I see what happens when a social force like feminism gets interpreted by a modern up-to-date American corporation.'

'It really makes you think, doesn't it?'

'I'll say. Or not think. It's double-think.'

'That's what you say now,' said Pistolet. 'After six months here you'll find it all completely logical.'

There was little else for Madison to do in the Cathedral except wait for Minnie Lu to summon him again. So when he met Cromwell in the hall and learned that Minnie Lu expected him the next morning at ten o'clock, Madison returned to the hotel and slept until six. Then he showered and shaved, alternating pulls of his razor with glances at the mirror that showed the television screen's broadcast of the local news. Traffic conditions seemed the reigning preoccupation. Wearing only a towel around his waist, he sneaked out to the ice-machine across the hall and filled his ice-bucket. He poured himself a large Scotch on the rocks and sat on the bed and thought about Sally Zehring's impending visit.

Stick to books; a safe topic, and Sally's chief passion outside the realm of Natural Language Processing and computational linguistics. Actually, an even greater passion than those two. How well-read she had always seemed, the English major from South Carolina – until, in her final undergraduate year at U.Va., she had discovered the beauties of phrase structure grammars in a beginners' linguistics course. Her grades had been so high (Phi Beta in English) that MIT had taken a chance on her fledgling interest and given her a full scholarship to do graduate work in linguistics. She had never looked back, but at least her love of literature lingered.

Thinking about the way love of literature had led Sally into linguistics made Madison consider how the process had worked in his own life. Initially, perhaps, linguistics had appealed to him as a method for looking at literature and language without using conventional criticism – his father's contempt for critics had stuck with him. Not all critics, though. The critics who were also poets had got his father's grudging respect: John Crowe Ransom, Robert Penn Warren, even Randal Jarrell – despite Jarrell's personal dislike of him. 'Few more unpleasant *personae* have been assumed by such a talented poet,' wrote Jarrell in an uncollected essay that left even the defensive Frederick Madison uncertain how to respond. 'Only Robert Frost has managed to combine such odious personal qualities with such near-perfect gifts for verse.'

There was suddenly a knock on the door. Madison was not entirely surprised to find it was Sally, arriving half an hour early.

'You look nice,' she declared.

He let her in and went into the bathroom to fetch another towel. 'Don't worry on my account,' she said when he returned. 'I've seen it all before, remember?' She stood at the end of one of the two double beds and swayed slightly, her long, full mane of blonde hair swaying too. On her next sway backwards she fell down heavily on the bed and her feet rocked into the air. She wore a white tennis skirt that seemed cut as high as possible; indeed, Madison thought, he could almost see possible. This was new: she was no prude, but had never been sexually provocative. Then Madison realised she'd been drinking.

'You're pissed,' he said.

'Not at you,' said Sally, kicking off both tennis shoes and tucking her feet sideways underneath her. She had grown up in Charleston and her voice was wide and sassy. Uncle Billie had once admiringly called her a strapping colt of a girl, for she was big-boned, with wide shoulders that tapered down to a thin waist, and high, round breasts. Her face was especially striking, for she had blue eyes

101

the size of saucers, a full mouth, high cheekbones, and a strong, straight nose. She could stop traffic any day, but charmingly, she never seemed to want to. Hers was a casually assumed beauty: sexy, unaffected, fun. Very stupid men usually assumed that she was stupid, too.

'I mean, you're drunk,' he explained.

She shook her head. 'Not really. Just prepared. An evening with the Empress is in store for this girl. It's a dry house and I need something to get me through three hours of ginger ale and pretzels.'

'If you're going to marry her son you had better learn to tolerate her hospitality.'

'I knew Jeffrey must have told you I was engaged. I like the house; it's the Empress who worries me. All evening I sit there feeling her eyes on me, knowing she's thinking "Why does my Sammy want to marry this white girl?" And she makes me feel cheap. Well,' she said, unfurling her legs, which were long and well-shaped, and lifting them high into the air for Madison to examine, 'if she wants cheap she can have cheap.' She sat up again. 'Can I have a drink, please?'

'Better not,' said Madison, starting to put on his clothes.

'You've lost weight.'

'A little. There's a lot of outside stuff to do around the house I've rented.'

'The English gentleman in his garden.'

'My mother was born there, you know.'

'Where, in your garden?' She laughed. 'You'll always be a Yankee through and through. Just like your father. Incidentally, I saw him last month.'

'Really?' He feigned lack of interest but found himself suddenly alert. How drunk was she?

'At a reading,' she said, and Madison relaxed. 'At Harvard. He was very good. I went up afterwards to try and have him sign my copy of *Blue Is Not Your Dying*. I would have asked him for news of you but the line was too long. Sanders Theatre was packed. He's very dynamic. Not as good-looking as you, though. You and your willowy good looks.'

Madison felt silly at how much this pleased him. 'Willowy? Is that a compliment?'

'Gary Cooper was willowy, so what do you think, you vain creep?'

Willowy; he had a thin, almost epicene countenance, inherited chiefly from his mother. His father was a hearty type; face fuller, nose broad, cheeks wide.

'When are you due at the Empress's?'

'Not for a while. I have time to talk.'

'You'd better sober up. What would the young heir say?'

'Oh, he's not even there yet. He's playing tennis. I was supposed to play with him but I said I had work to do.'

'Who wins when you play?' he asked, since Sally was very athletic.

She paused. 'Sammy does.'

'You let him.'

'Maybe,' she said coyly. 'But then, I used to let you win.'

'Horseshit,' he said, picking a tie from the drawer. 'I could always whip you.'

'I suppose that's true. But Sam has a better racket than you do. So do I, now. He gave me a Prince for Christmas.'

'Sorry; I meant to but forgot.'

She stuck out her tongue at him, then said, 'Why are you putting on your blazer?'

'To go out. I thought we'd have a drink in the bar downstairs. I know I'm not in Sammy's league but I can still afford to buy you a drink.'

She started shaking her head. 'I don't want to go downstairs. I want to stay right here. What's the matter, don't you trust me? Or don't you trust yourself?'

'I'm spoken for, didn't you know that?' Is that how he would describe his relationship with Catherine? God help him. And her, too.

'Jeffrey told me. But who wants to be spoken for anyway?'

'I do. And you do. Just not by each other.' This suddenly struck him as a very odd thing to have said. He continued heavily, 'You can't show up at the Empress's half-crocked with a bedroom look in your eyes.'

'Why not?' She blew him a soft kiss.

'I mean it.'

'All right. Just don't make me go downstairs to that terrible bar. I hate it.'

'We'll find another bar.'

'There isn't time. Just stop it, all right? We'll both be good as mice.'

Madison went to stand by the window. 'If you're staying, I'm going to have a drink. What do you want?'

'Scotch and water.'

'Forget it. I'll get you a soda.' He went out to the machine in the hall and bought a can of Coke and another of club soda. When he came back she was going through his drawers, much as she had always done in the past. Their mad and mutual intrusiveness; no wonder they hadn't survived – they had almost consumed each other. He mixed himself a stiff Scotch and soda and poured out her coke in a water-glass. He handed it to her. 'Find anything interesting?'

'Not much. No pictures of your girl. No love letters from me, either. What are you reading this for?' She held up a copy of *The Letters of Randal Jarrell*. 'Was he a friend of your father's?'

'He despised my father. Quite right, too.'

'You don't seem to think much of either of your parents.'

'I like them the way you like your future mother-in-law. I take it young Sammy is a model of filial piety?'

'Why do you dislike him so much? Is it because you went to school together? He says you used to persecute him.'

'He does? He was Mr Bad Ass, not me. I don't think he ever lost a fight. That's not why no one liked him. All he could talk about was his money, and his mother. He didn't even call her his mother – he called her The Empress, for Christ's sakes. Can you believe it?'

'Sure I believe it. There's a cult of worship in that clan and it's all centred around the Empress.'

'Don't you start calling her that, too. But Pistolet was the one who really hated Sammy at school. So why doesn't Sammy hate Pistolet?'

'Jeffrey never slept with his fiancée.'

'Sammy had it in for me long before he started going out with you.'

'Yes. He told me you threw him into a pond once, and when he challenged you to fight, you wouldn't. *Not* very brave.'

'I didn't have the money for the medical bills.'

She laughed briefly. 'Anyway, Sammy did want to go out with me, but you were in the way. Mister Consultant from Harvard.'

'Then I went to England . . . '

'What a coincidence. You went to England, where you were never seen,' she paused to finish her Coke, 'and as far as Sammy knows, never missed.' She stood up a little unsteadily and looked at her watch. 'Since you're playing Mister Well-Behaved I think I'd better go now. No point in getting in Dutch with the Empress if you're just going to rehash the past.'

'Wait a minute.' How could that be? Hadn't he been hired and sent to England as an investment for Ling Enterprises? 'Are you trying to tell me I'm in England because Sammy wanted me out of the way?'

'Of course not. You're there for a lot of reasons. But you're right, for Sammy it was important to get you away – *pour ne pas contaminer les autres*. And les autres, c'est moi.'

105

'Harvard Square was too close?' He thought of his junior professor's office just off Mount Auburn Street, near J Press. The second storey of a Federalist house; lovely, as the English would say.

'Ah, that's probably where Sammy came in. I bet he scoured the globe on your behalf, looking for a distant development post for you to fill. When Oxford opened up, he figured that would do. He would have preferred the Far East, but the Taiwan R and D subsidiary is strictly manufacturing these days.'

'But what about document-creation? Surely he could see the importance of it.'

Sally shrugged. 'He never thought it would get anywhere.'

Had Ling really never seen the promise of his project, was it all a ploy of Sammy's to get him out of Sally's way? He said bitterly, 'I suppose you're sceptical about my chances, too. And Pistolet.'

Again Sally shrugged. 'Don't take it personally. If anyone can do it, it's probably you. I'm just not convinced anyone can. Yet. And let's face it: for the last two years you've just kept your head down.'

'What should I have done?'

'The least you could have done is *name* your project. "Automatic text-generation" – that title would put anyone to sleep. Why not call it something simple – like the Creation Project? Something like that. Anything's better than "document generation".'

'If Sammy was just getting me out of the way, why didn't he go out with you as soon as I'd left?'

'He tried. He asked for a date about an hour after your plane left Logan for London.'

'And you said no.'

'Naturally. I was being faithful to you.'

'Not for long. You started seeing that jerk in hardware.'

Sally suddenly sat up straight on the bed. 'I can't believe you said that.'

'Why? It's true.'

'You bastard. I waited for you, and what happened? You never came back. And you didn't have to go there in the first place.'

'Sure I did. It was an irresistible opportunity.'

'And I wasn't.'

He shook his head. 'That's not fair.'

'Love and work,' she said. 'Freud says all that matters is love and work. But with you it's always been work.'

'I was being given the chance of a lifetime.'

'If you really felt you had to go to England, you could have come back. You told me you'd be gone six months; then it was a year; then it was indefinite. What did you expect me to do? Be a modern-day Penelope, weaving you synthetic sweaters to keep out the Massachusetts chill when you returned? I waited; in fact, if you ask me, I waited too long. At least that jerk in hardware, as you call him, never led me on.'

Madison sighed. The awful thing was that Sally was right. He could have asked her to join him in Oxford, but he had dreaded her saying no. Far better to make his breakthrough, then return in triumph and claim the girl as his reward. The next thing he knew, she had sent him a Dear John letter and started seeing Hilton in hardware. He had got so caught up in his work that he'd lost all track of time. Now he looked, and found Sally staring at him. He shrugged. 'Speaking of the jerk in hardware,' he said, 'whatever happened to him? Sammy buy him off or something?'

'Ralph, Ralph Hilton. He works for DEC now. He received a bad review from his Vicar – the only bad review in his group – and he got the message. Sammy helped make that happen, I'm pretty sure of that. Then since you were mad at me about seeing Ralph – I don't know why, I never would have seen Ralph if you had shown the slightest inclination to come back – the next time Sammy asked me out, I thought, why not? And the rest is history. Or history in the making.'

'The rough path of smooth love.'

'And yours is smoother?'

'No. But tell me, is Sammy *still* jealous of me?'

'I think he feels I'm over you emotionally. Besides, he knows you've got an English girl. I told him last week, after Jeffrey told me.' Now Sally stood up. 'I'd better be going. I'm late as it is. When do you leave for England?'

'Tomorrow night. I have a meeting in the morning with Minnie Lu.'

'About parsing? *Write Right*?'

'Yes, and about the timetable for my return. But if Sammy was so jealous I'm surprised he wants them to call me back now.'

'He probably doesn't know anything about it. You're not that important, you know. Like I say, I'm engaged to him and you've got yourself an English girlfriend. He thinks I'm over you.'

'You are.'

'That's what you think.' And she stood and faced him, and then reached her finger out and touched him very lightly right under the centre of his belt. Then she slowly ran her finger up along his chest to his chin. 'Tell me, is your girl an English rose?'

Catherine: pink cheeks, fair skin, thorny at times. 'Yes,' he said with an effort, trying to ignore Sally's moving hand. 'Come on, I'll walk you to your car.'

The hotel lobby was less crowded than on the previous night. A group of Ling salesmen sat on the over-stuffed couches of the foyer and looked with frank admiration at Sally as she and Madison walked by. Outside, the night was clear: the stars stretched out across a dark-blue canvas of sky.

Sally's car was classic R & D, an ageing Rabbit, which she had managed to park in the front lot. When she opened the front door Madison put his arms on its top and held it open. 'Are you sure you're sober enough to drive?'

'Absolutely. Nothing like a little heart-to-heart with you to make a girl sober up completely. Will I see you again before you leave?'

'Maybe tomorrow in the Cathedral. I only have that morning meeting. I was hoping to get away by lunchtime.'

'Then come and say goodbye before you leave. I'll be in my cubicle all morning. Promise?'

He paused. 'I promise. You sure you're all right?'

'Quit asking me that, damn you. You never used to show such concern.'

'Don't be sour.'

'I'm not,' she said, and got into the car and closed the door. She started the engine and then rolled down her window. 'It's just I can't help thinking once in a while that I may be making a colossal mistake.'

'What, with Sammy? Think of the money; that should help.' She winced. He said quickly, 'Sorry. I shouldn't have said that.'

She shrugged. 'Since when did that ever stop you?' And shifting suddenly into gear, she drove off.

8

When he arrived at Minnie Lu's office the next morning, her secretary told him to join her in Virgil Peabody's office upstairs in the Spires.

He rode the elevator and walked out into a large sunny

area with a stunning Rothko-like abstract on the far wall, a fiery orange sun against a background of cream. He tried to collect his thoughts as he came to the row of large offices set along the southern wall of South Nave. Virgil's secretary was absent, but his door was open; Madison stuck his head in and looked sideways down the length of Virgil's sanctum. Near the door were several Eames chairs grouped around a glass coffee table; a setting for relaxed conversations among the mighty. At the far end sat Virgil's desk, bare save for a single stack of papers, with the formidable figure of Virgil behind it. In front of him, her back to Madison, sat Minnie Lu; next to her was an unoccupied chair, presumably destined for Madison.

As he walked across the room, both Virgil and Minnie Lu were talking rapidly in Chinese. They could be calling him old puke-face for all Madison knew, feeling like a proverbial fly on the wall that had gone deaf. He would have given a lot for an intelligent simultaneous translation program; it was a pity that machine translation, after a false dawn in the 50's, was generally conceded to be decades rather than years away.

The two kept talking, Minnie Lu the more voluble. This gave Madison the opportunity to inspect Virgil Peabody, whom he had not seen for over two years – well before his recent and remarkable ascent to be the Head of Marketing and R & D, the third most important person in the company after the Empress and son Sammy.

Madison's first introduction to Virgil had been as a consultant, up from Harvard for the day, in the company of the Welsh Lunatic. He had expected to meet some relative of Endicot Peabody, former governor of Massachusetts and a childhood friend of Madison's father; but Virgil, like Minnie Lu, was first-generation Chinese-American, a native of Shanghai brought to America as a teenage boy in the late 1940s, a scant three miles ahead of marching Mao militia. Despite a first-rate Chinese degree in engineering,

Virgil's father had been forced to work as a waiter in Boston's minuscule Chinatown; he never managed the crucial Step One with English. Virgil himself was not in any sense a native speaker of English, but in technocrat-speak he could hold his own with the company's finest assassins of the language.

Virgil was highly intelligent, with the concomitant corporate virtues of exceptional technical skills, unswerving loyalty to the Lings, and a capacity for ruthlessness so famous in the company that its victims were always half-surprised that anyone could so magnificently live up to his reputation. They would have done well to remember Minnie Lu's oft-quoted observation: 'When Virgil cut you, you no bleed.' He had made it to the top despite other equally manifest shortcomings – coldness, difficulty in communicating, an uninspiring manner, and a pretty revolting physical appearance. He had a short, squat frame, a habit of sucking his teeth, and notoriously bad breath.

Yet he was now in the public eye; Madison had heard that someone was helping to write Virgil's speeches, and the clean-up act extended to his appearance. He wore a grey suit of unremarkable check; gone the maroon polyester that had once been a Virgil trademark. The hair was shorter and combed back with the assistance of grease, but the glasses remained defiantly thick, the simple black frames saying menacingly, *I am watching you*.

By the time Madison reached them, Virgil and Minnie Lu had decided to take notice of him, Virgil by staring coldly at Madison before standing up and walking to the windows, Minnie Lu by turning her head and suddenly speaking in English. Madison sat down carefully as she began.

'I tell Virgil,' she began, 'what you and I discuss two days ago. It is time you return.'

'Well,' Madison said tentatively. Virgil suddenly piped

up from the window, 'We need your help here most badly.'

Clearly, to Virgil's mind this was sufficient reason for any employee to uproot himself. Madison wondered how best to make it plain that for him it wouldn't do. '*Why* is it so important to have me back here?'

Virgil looked annoyed and turned to Minnie Lu, who frowned. Virgil was unaccustomed to such heresy; this at least was what Minnie Lu's scowl at Madison suggested. 'It best for you to be here,' she hissed.

'Perhaps,' said Madison, thinking that was his own look-out, not hers. 'But what I'd like to know then is why, from your viewpoint, you want me *here*.'

'Because,' said Virgil with a sigh, still staring out of the window. Madison waited. 'Trouble ahead for company. We need something very new. So we try *Write Right*. Maybe that will help us.'

Madison said, 'Document-generation – what I'm calling the Creation Project – would be more help still. You know that, Minnie,' he said, turning to her.

She looked for guidance to Virgil, who continued to stare moodily out towards Boston. Suddenly he clapped his hands together and turned around to face Madison, who wondered whether this dramatic gesture had been taught to Virgil in a seminar on leadership. Ling was a great company for employee courses: from the lowliest secretary to the highest Bishop, no one was safe from these ancillary programmes of education. 'You have had your chance. And now have nothing to show.'

'I'm close. Very close. All I need's one more year.'

'You don't understand,' Virgil said sharply, his voice rising. 'We are in big trouble. Next quarter, next quarter, I tell you, Ling Enterprises for first time in history . . .' his voice suddenly trembled ' . . . Ling Enterprises will *lose money*.' There was a stunned silence as Virgil went and sat down at his desk, and twiddled his thumbs in a slow butterfly rotation. Madison had never seen menacing thumbs before. 'Leave us for a minute,' Virgil said quietly to Madison.

Outside, Virgil's secretary had returned to her desk, an Asian woman in a pink suit. He smiled abstractedly at her when she looked up, but she ignored him and kept typing. It was still called typing: Madison tried to think of a new verb – 'to word process' had not, thank God, quite entered the language.

He was dazzled by Virgil's news. Fiscal quarters came and went, some good, some less good, a business boom here, a flat spell there. But what was never in question was the fundamental bottom line: the plainest purity of all – *profit*. This was hi-tech, after all: Information Technology, the Computer Age; this was the America where everyone, but everyone, lived in the black. Or died. *Lose money*? Things must be tough in the Cathedral.

'Hello, Robert,' said a cool voice behind him, and he turned around to find the large figure of Sammy Ling. He was elegantly dressed in a black pin-stripe suit and white shirt, and an orange and blue tie. He was at least a couple of inches shorter than Madison, and made to look shorter still by a bald patch that expanded each year, crowding the remaining strands of hair that he pasted back, somewhat desperately, in furrows above his ears. Sammy was heavy-set and powerful; in Britain he would have looked an obvious rugger player, key member of the scrum. It was not surprising that he had been a three-year football letterman at school.

Madison looked at Sammy; Sammy looked at him; there was, despite the new hiccup in the company's fortunes, about a billion dollars difference in the capital worth of their respective stares, which perhaps explained why Madison made an effort to conceal his hostility, and Sammy didn't bother.

'So how is life in England?' asked Sammy with a studied informality.

Madison shrugged. 'Busy.'

'I hear you're doing good work over there.'

Madison said nothing, content to let Sammy patronise someone else. He must have been staring at Sammy's tie, for suddenly Sammy said, 'You like the new design?'

'What?'

'Of the tie. The school tie. Not bad, don't you think?'

Such was his loyalty to the old school, Madison hadn't even recognised it.

'We had it redesigned last year,' Sammy was saying.

'*You* did?'

'We did. The trustees. I'm a trustee now,' he said proudly.

'Really?' Madison sensed he sounded inappropriately disbelieving but could think of nothing else to say. He added belatedly, 'Congratulations.'

'Thanks,' said Sammy, looking at his watch and preparing to move away. 'And by the way, congratulations to you, too.'

'On what?'

'On your engagement, of course. Sally told me about it. I think that's terrific, old Yankee stock like yours marrying someone from the old country. England, I mean. It's great news.' He punched Madison sharply on the arm like a third-rate jock, and walked away before Madison could say anything. Why had Sally told Sammy Ling that Madison was engaged? It wasn't true and she knew it.

'Come.' It was Minnie Lu in the doorway; she must have been standing there, waiting for Sammy Ling to finish. He followed her back in, to find Virgil looking impatiently at a memorandum. As he sat down, Virgil looked up and said simply, 'Six months.'

'I beg your pardon?'

'We give you six months to succeed. You bring back a generation program this autumn that we can ship by Christmas, and you can do whatever you like. Stay there;

114

come here; etcetera. You be a hero. Otherwise you come back and run *Write Right* – and right away.'

Madison sat quietly for a moment. Then before Virgil could dismiss him he tried the tack he had taken with Lewis Llewellyn Thomas. 'What would happen if I couldn't come back just then? For personal reasons, say.'

'Personal reasons.' Virgil almost snorted, such was the rush of air that came out of his nose and mouth in derision. 'Naturally, we respect *personal* reasons. We would say, fine, okay, *personal* reasons keep you in England. *Personal* reasons mean you cannot return to work here and be responsible employee. We would say all these things in polite manner and then,' said Virgil, pausing while Madison waited – until suddenly Minnie Lu piped up and said, 'And then we terminate you!'

Part Three

1

On his first morning back in his UK office Madison carried the *Collected Poems* of Frederick Madison into the office and plopped it down on Dorothy's desk. She looked warily at him.

'I'm afraid I have rather a large typing job for you.'

'Not that?' she said, appalled.

'I'm afraid so.'

'Which part of it?'

'All of it,' he said, unable to repress a smile. 'I'd like it in three files.' He picked up the book and began marking the contents pages with a pen. 'File one should be the first two collections – marked here – chiefly his war poems and juvenilia. File two is the mature Madison, his next four volumes of verse. File three are these last three collections marked here; my old man's thoughts turn towards senility, impotence and death, only spasmodically disgorging hints of his earlier bravado. He is growing tired, the careful reader sees, but a Yeatsian flame of quivering strength persists.'

'Is this for the company,' she asked crossly, 'or just for you? Because if you expect me to do personal work – '

'I expect you to do whatever I tell you to do.' He was almost as taken aback as she was by his new assertiveness. 'Now listen carefully. Skip the titles for now, type only the words, and don't bother at all about the punctuation. I just want the words, pure and simple; I can convert the spaces later and have carriage returns between each word. Don't worry; you can run the spelling checker at the end.'

'Isn't there some other way to do this?'

He shook his head. 'Volumes of poetry are not often available in machine-readable form; my father, goddamn his ornery soul, is for once no exception. And I haven't got the time or the budget to OCR it.'

'To what?'

'Scan it. With an optical character reader.'

'So this *is* a personal job,' she said, returning to that line of defence.

'Not in the slightest.' He adopted an air of wounded hauteur. 'I would never ask you to do personal work for me in company time.'

'Catherine does. She asked me to get your dry-cleaning last week.'

'Most improper. Next time, say no. Now get started, we haven't got much time.'

In the event, it took over a week, and Madison had to supplement Dorothy's grudging labours with two typists from an agency. The spelling verifier alone took two hours to process the files, and it was not particularly useful: he was surprised to discover his father used many proper names in his poems, none of which belonged to the spelling program's dictionary and were thus flagged, wrongly, as spelling errors.

During this week Madison worked hard on the tools he would need to massage all this data. He took a subset of the original parser Pistolet had built, rewrote it in the A.I. *lingua franca* LISP, then recompiled it into the faster language C, and had it ready to run on his own souped-up desktop machine. The parser would scan the words in the new database, then assign appropriate grammatical information to them, based on the generalised lexicon Wellington had assembled two years before and a schema he took from the work of Verlinimmö, a Finn. Why so many outstanding linguists were Finns had never been satisfactorily explained to Madison. They had an insanely complicated language, virtually incapable of being learned by outsiders, but then so had the Basques, and the Click people of the Kalahari – and neither group had produced memorable linguists.

The analyser contained a disambiguity sensor to cope with words of multiple grammatical category: for example, 'sleeping' as an adjective in 'Lay your sleeping head, my love', or as a participle in his father's poem 'You at peace and sleeping calmly'. After this, a frequency analyser went to work. In his academic days Madison had scorned this kind of computational linguistics as old hat, pedestrian, but recently he had come to see it as a mine of information, especially when enhanced by a few extras. He now knew not only which words his father used and how often, but also what kind they were – the Romance-Latinate percentage of his vocabulary, the preponderance of certain function words ('a', 'the', 'of', etc.), the 'readability level' of the work as a whole. Later, when it came to generating text, he could specify the diction he wanted, although it was not clear he could be specific enough. He would soon find out.

It was at the end of the next week that the phone rang late in the afternoon. It was Pistolet.

'Yes, Jeffrey,' he said a little tetchily; he did not want to be distracted and would in any case see Pistolet in London the following week at the A.I. conference.

'Sound more cordial. Long time no hear. I mean, silence is golden but she's only a platinum-blonde.'

'What a pleasure to hear you,' said Madison.

'Go on, ignore us. Sally moves steadily towards the marital tea-ceremony and I'm buried by top-down theorists. Not to mention Ryerson.'

'What about him?'

'He's all over my ass like an erogenous mosquito-net. Maybe he wants to harass me.'

'Complain to the Blue Rinse Lady.'

'Are you kidding? We're hoping she'll self-destruct. Anyway, what gives? Is life getting you down? Cheer up; at least you're still alive.'

'So what, you're alive too, or at least, up to a point.'

'And that point taken. But some people *aren't* alive. As of last night, one of our colleagues is no longer with us.'

'Another car accident?' asked Madison. Route 128 had been known to claim the odd employee.

'Nothing so drab. This was strictly a Third World event. Hang on – is South Africa the Third World?'

'Hardly. I thought we didn't do business with them.'

'We don't, even though the government has kindly offered our Chinese executives honorary white man's status. Big of them, don't you think? They do that with the Japanese, apparently, ever since they started buying their cars.'

'So?'

'So, it's ironic that having sent two executives to Johannesburg to reiterate our lack of interest in doing business there, one of them should get blown to bits in the lobby of his hotel by an ANC bomb. Our guys weren't even the enemy; one of those freak accidents so beloved by revolutionary movements.'

'Jesus.'

'I'll say. The flags are at half-mast on top of the Cathedral.'

'Is everyone upset?'

'I wouldn't go that far. Even funeral clouds have their silver lining. You remember Operation Trojan?'

How could Madison forget? It had been a talking database that was supposed to double the company's revenues in two years – and this in the early days of text-to-speech recognition. The problem was, the database hadn't known when to shut up; customers had to turn off entire systems just to get this one application to be quiet. Ling had sold only six packages in eighteen months, and for a while the Empress had threatened to shut down the entire A.I. group.

'Well, the guy who got iced in South Africa was the marketing genius in charge of that one. See what happens to you when you fuck up badly enough.'

'Don't be so tasteless.'

'All right. But seriously, his family is looking at something like eight hundred K in compensation. If I were married I might tell my wife to hope for a bomb, too.'

'You nervous about flying here?'

'Not me,' said Pistolet. 'It's the others; they are actually taking protective sessions with Sammy's bodyguard.'

Alarm bells rang for Madison. '*Others*?'

'Yes, even Sally. Though you've got to admit London is a serious terrorist target. Not for the ANC, maybe, but there are lots of other twisted characters hanging out there. The IRA, and the INLA, and the PLO, and the USO, and the GPO – '

'Yeh, and the BO,' said Madison curtly. 'Cut it, will you. What's this got to do with Sally? Why are you talking about London and her?'

There was a silence on the other end. It was difficult to detect conversational nuance over trans-Atlantic lines, but Madison sensed that Pistolet was considering which tack to take, which high line of insouciance mixed with provocation would work best – work, that is, to get a rise out of Madison. 'You tell me,' Pistolet said lightly. 'You're in a better position to recommend a London hotel than I am.'

'To Sally? I thought only you were coming to this conference. She's coming over here, too?'

'*Absolument*, daddy-o. Along with me, and Greenfield, and the Blue Rinse Lady herself. Week after next. Same as me. Enjoy, as Greenfield would say.'

123

'Why are *they* all coming over?'

'Because Lisa has taken to A.I. with a vengeance. She's decided it's the wave of the future and wants Ling at this conference, waving the flag. She can't fly over everybody in the A.I. group, so this year it's the Natural Language group's turn. She's probably trying to boost our morale. The parser isn't getting any faster.'

'Don't mix so many metaphors. You're all coming, I can't believe it.'

'Start keeping the faith. But don't worry, Sally's not coming to see you. Catherine or Clytemnaestra or whatever her name is hasn't got anything to worry about. Sally's really and truly engaged now: it's official. She'll be all business with you, boy, don't flatter yourself.'

'It's official?' This came as no relief.

'The wedding's on the day after Hallowe'en, which seems appropriate, considering the horror story she's about to become a part of. A big affair: Dedham Church; the cream of Boston society. Sally said I had to liven it up by throwing confetti, but I said it would be more fitting to throw rice. Fried rice. She didn't think this was very funny.'

'It's not.'

'Of course it's funny. Don't go all pious on me. I've got to run: I just wanted to fill you in on our tragedy in Jo'berg and our impending arrival. In five minutes the Blue Rinse Lady wants me to go over my astrology demo and explain how it works. Got any useful suggestions for that?'

'Yeah, 'fess up.'

'Thanks. I tell Minnie Lu you're a genius and this is the thanks I get.'

'You told Minnie Lu that? Really?'

'No, not really. Why try and make the Dragon Lady laugh? See you at dinner next Tuesday night. Lisa will be there, so consider it a command performance. So long.'

Madison went home and found Catherine hanging curtains. 'Where's the whisky, Robert?' she asked, and he went and made her a drink. Bringing it back, he explained to Catherine that Tuesday's trip to her Granny was off.

She responded stiffly. 'Why do you have to be in London on Tuesday?'

'Because my boss says so. Pistolet was supposed to come alone to this conference, but now most of the Natural Language group is coming. So I have to be there as well.'

'Exactly who are they sending?'

'Someone named Greenfield. My new boss, Lisa Adams.' He paused. To hell with it; there was no reason to lie. 'And they may send Sally Zehring.'

Catherine looked at him. 'Isn't that the girl you used to go out with?'

'Don't worry about it.'

'Worry? Why should I worry, darling? From the little you ever said about her, she doesn't sound much of a threat. Not that I wouldn't trust you anyway. She sounded pretty common to me.'

His least favourite expression, perhaps because it had been a staple of his mother's repertoire – 'Rich but common,' she'd say of new arrivals in Vermont; 'He was rather a common, funny little man,' she might say of the plumber.

'Her breeding's just fine, Catherine,' he said sarcastically. 'Her uncle didn't play golf but he was on the Supreme Court of Louisiana.'

Catherine laughed a little falsely. 'Very prestigious, I'm sure. Don't you Americans laugh at those funny little Southern states?'

Madison stretched his legs under the table. 'There are plenty of racists in the North. Once you meet some Southerners you realise they're not all half-crazed illiterate crackers.'

'This woman read poetry to you before bed, I suppose,' said Catherine, who was defensive about Madison's

125

excessive education. She had exactly one A-level to her name.

'Erotic verse.'

'Charming,' she said, not looking bothered, which in turn bothered Madison. Did he want her jealous, worried about Sally's appearance in his life? Probably; there was something annoying about a totally complacent partner.

'She's perfectly nice,' he added, unsure why he wanted to keep on the subject of Sally.

'I'm sure,' said Catherine again, and he could tell she had already tuned out, with the vacant look that usually arose if he started talking about neural networks or parallel processing. 'What shall we have for dinner?' she asked, her voice brightening.

When Dorothy and the temps had finished the entry of his father's poems, it took only a matter of hours to sort the words and run the analytic tools he had developed for them. The total numbers were unsurprising, but broken down into the three compartments he had specified of early, middle, and later work, there were some interesting differences. In the early work, for example, there was a smaller proportion of articles, particularly 'the'. This was Auden's influence, Madison felt sure, however much his father denied it; the Yorkshire habit of saying 'went down pit', not 'went down *the* pit' transmogrified into the curt clipped voice, almost Germanic, of the younger Auden. Madison's father had written about such different topics – the war, rural life, heterosexual love – that the influence had rarely been detected.

In the middle years there were many more proper names – the words Vermont, Maine, then a host of Italian place-names – statistically significant enough to warrant inclusion in the domain-specific lexicon he would use in the generator. Here too the Romance-Latinate percentile swelled, reflecting the growing lushness of diction, his

126

father's movement away from the starker Anglo-Saxon vocabulary (often very Frost-like) of his early work.

He ran the parser overnight through the entire list to assign each word to its appropriate grammatical category. Unfortunately, his father seemed to have a propensity for words that doubled as nouns and verbs, a trait that would have stood him in good stead in the computer industry. He's as bad as Sammy Ling, Madison decided.

2

Ling was not a merchant bank, not its employees merchant princes. For them the confines of a Holiday Inn or Sheraton were ample, indeed luxurious. There was no demand to go further, to stay in the Ritz, spend ninety dollars on dinner, use a helipad.

All of which, during his tenure at Ling, Pistolet had managed to do. Now Madison found him in a large corner room of the Hyde Park Hotel, overlooking the park, dressed in a kind of preppy overdrive: a navy-blue Lacoste shirt with a red-and-blue-striped Brooks Brothers tie, chinos with a striped cloth belt, and Bass Weejuns with argyll socks. Capping everything was a sports jacket of red check madras. Madison felt staid in his blazer, grey flannels and brown brogues.

Room service had been up with a supply of mixers and ice; Pistolet's one gesture towards economy was to bring his own booze – a duty-free quart of Chivas Regal. He poured them each a tumblerful of whisky, threw in some ice, then tried insincerely to add some soda. 'Tell me how you'll get this place on expenses,' Madison said.

Pistolet smiled. 'London's very crowded this time of year, you know. I persuaded Lisa Adams this was the only hotel with available rooms. She may have thought the price I quoted was in dollars, not pounds.'

'That's because you *told* her it was in dollars,' said Madison as he sat down by the window and admired the view of Hyde Park. 'So what's the agenda?'

'Nothing too strenuous. The conference tomorrow; a quick visit to you the day after; then a late-night flight back to Boston. You'll be spared Lisa Adams the day after tomorrow; she's got to see European marketing in Paris and will fly back from there. Though, so far, she's been pretty relaxed; she even got half-looped on the plane-ride over here.'

'I assume she's joining us tonight?' When Pistolet nodded, Madison added, 'Can we shake off the others?'

'If we dump Greenfield on Sally, she'd never forgive me. Anyway, who wants to? The Blue Rinse Lady alone is a terrible prospect. She still wants to know the secret of my astrological demo. I've managed to persuade her it's not commercial, but she's pretty insistent on getting a copy for personal use.' He started pacing in the narrow space between his bed and the wall. 'She didn't bring it up on the plane, but she's bound to tonight.' Pistolet stopped pacing. 'We need outside intervention to save me from the Blue Rinse Lady. Where's your friend Kaminski?'

'Funny you ask. I think he's down here at his flat tonight.'

'So call him. We need him.'

'What do I tell him?'

'The truth, of course.' He began pacing again. 'He's no fool, even if he is your friend. Tell him dinner is free at the restaurant of our choice. In delightful company: my wit, Sally's brains and, let's be honest, her boobs. Do you think women have any idea how men really talk about them when they're not there? I mean, even educated, sensitive men like us. Or me, at any rate. Best of all, from Kaminski's point of view, the charms of the Blue Rinse Lady. You said yourself the woman was attractive. I have a feeling he'll go for her. And her for him. Or she for he. Is my grammar right?'

'Your reasoning is. Even if they don't like each other, you've got Lisa Adams off your hands.'

'Cynical, cynical.' Pistolet swallowed some whisky. 'But right.'

It proved easy to persuade Kaminski to join them; he came to the hotel lounge, where Pistolet and Madison were continuing to drink. 'So who else is here?' he asked as the waiter brought him his own drink, a vodka and tonic.

'Wait and see,' said Pistolet. 'Goodies from America.'

'Actually, an Antipodean arrival,' said Madison, thinking of Lisa Adams.

'If she's anything like that,' said Kaminski, pointing to a woman in silk-satin pyjama trousers at the reception desk, 'I'll be perfectly happy to show her the ropes.'

When the woman turned around Madison saw it was Sally Zehring. When she saw them, she smiled and came over. 'Hello, Robert,' said Sally, and kissed him carefully on both cheeks.

'How European!' cried Pistolet. 'Waiter, a Cinzano for the *signorina*.' The joke was lost as a waiter nipped forward, nodded at Pistolet and set off smartly for the bar.

'Keep it here for me,' Sally declared. 'I've got to go upstairs and change.'

'You look fine as you are,' said Madison, remembering how her quick changes could take an hour.

'Why, thank you,' she said. 'With any luck I'll look even better once I shower.'

And so she did when she reappeared, half an hour and two rounds of drinks later, in the company of Lisa Adams. The Blue Rinse Lady was looking relatively low-key: no hot-pants, no leather, just a sleeveless dress of white

129

linen that highlighted her tan. She must have recently gone to the hairdresser, for the blue-rinse streak in her blonde curls quivered in the lobby light like a feminist hologram. Kaminski seemed impressed; Lisa looked him up and down carefully when introduced.

Sally was also wearing a sleeveless dress, but it was slinkier, in black silk that showed off her curves. She wore heels, and a fair amount of jewellery. Of the men present, only Kaminski, trendy in a suit of double-breasted pin-stripes that he had not yet had time to rumple, looked suitably attired to escort the two women.

The five of them went out and crammed into a cab. Pistolet and Madison were the two tallest, but sat scrunched up on the jump-seats. Kaminski sat beaming in between the two women.

'Where is Greenfield?' asked Madison.

'Not well,' said Pistolet. 'Jet-lag *par excellence*. He's sleeping in his room.'

They ate at a bistro in the West End, sitting at a long table at the back. Pistolet took command, putting Kaminski and Lisa Adams across from each other at one end, and Sally at the far end against the wall. He pointed a finger as Madison began to sit in the middle. 'Where have your manners gone? Move down one. You and Sally should have a lot to talk about.'

'I need a drink,' said Lisa Adams, confiscating one of the two bottles of white wine the waiters brought. Pistolet sat in the middle, unpaired, and began talking. 'Jet-lag,' he was declaring, 'there isn't any such animal, whatever Greenfield says. It's just an excuse by the sedentary to catch some extra zee's. The best way to avoid it is to party, party, party.'

Madison looked at Sally and smiled. 'To listen to him you'd think he did nothing but travel. I bet you this is his first trip out of the Cathedral since he last came over here.'

'Was he this manic then?'

'He was worse. He tried single-handedly to change the licensing hours of the pubs.' He moved his feet and accidentally kicked Sally lightly in the process. Madison peered under the tablecloth at her feet. 'Sorry about that, but at least you've learned to keep your shoes on in a restaurant.'

She nodded. 'Ever since you hid them under the couch at that Chinese restaurant in Boston.'

'How did I know the fire department would show up?' Sally had hopped around shoeless on a pavement in Back Bay for half an hour before a false alarm was declared.

Pistolet now turned his attention to them, Kaminski and Lisa Adams having found the topic of direct mail in common. Madison sided with Sally against the exuberant zaniness of Pistolet, an alliance that dated from the days of their romance. Pistolet was in high gear: 'You and Sally should see more of each other,' he said, ignoring Madison's hostile eyes. 'But then, neither of you is a big traveller.'

'And you are, Jeffrey?' asked Sally.

'Of course not,' he said as he poured himself more wine and ordered another bottle from the waiter. 'I only travel when I have a reason.'

'What, when your signs are right?' asked Lisa Adams, eavesdropping. 'That's one area where your program will help, Jeffrey.'

'Will?' queried Pistolet. '"Might have" is more like it. Now that Blackburn's gone.' His tone suddenly shifted to the lachrymose.

'Who was Blackbird?' asked the Blue Rinse Lady.

'Blackburn. Robin Blackburn,' Pistolet said slowly. 'Perhaps the finest software engineer ever employed in the Cathedral. A man of truly remarkable gifts.' He paused and pointed a finger at his temple. 'If not quite all there.'

'Typical R and D space cadet,' she said dryly. 'What happened to him anyway?'

'It's a long story,' said Pistolet, with no intention of stopping. 'Robin Blackburn was a coding genius, but also the most absent-minded man I've ever met. I mean, really out to lunch. I speak with some authority, comrades, because he and I were partners in many a project – the Omega translators, the Persimmon pre-parsing code. Before your time,' he said to Lisa Adams, 'but you remember, Robert.'

Madison could only stutter a brief affirmative. He had heard of none of these projects, nor, for that matter, of Robin Blackburn.

'Anyway,' continued Pistolet, looking askance at Madison, 'some time ago Robin Blackburn was sent by Minnie Lu to Berlin to inspect a new document architecture. Extremely hush-hush. It was created by two young wizards at the Technology Institute there, and if it did what they said, this architecture would revolutionise text storage and retrieval, making an editor run like lightning. Blackburn was to examine the system; if it passed muster, Ling would release monies held in escrow to the young Berliners, and Blackburn would fly straight home with the source code. The muckety-mucks in the Cathedral were extremely paranoid about the whole thing; they actually contemplated having Sammy Ling's bodyguard go with Blackburn, but finally calmer heads prevailed and they sent him incognito.

'Blackburn flies in to Berlin, goes to the meeting, and lo and behold, the architecture really does seem to work. Blackburn is very excited, he phones the Cathedral, they release the money, and he runs to catch his plane, taking the source code with him. For once Try Walking Across was on time and he just makes his flight. The plane takes off, climbs to thirty thousand feet, and then Blackburn discovers that in his rush he's left his

132

passport in the Berlin terminal, probably on a counter in duty-free.'

'Wow,' said Lisa Adams. Kaminski looked rather more sceptical.

'Blackburn was flying to Boston, but he had to change planes in London. When he gets there, he goes up to passport control with twelve pieces of identification: company ID, driver's licence, credit cards – you name it – and says to the guy behind the desk, "I've lost my passport, but I can prove I am who I say I am." The man takes one look at this high-tech goofball and says, "Not to me you can't, not without a passport, anyway."

'Blackburn makes the fatal mistake of losing his temper. He was usually a shy, retiring kind of chap,' Pistolet said, stressing the quaint sound of 'chap', as if to show how well he was adapting to his English environment. 'But he was furious to have his integrity questioned. Officialdom meant nothing to Blackburn. And once you're rude to a passport official, it's all over: there was no way the official was going to let Blackburn into the country, not even long enough to buy a ticket and go back to Berlin to find the passport.'

'So what happened?' asked Lisa Adams.

'They put him in a holding cell for two days, entirely incommunicado,' said Pistolet, 'during which the Cathedral went absolutely apeshit. You'd have thought it was a Len Deighton movie – they decided Blackburn had gone AWOL and joined the oppo.'

'Oppo?' asked Madison.

'Isn't that what they call the enemy over here? You know, Big Blue, DEC, Wang, Hewlett Packard. Anyone with the dough to buy out Blackburn. Now, back at Heathrow a bedraggled Blackburn is called into a little room where the men of Her Majesty's service are going to decide his fate. He's quite desperate by then, poor guy, and willing to do anything. "Please," he begs the officers,

133

"just call my employers. They'll confirm my identity. Call them in Massachusetts." "Ring your employers?" the officials say. "Don't be daft. Our expenses don't run to that." "I'll pay for the call," Blackburn announces, and the Brits, being the cheap bastards we all know they are (sorry, Kaminski) get excited and say, "He'll pay for the call!" And off they go to ring Massachusetts.'

'Oh no,' said Madison, fairly sure of what was coming.

'Olney picked up the phone in Personnel.'

'How do you know it was Olney?' asked Madison sourly.

'I don't. Maybe it was Macaulay or Smith. What's the difference, Robert? Anyway, Olney picks up the phone and hears a British voice on the line, saying, "This is the United Kingdom Immigration Authority, do you have someone working for you by the name of Robin Simon Blackburn?" And Olney, brilliant scientist of human nature, thinking Blackburn's now with the enemy, suspects an elaborate trick. Any minute, he decides, the voice will start demanding ransom money. So he says tersely, "We have no record of anyone by that name in our employ." And before he can ask the voice anything, the U.K. authority simply says, "Thank you," and hangs up the phone at this end.'

'So how did Blackburn finally get out?' asked Lisa Adams.

'We don't know that he ever did. He was in detention at least a week later, because someone from Ling Britain who was flying out of Heathrow saw him during his daily exercise round. Apparently you get an hour, in the company of two guards. This English guy in turn told his pals travelling to Europe to keep an eye out for poor Blackburn; they started leaving stuff for him – a clean shirt, razor blades, that kind of thing. But then one day they discovered their last bit of contraband had never been picked up – I think it was a tube of toothpaste.'

'So he got out,' said Lisa Adams.

'That's what everyone at Ling thought,' said Pistolet. 'But he never turned up.'

'He must have sold out to the enemy after all, or else he would have returned to the States.'

'Maybe,' admitted Pistolet, 'but then there were the postcards. Addressed to Olney, Macaulay and Smith at the Cathedral: "I'm still here," the first one read, "why did you betray me?" They were postmarked Heathrow. There were also sightings.'

'Sightings? Sounds like a UFO,' said Kaminski.

'Not far off. You'd be rushing through Heathrow with just enough time to stop at the duty-free store, and you'd look up and there he was, on the far side of the register, Blackburn, the Man Who Didn't Make It Through Passport Control, ambling through the departure lounge. By the time you got through the queue, he'd be gone.'

Pistolet assumed an air of gravity, concluding, 'So that's how Ling lost out on the next generation's document architecture.'

'Fuck that,' said Lisa Adams in a rush of pent-up agitation, 'it's the astrology code we need.'

Pistolet threw his hands up with an air of futility. 'Gone too, gone with the wind. Blackburn wrote twice as much of the code as I did. He,' said Pisolet with atypical modesty, 'was the moving genius behind the astrology project. Which is why,' he said, staring earnestly at Lisa, 'though you were kind enough to credit me with Astrologer, it is, alas, Blackburn alone who could really help you. Until we find him there will be no future for the program.'

'I'll find him,' Lisa Adams declared, and stood up. 'I'm calling People Resource right now and telling that asshole Olney to straighten this out.' She walked away intently.

Madison eyed Pistolet, and after a long pause, said, 'There had better be a Blackburn somewhere, Jeffrey.'

'There is,' Pistolet confidently replied. 'He left Ling two

years ago to bum around Europe. God knows where he is now – they'll never find him. He was a real douche-bag, too. Didn't know C from COBOL.'

'Careful,' said Sally, for Lisa Adams was returning.

'Someone's on the phone so I couldn't get through,' she said, sitting down. 'But I will.' And she began talking to Kaminski again about long-term debt, while Pistolet listened politely.

'How much longer do you have?' Sally asked Madison as their food came.

'For the company? About five months, according to Minnie Lu. She said six, but that was a month ago. A lot could happen during that time.'

'Do you think so?' Her tone made it clear the question was rhetorical. 'I don't think Minnie Lu or Virgil are very likely to change their minds.'

'You have that on high authority?' he asked sarcastically.

Sally didn't seem flustered by this allusion. 'Sammy? No, I wasn't referring to him; at least, he's never mentioned it to me. As I said back in Madison, Robert, Sammy isn't jealous of you any more. He's not as insecure a man as you make him out to be.'

'*I* do? You're the one who suggested he was obsessed by supposed prep school slights. If I were him, I wouldn't be telling my fiancée how some adolescent crap has haunted me ever since.'

'Why do you still hate him so much?'

Madison scoffed. 'I don't hate him. Don't be ridiculous. I simply don't respect him, which is *not* the same thing.'

'If you didn't hate him you wouldn't be so uncharitable about him. It's not easy being Sammy Ling.'

'He gets rewarded. And it's not as if he's had to push for the rewards.'

'Oh, and you did, I suppose?'

Pistolet returned his attention to them as he heard

136

Sally's voice rise. 'Enough, you two. No heat tonight, okay?' He addressed the table at large. 'Who wants dessert? No one? Fine. Let's get the bill and boogey. I haven't come four thousand miles to hear these two spat.'

'Where are we going?' asked Kaminski. He and the Blue Rinse Lady seemed deeply engrossed.

'I know a place,' said Pistolet.

Madison groaned. 'What *kind* of place?'

'It's entirely respectable.'

'I'd take you to Annabel's,' said Kaminski, 'but it's closed for redecoration. So much for my four hundred a year.'

'Four hundred pounds,' murmured Lisa Adams appreciatively.

'I write it off, of course,' said Kaminski, and she nodded sagely.

Led by Pistolet, they walked along Park Lane to Piccadilly, then turned down a side-street near Fortnum's. It was cooler now and they walked briskly, past a shirt-maker off Jermyn Street, a bistro, and a vendor of military paraphernalia. It did not seem ripe territory for nightlife, but suddenly Pistolet stopped before a canvas awning, painted green, that said The Go-Go Club. 'Here we are,' he declared.

Inside, only a few tables were occupied. They were ushered past a long mahogany bar to a smaller, darker room at the back. Kaminski ordered some white wine. Madison soon realised that almost everyone was getting tight, especially Pistolet; only Sally, who was drinking more slowly, seemed sober. Kaminski and Lisa Adams had clearly established emotional as well as fiscal rapport; they sat down together as a matter of course. Pistolet announced he was going to stand at the bar ('check out the prospects'), so Madison found himself again sitting with Sally. Music was playing from hidden speakers, and soon Kaminski and Lisa Adams got up to dance. Madison and Sally watched with fascination as Lisa Adams put both arms around Kaminski, then cupped her hands behind his neck and pressed him towards her. Kaminski himself seemed unsurprised by this display, and smiled mildly. They moved slowly around the dance-floor, stubbornly adhering to a leisurely tempo even when the tape began to play aggressive rock-and-roll. The club was filling up; a boisterous bunch of Yuppies occupied the table next to theirs. They looked like ad people, or PR types out for a good time after a successful launch. They certainly made a lot of noise.

Madison and Sally made desultory conversation for a bit, then 'Are you going to have a fuck?' she seemed to ask over the din.

'What?' he shouted back in surprise.

'Are you having any luck?' she said more clearly. 'You know, with Creation.'

'Not a lot. But I'm hoping that may change.' He leaned forward and shouted, 'I think I've found the right domain.' He told her at some length about his choice of his father's *oeuvre* as guinea-pig. It was hard to make himself heard, especially as a man in a white suit at the Yuppies' table kept shouting about a priest. Finally Madison picked up a paper napkin and took out a pen to sketch his plan, but Sally put her hand on his wrist. 'Don't bother,' she said. 'It's too noisy here. Tell me tomorrow. Let's go,' she said. 'I need some sleep.'

The man at the next table was growing angry. 'I don't care if he is a priest,' he was shouting. 'They ought to throw him out anyway.'

Another man at the table, whom Madison couldn't see, began to chant, 'Fish, fish, fish.'

'Sh-sh,' hushed his female companion, looking at Madison in a half-embarrassed, half-delighted way.

'Father O'Hara's a dirty old man. Father O'Malley's a goat in disguise,' said the invisible man.

'I've never seen a priest like that before,' said the woman.

'What in God's name are they talking about?' Sally asked.

'Who knows? They're all drunk. Let's get out of here.'

Madison paid the bill, after looking vainly for Kaminski and the Blue Rinse Lady. It would be interesting to see if she queried the tab when it appeared on his expenses. He and Sally walked into the front room, to find a small commotion in progress at the bar. A barman was tugging at the jacket of a man sitting on a bar stool; next to him sat a young woman with hennaed hair and a green miniskirt who was leaning away, looking frightened. On closer inspection, the man on the stool turned out to be Pistolet, who had removed his tie and added to his Lacoste shirt the extra sartorial touch of a priest's collar.

'Oh God,' said Madison. 'I'd better try and save him.' He walked across to the bar and addressed the barman. 'What's the matter with this man?' he demanded.

'Nothing to worry about, sir,' the man said, now waving to a bouncer at the front door to come and help him. 'The good Father here has been over-indulging himself. I think it's best to put him in a taxi and send him home.'

'Father Pistolet,' Madison said sternly, addressing his friend. 'Have you been misbehaving yourself?'

Pistolet was just sober enough to manage a rapid shake of his head. 'No, my son. Scout's honour,' he added inappropriately.

'For a man of the cloth he's got very clammy hands,' said the young woman in green, as her fear dissipated. She now seemed intent on continuing to play a part in the proceedings. 'I thought RCs were meant to be celibate.'

The tag 'RC' seemed to spur Pistolet, himself half-Catholic on his father's side, into action. He shook free of the barman and the recently-arrived bouncer and stood with his feet balanced on the lowest rung of the bar stool. He loomed over everyone, balancing himself with one hand on the bar, the other stabbing out into space above their heads as he began to speak:

'I am a Vicar from Ling Enterprises.'

Madison kept himself from pointing out the untruth of this. How could he explain to an angry barman, what his friend really meant? Two large men at a table stood up and applauded. 'Encore!' they shouted. Moved, Pistolet began again:

> Hath not a priest passion?
> Hath not a cleric cravings?
> If you tempt us with the same means,
> do we not heat, in winter,
> summer, and Fall, and do we not prick
> or wish to prick the virgin's blood?

Here the bouncer was joined by a colleague; this reinforced enforcement lifted Pistolet high into the air as the hands of the heavies held him up by his armpits. He was singing now, to the tune of 'When You're A Jet' from *West Side Story*:

> When you're at Ling
> you get down on your knees,
> you say, 'Sun God, I'm grateful,
> o' Empress, I'm pleased.'
> When you're at Ling
> you say 'Sammy, our care
> is to make you more money,
> through third-rate hardware.'
> The COBOL's buggy . . .

His voice grew strangled as he was carried from the room. On their way out, Madison and Sally met the bouncers on their way in. Pistolet they found sprawled on the pavement, waving his legs in the air and now singing to the tune of 'Mammy':

> Sammy, how I love you, how I love you,
> my dear old Sammy.
> You've got Caucasian skin,
> your eyes are not quite thin
> enough to pass as Asian.

'Hail a taxi, will you?' said Madison to Sally. 'I'll try to get Father Christmas here back on his feet.'

'Hath not,' Pistolet struggled to say as Madison lifted him up under the arms.

'Shut up, Jeffrey,' Madison ordered. 'We can't take much more of this.' Sally had managed to find a cab at the corner and helped Madison load Pistolet into the back seat. Pistolet sang '"O the mad dogs of Bitely, they wear their learning lightly",' then suddenly fell asleep.

'What a jerk,' said Madison uncensoriously.

Sally laughed. 'It's just like old times.'

At the hotel they managed to pry Pistolet out of the taxi, into the lift, and up to his room. He collapsed on his bed in a heap. 'I suppose we can't just leave him like that,' said Sally. She pulled off his shoes while Madison managed to work off the madras jacket. The priest's collar had a Velcro strip at the back which Madison pulled off with a rip. He held the collar up in the air. 'I always wondered how these went on.'

'What did you think, they came in one piece?' Sally giggled again. 'Did you believe priests pulled them on over their heads or something.'

'I guess so. Like putting on a doughnut. You know, put your head through the hole.'

Sally giggled, but seemed to catch herself. 'It's almost two o'clock and I'm due in the hall at nine.' She started to go to the door.

'Wait a second,' said Madison. 'What about me?'

'What about you?'

'I was going to stay at Kaminski's flat if I missed the last train, but I can't go there now. I'm sure he's got the Blue Rinse Lady with him.'

'So stay here,' she said.

'I can't stay here – I'm not sleeping in the same bed with this guy. Even if I were inclined that way, he takes up all the room. I mean, look at him.' He pointed down at the recumbent Pistolet, who had indeed managed to corner all but a corner of the double bed.

'Can't you sleep in one of these chairs or something?'

'Thanks a lot. I come all the way down to London to show you the town and you're going to make me sleep in a chair. I need some sleep, too, you know; I've got to be at this convention myself.'

'What am I supposed to do about it?'

'Let me sleep in your room. I bet you it has two beds, you always took two beds.'

'It does, as a matter of fact. But I can't let you sleep there. What would people think?'

'What people? It's two in the morning, for Christ's sakes. I just want to go to sleep, then get up and get out of here.'

'I don't know. How can I be sure I can trust you?'

'What? Who visited whose hotel room back in the States? I was a perfect gentleman there; you were the one making advances.'

'Not really, I just had too much to drink. Like you've had tonight.'

'Oh for God's sakes, just let me use the other bed, okay? You can trust me. No one's ever going to know – not Sammy, or my fiancée, or even Pistolet – I'll tell him I went back to Kaminski's. Not that he's likely to ask.'

Sally still hesitated, and Madison used this as an excuse to open the room door and move out into the hall. She followed slowly, saying, 'No funny business now, you promise?' Down the hall a porter moved from door to door, collecting breakfast orders left hanging around the doorknobs. He ignored them as they moved towards the lifts.

'Where are you going?' asked Sally, stopping by a door.

'Oh, are you on the same floor?'

She took out a key from her handbag and opened her door. 'No funny business, now,' she repeated. As he followed her into the room he saw the porter down the hall. He looked away from Madison's guilty gaze but murmured audibly, 'Good luck, sir,' as Madison entered her room and closed the door.

Sally went quickly to the far bed in the room, as if to claim it, while Madison crossed to the window and pulled back the curtains. He looked over Knightsbridge, quiet and deserted at this hour. He was unable to open the window and could hear nothing but the low hum of the air-conditioner.

'You do what you want,' said Sally, 'but I've got to get some sleep.' She went and took a nightgown from the dresser's middle drawer, then walked into the bathroom and locked the door behind her. Madison heard water run, then the sound of Sally brushing her teeth.

He looked around the room, which already had stray articles of Sally's scattered about: a brush and make-up bag on the bureau top; a paperback on phrase structure grammars lying face down on her bed; a green address book on the night table; a half-empty bottle of Evian water on top of the television. Not for her the methodical orderliness of Catherine; Sally was neat when needed, but not obsessed.

The sight of the water bottle made him thirsty. He found a mini-bar in the tiny hallway by the room's door and poured himself a Scotch and soda with two of the miniatures and a bottle of Perrier. Sipping his drink, he sat down on the bed and looked through Sally's address book, turning at once to the listings under L. He had counted a good ten numbers for various Lings when the bathroom door opened and Sally came out. She wore a simple white nightgown and had brushed out her hair: it flowed in a gold mane half in front and half behind her shoulders. 'What the hell are you doing?'

'How many phones does Sammy Ling have?' he asked mildly, taking another sip from his glass.

She came and took the address book out of his hand. It was impossible to tell if she was truly angry, since in the past they had rifled each other's belongings as a matter of course. She got her brush and sat down on the edge of her bed across from him, slowly stroking her rich blonde hair. 'Let's see,' she said calmly, 'there's one phone for the public which the secretary answers, then another that's not listed in the corporate directory. Then there's his direct line; it's on his desk. Then there's two at home; same distinction. One for the car, and another for the chauffeur to find out if his flight's delayed. Finally, there's one in the helicopter. Of course.'

'Of course,' said Madison, loosening his tie.

Sally smiled and started brushing the hair on the other side of her head. 'Poor Jeffrey. He may have thought that ridiculous story about Robin Blackburn convinced the Blue Rinse Lady to forget about the astrology program, but I doubt it. She'll keep on at him about it until she finds out he's hoaxed her. Then his goose will really be cooked. It won't need Sam to fire him: Lisa will get to do it all on her own.'

'She's terrible.'

Sally put her brush down on the night table, pulled back the covers and got into bed. 'Why don't you turn off the overhead light and go to sleep?'

He turned on the bedside lamp, then went to the door

and hit the main switch. Sally plumped a pillow before laying her head on it and looked up at Madison in the dimmed light of the room. 'About Jeffrey, I don't know what to say. Lately he's been drinking far too much. He's never taken my advice, even if we are friends. And I can't talk to anyone else about it. You know what People Resource are like. Jeffrey's such a thorn in their side that they'd love to have something on him. Would *you* trust Olney?'

'Couldn't you talk to Sammy? Surely he knows how talented Pistolet is. He wouldn't want to lose him.'

She shook her head emphatically. 'He's very prudish about drinking. You'd almost think he was actually Chinese, the way he behaves. He doesn't even like me to drink a glass of wine when we have dinner in a restaurant.'

'That must be a considerable sacrifice.'

'It is. How about you? Are you drinking much these days?'

He held up his glass. 'Cheers,' he declared. 'No, tonight is pretty unusual. I don't drink much any more, probably because I'm no longer in the vicinity of Pistolet. I have a drink or two when I get home from work most nights. But that's about it.'

'You must be happy now.'

He looked at her for a moment before responding. 'No, I was happy when I knew you.' He walked over to the window and tried to decide if the filtered light against the bedroom wall was refracted moonlight or from street-lamps. He looked over at Sally and saw that her eyes were closed. 'You listening?' he asked, and she nodded in response. He took off his jacket and tie and draped them over a chair-back, then went to the bathroom and chewed some of Sally's toothpaste, remembering that even when they had been lovers she had balked at his using her toothbrush. When he came out, Sally's eyes were closed.

'You still awake?' he whispered, and she murmured. 'How about you?' he asked. 'Are *you* that happy these days?' At first he thought that she had fallen asleep, but then she shrugged very slightly, barely enough to move the pillow beneath her head.

'I know what you mean,' he said, and walked to the window again. 'Sometimes I almost envy my father. Here we are, good at what we do, educated, well-paid. And yet don't you feel powerless?' He turned around to look at her face in the dim light. 'You awake? Of course you are; you're just pretending to be asleep. Otherwise I could talk about things and you wouldn't bat an eyelash – like whether Sammy wants to sleep with two goats and the Blue Rinse Lady. All at the same time.'

A small smile appeared on Sally's face, which expanded slightly as she kept breathing steadily. 'I knew you were awake,' he said. 'You can't fool me.' He turned again to look out of the window. 'Where was I? People are always asking me whether I regret leaving Harvard, don't I hate working for a big company? And isn't it terrible working with computers? – as if the machines are to blame for the corporatisation of America. But computers aren't centralising at all; I can now put more power in a chip the size of my thumbnail than you could in a room full of refrigerator-sized machines thirty years ago. That's not centralising; that scares the corporate clones to death – they don't like the autonomy of that kind of power; that's half the reason it took so long for the microcomputer to emerge.

'I suppose I shouldn't be so contemptuous. If I were more normal, perhaps just less privileged, I'd have stayed at Harvard, taught my courses, made a living, and that would be that. Instead I came over here, seduced by the opportunity to do something unique. I should have known it couldn't last, not in corporate America anyway. You know, once, when I was in college, I asked my father why

146

he lived in Europe – I was being snotty, you know, "The twenties are over, old man, what are you doing there?" – and he said, "Son, America has become one big corporate buzz-saw." Now I think I know what he was getting at. America is becoming one big *opolis*, one vast corporate world. Ling, big as it is, still has some distinctiveness – but not for long. It will get swallowed up by something bigger. Or if the Empress is too proud, or Sammy's too stupid, and they try to stick it out, well then, *whoof*, the company will go caput.

'So what do you do? If you're lucky, you make enough money and build yourself a wall. Then you don't care who controls what, so long as you're not working, and you own your paddle tennis court, and the golf club lets your friends in. But it takes a lot of money to build a wall like that; more than I'll ever have.'

He finished his drink, then took off his shirt and trousers and placed them on the chair. He looked over at the bed. Sally was still lying on her back, a sexualised vision with gold hair floating down on the folded-back white sheet. He felt himself grow slightly excited and thought intently of stray asexual subjects – hitting a golf ball with a five-iron, the noise of the traffic outside in the night. He moved slowly and quietly towards Sally's bed and stood looking down at her. 'I'm not trying to scare you. It won't matter for you at all, I guess. If the company gets sold, Sammy will make out just fine. Fine? More than fine. I wouldn't mind retiring with a billion dollars.

'But I hope you know what you're doing. For that matter, I hope I do, too. It's seemed so long since we were together. Being over here has distanced it from me. And now, seeing you, and Jeffrey behaving like he always did, brings it all back. You really hurt me, Sally, as badly as – well, as bad as when my father left. And the awful thing is, I can see now that it was *my* fault. I was so busy feeling wounded that I couldn't see that it was self-inflicted. I should have come back, but I got swallowed up by my work. Creation – it's been more like Destruction. I know that now, seeing you.

'I could have done without it, to tell the truth; I was worried I would feel this way. Don't you feel it too, Sally?' He looked intently through the dark at her face, eager to discern any sign of assent. 'Just tell me if you feel it, too. Then I'll let you go to sleep. Simply say yes or no, that's all I want to hear.'

He stood staring, listening to the even breathing below him, until finally, reluctantly, he got into his own bed and almost instantly fell asleep.

3

When he awoke, Sally had finished dressing. 'What time is it?' he asked, sitting up.

'Almost eight thirty. I was going to let you sleep. Are you hung over?'

'Not really.'

'Jeffrey must be.' She picked up her handbag. 'Stay as long as you like. I've got to run; the show starts at nine.'

Madison said, 'Wait a minute.'

She stopped and looked impatient. 'What is it?'

'I mean, when will I see you again?'

'I should think in about two hours. I'm meeting someone from Siemens between ten and eleven, about machine translation, then I'm just going to walk around the hall. You'll find me; there can't be that many people attending an A.I. convention.'

148

'You'd be surprised. If I haven't found you by half past eleven, meet me by the front door.'

'Why?'

'You said you'd listen to my problems on Creation. So I'm taking you up on the offer.'

As soon as she left, Madison got up and showered and shaved (borrowing Sally's razor). He felt grungy, putting on old clothes, and borrowed a pair of purple socks from one of her drawers. He rang Pistolet's room but there was no answer. Resisting the considerable temptation to poke some more through Sally's belongings, he left the room and went downstairs to the lobby.

He felt no need to hurry to the conference centre, and decided to walk there. He set off along the edge of Hyde Park. Spring was advancing: bulbs had flowered in ordered profusion throughout the park. The temperature was beginning to climb, creating the usual illusion that summer would follow. Skirts were shorter, men were no longer wearing overcoats. Everywhere, happy clichés abounded.

Still dawdling, Madison walked north at the east end of the park and continued along Piccadilly until he turned down St James's. As he neared the white façade of Boodle's, he passed an old-style pharmacist and saw a familiar figure at the counter. He waited until Pistolet emerged, somewhat unsteadily, carrying a small paper bag. He showed no sign of surprise at finding Madison there. 'Christ, why didn't you stop me last night?' he said. His voice was ragged and hoarse. 'That Frascati was lethal.'

'The boozer always blames the brand. I rang you earlier, but no luck.'

'That reminds me, someone called you this morning.'

'What? When?'

'Very early – too early. In my room. I wasn't in best

149

form. I suggested they try Kaminski's – isn't that where you were staying?'

Madison nodded slowly and said, 'Who was it anyway?'

Pistolet shrugged. 'Some woman. Probably your English lady-friend. Once I said you weren't there, she didn't stick around to chat.'

Pistolet extracted a dark medicinal bottle from the paper bag, which he crumpled and chucked neatly into a litter bin as they came to the corner. Madison took the bottle and examined it closely. 'The Authentic Pick-Me-Up', read the label. In minute type, specific instructions followed. 'What's in this stuff? "By appointment to HM the Queen Mother", it says, for Christ's sake.'

Pistolet shook his head gingerly. 'The chemist – is that *really* what they're called here? – was pretty close-mouthed. But he seemed to be hinting that a large part of it is pure alcohol. In which case, why don't they open their goddamned pubs a little earlier and let me chase the hair of the dog in style?'

'You're supposed to mix it with water,' said Madison, still reading the label. He handed the bottle back to Pistolet.

'I know. But when I hit him up for a glass of the local *aqua vitae*, the man looked at me like I was asking for a vaginal deodorant. You don't happen to have a spoon on you, do you?'

Madison went through an elaborate pantomime of checking his pockets. 'Damn. Only yesterday I had my spoon right here in its usual place. Whatever could I have done with it?'

'Thanks a lot. I've got to find some water. I don't care if this stuff is pure alcohol, it smells awful. I've got to cut it with something.'

'This is Clubland,' said Madison as they neared Pall Mall. 'Any gentleman buying this potion would have a club within spitting distance in which to imbibe it.'

'"In which to imbibe it." Jesus, Robert, you didn't use to talk like that.'

'Sorry. But you didn't use to drink like that, either.' They walked along Pall Mall, past an angling shop where he had gone with his father to buy a fly rod almost a quarter-century before.

'Where are we going to find some water, Robert?' Pistolet looked around at the grey and faded yellow stone that lined the Mall – faceless, impersonal, daunting, and bone-dry. 'Hasn't the Somerset Club reciprocal privileges with one of these outfits?'

'Since when are you a member of the Somerset Club?'

'My brother is. Or at least, he was, until he forgot to pay his dues three years running.' He pointed to a ponderous portico across the street that Madison knew belonged to the Reform Club. 'I don't suppose that fraternal link would buy me a beer in there. Or even a glass of water.'

Madison was thinking of his father's fly rod. It had been a brush rod, the same height as his father, though it had towered over the eight-year-old Robert. His father had paid cash, in the old money – there had been a threepenny-bit in his father's change. It was gold and oddly shaped, hexagonal, with the Tudor portcullis stamped on one side. 'A reward,' his father had said, handing it over, taking the rod and moving his little boy out of the shop and virtually straight across the street – to the boy's eyes almost a boulevard in its width – into the confines of . . . The confines of what? He racked his memory; there had been tea, served in a large room full of . . . Full of what? 'Full of sleeping dinosaurs,' his father had said, 'who have never been anywhere.'

'Let's find a café,' said Pistolet. 'I'll buy a steak if I have to, anything for some water to get this stuff down. I feel terrible.'

'Hush,' said Madison. He began to cross at a zebra crossing. 'Come with me.'

'Where are you taking me?'

'"Come fly with me, come fly, come fly away",' sang Madison, thinking of Pistolet with fedora dancing around the conference room in the Cathedral.

'Would you slow down? What are you doing?'

'*Suivez-moi*,' said Madison, usurping Pistolet's usual ebullience. He marched ahead of his friend to a large building of painted stucco, difficult to date but probably early nineteenth-century, the building blocks edged by more than a century's accretion of dirt. The two walked through a stone porch and tall mahogany doors into the lobby of the Travellers' Club.

They had walked up three steps when a porter emerged from a glass-and-oak lodge. 'May I help you?'

Pistolet sighed, still in the dark. Madison said, 'I'm here to meet a member.'

'His name, sir?' The porter was polite enough to mask most of his disbelief.

'Frederick Madison. I'm his son. We may be a little early for him.'

'I hadn't realised Mr Madison was in England. If you care to wait in the main room, sir, I'll tell him you're here when he arrives.'

'He's just arrived,' Madison lied, and led Pistolet into the main room. He sat down heavily in a leather chair. 'You go find a men's room and take your medicine. I'll wait here.'

There was no one else in the room. Madison scanned the *Financial Times* while he waited. Pistolet came back and sat down next to him. 'Better?' asked Madison.

'I'll live. Just. Where are we?'

'One of my father's clubs. He's not as avid as my uncle, but he does belong to quite a few. After his African escapades in 1940 he was made a member of the Explorers' Club in New York. They have reciprocal privileges with this place.'

152

Pistolet said, 'I think I'm going to survive this hangover after all. Let's head out. I was thinking of asking you if we could put a drink or two on your old man's tab, but it's a little early, even for pink gin or whatever they drink here.'

They left the club under the curious gaze of the porter, and kept walking east. 'Did your father take you there often?' Pistolet asked.

'Only once, when I was a little kid. I remembered it because it was on a trip to visit my grandparents – my mother's parents. He hated them.'

'I always forget you have English relatives.'

'I don't any more. They died when I was eleven. They were pretty stiff, at least they seemed that way to me. My mother was an only child so I don't have any close relatives over here at all.'

Pistolet was not so revivified that he was capable of walking very fast, and Madison was growing tired of slowing down to accommodate him, so they compromised by hailing a taxi, which quickly deposited them in front of the conference centre. As they arrived, Pistolet whistled appreciatively. 'The Houses of Parliament. And Westminster Abbey. They're real.'

'Not so. High-resolution graphics of astounding pixel density have been placed over the windows. You are not in a London taxi; you have not left Boston. Instead a vast series of optically-stored images have been played to you in a small simulator chamber at Logan Airport.' This was a Virtual Reality game they had played before.

'How do you account for the Travellers' Club, then? That seemed spontaneous enough to me. Or the bouncers last night. My back's still hurting from the sidewalk.'

Pistolet let Madison pay for the taxi and asked, 'What is that?' of the modern building before them. Large windows had thin mullions of bone-coloured concrete that contrasted with the dark reflecting glass of the panes.

153

On the higher storey the windows caught the neighbouring Abbey in distorted reflection.

They ducked and weaved their way through traffic, and entered the building. In the lobby, it took ten minutes to register, a procedure made lengthier by the exceptional security-consciousness of the convention's organisers, who wanted multiple confirmations of identity. After registering, Madison paused at a large message-board. This ran entirely against the grain of the proceedings, since it held hand-written messages on folded scraps of paper; the only electricity here was static, caused by the thick green felt of the board. Scanning the M's, Madison found to his surprise that there was a message with his name on it. On a scrap of paper was the simple request, 'Please ring Kaminski.'

Who answered after three rings. 'You got the message.'

'Is something wrong?'

'Lisa won't be making it to the centre, I'm afraid.'

'What's the matter with her?'

'Seems to be something she ate.'

'What did you give her for a nightcap?'

Kaminski was not amused. 'We each had one small brandy. And I feel fine.'

'So what's the prognosis for Lisa?'

'She's in bed for the moment, and I imagine she'll want to stay there for some time.'

'At the hotel?'

'No. Here,' said Kaminski a little reluctantly.

'Well done.'

'She's ill, I tell you. The point is, she won't be at the show, and she wanted you to know that.'

'I'll tell the others.'

'That's not all. She was supposed to meet someone from IBM. She told me to tell you to have Pistolet meet them instead. He's to meet a man named Magnusson at the IBM stand at noon.'

'I'll tell him,' said Madison, surprised and a little offended that she had asked Pistolet, not him, to substitute. 'You look after Lisa and I'll check back with you later. Tell her we'll see her when she returns to the hotel.'

He hung up, and explained things to Pistolet, who was not pleased. 'How fitting. International Bowel Movement strikes again, and just on the day when I feel like crap. I wonder what the Blue Rinse Lady is up to.'

They walked up a burgundy-carpeted staircase, stopping on the landing to look out over the square at the Abbey. They could see people inside the hall, partly obscured by booths, but their own progress was blocked by a wooden carousel that resembled the metal detectors used at airports. A young woman and a young man, each in blue blazer and grey slacks, tended this curiosity and monitored a screen.

'Do we empty our pockets first?' Madison asked them.

'Just a precaution, sir. If you could stand on the line right here,' the man said, pointing to a strip of yellow tape in front of the contraption, 'then simply state your name as it appears on your badge.'

'What for?' Pistolet asked.

'This machine makes a voice print,' said the young woman. 'On this monitor here you can see it etched. We've stored the prints of everyone who's come through here.'

'Really?' said Pistolet. 'Can you call up someone named Sally Zehring's print?'

'I couldn't do that. They're all meant to be confidential.'

'It's confidential, but you won't let me into the hall until I give you mine.'

'That's right,' said the woman cheerfully.

'Bite the bullet, Jeffrey,' said Madison, and stood up to the line. He said his name calmly, and watched as a pink line pulsed on the monitor and streaked across the screen like a pale carnation's electrocardiogram. This seemed to mean he was who he said he was, for both guards nodded approvingly. Pistolet followed, intoning, 'Jeffrey Pistolet' in a rough, hurried voice. His line ran well below Madison's, which was still casting a faint pink hue that only slowly receded from the pixels.

They walked through into the hall, Pistolet complaining about the waste of time. In front of them lay an area given over to Expert Systems, where a series of black metal desks was positioned in a wide semi-circle around a large screen. On each desk sat a colour monitor and a keyboard, linked to a VAX computer that sat under the screen. A man in a double-breasted suit was exhorting members of the audience to sit at terminals. He spoke in a loud French accent to the people at the terminals and the crowd of spectators gathering behind them.

'We are talking about shell,' the flamboyant Frenchman announced in a high and penetrating voice. 'Let us commence with ze forward chaining, yes? Ze data I want you to enter is completely straightforward, we all agree. Follow ze prompts on screen.' The guinea-pigs began to type, and on the large screen a weird map of many bright colours began to appear in dots, accumulating slowly – much as a painting, viewed from too close, takes shape as the viewer slowly moves back.

'What is the data?' Madison asked a jolly-looking woman in a trouser suit.

'People's food preferences. It uses that to chain forward and provide calorie and nutritional analysis. Then the inference engine constructs a profile diet and fitness programme based on your tastes.'

'Wait a minute. Who is this guy?'

'Vachon. Jean-Michel Vachon.'

'He sounds familiar. Is he well-known in Expert Systems?'

The woman laughed. 'The designer isn't even here.

Vachon used to be a famous chef in Paris. When his wife died from cholesterol poisoning, he turned completely against *haute cuisine*. He's become a health fanatic, and goes around trying to persuade restaurants to serve healthier food. He liked the sound of this program, I guess, and the designers must be happy to have him – he's a terrific huckster.'

'*Pamplemousse*,' Vachon suddenly squealed as a selection appeared on the large screen. 'Not good for you. Too much azzid.'

A man at a terminal sheepishly altered his choice to bananas.

'Much better,' Vachon declared.

'Madison, come here,' said Pistolet, appearing at his side. 'There's something you've got to see.'

'This is pretty remarkable, too.'

'Nothing on what I've got to show you. Come on.' He led a sceptical Madison through the crowded hall until they came to an open area which held small round tables and white garden chairs. Here the floor was uncarpeted, and painted with a clever *trompe l'oeil* effect of paving-stones, which gave a synthetic tap to Madison's heels as he crossed the floor. The overall effect was of an Italian café on the perimeter of a piazza, but here the view was of Westminster Abbey, not the Doge's Palace or St Mark's.

Pistolet sat down and Madison joined him impatiently. 'Jeffrey, we only just arrived. I don't need a break yet and neither do you.'

'That's what you think,' Pistolet said, and snapped his fingers loudly in the air. 'But actually we're working. Wait until you see the waitresses.'

'Is that all you ever think about?' But Pistolet's preoccupation was justified by the waitresses. There were three of them, and striking in appearance, though very, very short – none was taller than the table-top at which Madison and Pistolet sat. Although their arms were stunted and their legs mere stumps, they possessed a certain limited but palpable grace when they moved. Which they did now; with a squeak and a beep and a monotone hum, they moved out of the serving area towards the sparsely populated tables.

'What is this about?' demanded Madison.

'Robotics is often associated with A.I.,' said Pistolet casually; he seemed to have regained his usual jaunty composure and his voice was gradually reassuming its standard crooner self. 'A little tacky, perhaps: it smacks of the assembly line – *un peu appliqué* for the rarefied likes of you and me and the MIT brigade. But let's face it: right now, it's the only section of A.I. that's even close to making money. Try interesting General Motors in parsers. They don't care that their executives can't write; illiteracy masked in flannel has become virtually a status symbol. But show them a sweet young thing like Elsie that can do sixteen hundred rivets in an hour, and they'll be lining up outside your door.'

Elsie was green, and the fattest of the three; she stopped just short of their table. Unlike her movie counterparts, Elsie had no flashing lights on her physiognomy. 'What can I get for you gentlemen?' The voice was husky and Bacall-like, by no means mechanical.

'Pattern matching?' asked Madison of Pistolet.

'For what? Oh, you mean the gender. Yes, it has extraordinary powers of feature-extraction.'

Elsie lowered her head slightly. 'The menu is as follows: light refreshments, snacks, and various beverages are available.'

'Sounds just like British Rail,' said Madison. 'Coffee for me, please.'

'Gin and Tonic. Lots of ice. Schweppes for the tonic,' said Pistolet.

'The bar is only open after twelve hundred hours. At

158

present only soft drinks are available.' Elsie did not bother looking at a watch since she didn't wear one.

'Oh come on, Elsie, do us a favour,' said Pistolet in a passable imitation of a grovelling Cockney.

'Do not importune me, please.'

'Is that what you call it? Please, luv, give us a nip or two.'

'Do not become familiar,' said Elsie resolutely.

'Aw shit, so give me a coffee too.'

'Is that the future, then?' asked Madison when Elsie had brought them cups of coffee and turned her attention to other customers.

'Probably. Management in restaurants will love it. No bitching about tips any more.'

Madison looked at the digital clock pinned to a black trellis that separated the kitchen area from the customers. It was twenty minutes past eleven. 'Have you spotted Sally yet?'

'Relax. She'll show. I'm very impressed by your reinterest.'

'*Re*interest? God, you massacre the language.'

'Only in imaginative ways. Why this concern for Sally? At the Cathedral last month you were strictly Mr Ice-Man, lots of "I am involved: do not touch" signs. I'm glad that's over: you made a pretty beat kind of prig. So why the solicitude now? Isn't it a little late to start showing some interest again? Wouldn't Catherine be down on this kind of behaviour? – she might even decide you weren't of the right class after all.'

'I'm simply meeting Sally to talk about my work. She offered to discuss my project.'

'More power to her, then. You know I can't follow you there. Sally's the one with literary pretensions. She's even read your old man's books. That's not for me. Give me some text and I'll unravel it any way you like. But don't ask me to try to *make* the stuff.'

'Is that because you think it can't be done?'

Pistolet dumped three sugar cubes in his coffee before replying. 'I don't think you can do it alone – at least, not in the time Virgil's given you. But I expect it can be done. I just don't know why it *should* be done. I mean, what's the point? You've never really told me what the point is supposed to be.'

'I've got to go.' It was nearly eleven thirty. 'Where are you going to be?'

'Probably right here. Elsie should start serving drinks at noon.'

'What about the man from IBM?'

'Christ! Thanks for reminding me.' He stood up. 'I'll come back here after I see this guy. Come and find me.'

On his way out, Madison was made to pass through the voice machine again; fortunately, his two prints were more or less identical. He found Sally outside the front doors, looking abstracted. 'Sleepy?' he said, coming up behind her, and she jumped.

'You scared me,' she said. 'I was thinking.'

'That's good to know. How was your meeting with the German machine translation people?'

'Pretty disastrous. There was only one of them, a little man in a turtle-neck. He didn't know very much English and I don't speak a word of German.'

'All the more reason for machine translation.'

'His program works, but in a very limited way. If you were doing a tremendous amount of translation it would be useful in cutting down the donkey-work. It translates about sixty per cent of the text correctly – useful for technical documents. Effectively, it's giving you a rough draft.'

'Thank you for the report. Why were *you* meeting this man?'

'I was asked to by Virgil Peabody. Since I was here, I guess he figured why not kill two birds with one stone.'

Madison didn't say anything. Virgil wasn't stupid: why not involve his boss's future wife in projects? Sally looked

160

at him alertly. She said, 'I know what you're think-ing.'

'I bet you do. Come on, let's get away from the future for a while.'

'To the Houses of Parliament?'

'No. We need peace and quiet, away from the mad-ding crowd.' He started walking, and she followed him grudgingly as he crossed the street. Away from Parlia-ment, through a small entrance into the south transept of Westminster Abbey, deftly avoiding a large group of Japanese tourists on their way out.

'We were going to talk about your work,' said Sally.

'Yes. I'm a little blocked. I was hoping you could help.'

'What seems to be the problem?'

'It's the generator, really. It never captures the essence of whatever domain I'm trying to generate.'

They had moved into the east transept. 'You say domains,' said Sally. 'I assume you mean kinds of writing, like business letters, or legal documents.'

Madison nodded. 'Yes, I've tried all those, and others too.'

'What about individual writers?'

'Funny you should say that.' And Madison briefly explained his efforts with Updike and golf, a one-day stab he had had at a Zane Grey Western, and finally the process by which he had hit upon his own father's work as an ideal constricted domain.

'And?'

'The results are pretty poor. I wasn't prepared for the problems of poetry: in some ways they may outweigh the advantages.'

'How's that?'

'Well, there's no typical knowledge base to put in; terms and definitions have to be general. My father's written about all sorts of subjects: Europe, the War, love, sex,

161

nature – you name it. I can't just enter twenty thousand facts and call it a representative knowledge base. I can't stipulate a setting for any given poem with any accuracy, I can't really say this poem must be set in the Midwest, or only after the year 1915. My father's all over the place.'

'And your daddy's got those monologue poems, with all those voices. Like this guy here.' She pointed to a relief of Robert Browning.

'So far, all I've got is some frequency analysis, and a vocabulary range, and a few rules about form – you know, negative rules – no sonnets, or villanelles, no forms my father never used.'

'You need a way to get across what's unique about his writing.'

'It's hard. Look at him,' and he pointed to a plaque commemorating Dylan Thomas, 'and look at him,' and he pointed to one in the floor for T.S. Eliot, 'they're absolutely different poets. But how could you convey this? I could try: Thomas is effusive, romantic, lush; Eliot is stark (especially later on), yet quirky. But that's hogwash. If I tried to imitate them with that kind of information, what I'd get would either be unrecognisable, or bad parody. You know, "I count my life in finger bowls" or "The force that through the green fuse is celery".'

'In a sense, what you're looking for is a kind of literary fingerprint. Like the voice print back there.' She crooked her head in the direction of the hall. 'A unique composite.'

'But I want to reflect the domain, not *be* it – I mean, not be what it has been.'

'Don't go non-modal on me. I'm not talking about duplicating past creations: this is *possible* worlds, or impersonations if you'd prefer. A voice indistinguishable from the domain, but saying things that haven't been said before. I know that. Any reader will say, sure, that's him, that's Frederick Madison, because the poem you generate will have his name written all over it. Even though he didn't write it.'

'Any suggestions?'

She sat in one of the pews at the end of an aisle, discouraging him from sitting next to her. She propped her chin on one hand. 'How about stylometry?'

'Usage analysis? Diction studies?'

'Something like that, but a bit more, too. Statistical analysis of that loosely-labelled thing called style. Stylometry. Stylometrics.'

'All I know about it is that literary people look down their noses at it for being too computational, and computational people think it's too vague and literary.'

'It has its weaknesses, but more in how it's used than what it consists of. Fanatics keep using it to try and prove that X didn't write whatever he's said to have written.'

'Richard Nixon wrote most of Shakespeare's plays.'

'That kind of thing. That's not really what you're looking for – you want it for the generative side. You're using the tools to *build* a style, not recognise one.' She paused and laughed. 'I'm not sure anyone's tried it before.'

'I haven't got much time.'

'No, you haven't,' she said.

'I haven't got much help, either.'

'That's true, too.'

He looked at her sideways. 'Any chance of a hand?'

She sighed. 'I'm supposed to be taking on some special projects. Sammy wants me more involved in management. Go ahead and laugh: you're not the only one.'

'I'm not laughing. It's not as if he's marrying a dumb blonde.'

'Thank you for the vote of confidence.' She stood up and left the pew. 'I'll send you some literature when I get back. There isn't that much to cover. Most of it is of the why-Nixon-wrote-Hamlet variety.'

'So you'll help me?' It suddenly seemed very important.

She sighed. 'I guess so. But don't you dare tell anybody. And that includes Jeffrey.'

'Why not?'

'Who's being naive now? Or is this just your typical bullshit? Sammy doesn't want you to succeed. You must know that. And deep down, he probably hopes you'll leave the company when they insist you come back to Massachusetts. If you come back to the Cathedral, the last thing he'd really want is for us to work together.'

'I thought he wasn't jealous any more.'

'He's not, really. At least not in his rational mind. Deep down, he is.'

'When they re-entered the conference hall there were fewer people milling around the exhibits, and the restaurant area was full for lunch.

'Have you seen much of this show?' asked Sally.

'Not really. How about you?'

'No. I had the German man to see. But we'd better look around. There's nobody else to report back on it; I don't trust Jeffrey to take notes.'

They walked around, looking at the state of the art. It was an enormously eclectic display, connected by the tenuous thread of 'intelligence'. They saw various Natural Language products, usually sophisticated front-ends, some with voice recognition, that let users instruct machines in natural English commands. There were Expert Systems for a spectrum of problems, some obscure, some not, from real estate appraisal of seven-figure properties to the medical packages telling colds from cancer. There were ergonomic displays – that odd hybrid of cognitive psychology and common sense – wrapped in jazzy modules: keyboards tilting to fit various-sized hands; 'notepads' with a light pen that threw up a scratchpad memo in highlighted purple on a six-foot monitor; a liquid crystal display screen that magnified dramatically, suddenly expanding an 18-point typeface to 256-point, until the dots of the serifs on the letters were inflated balloons on the screen.

'I wonder if any of this is actually being sold anywhere,' said Sally.

'Moving like hot cakes,' said Madison in a deadpan voice. 'Speaking of which, what about food? I'm starving.'

'Let's eat, then. But where?'

'You'll see. My new friend Elsie will look after us.'

And it was Elsie who waited on them, suitably impressing Sally with her prowess. 'Does she do housework?'

'Don't tell me the Lings are short on maids. I would like to know, as a matter of fact, where you and Sammy propose to live. Assuming it's not in the Spires back in the Cathedral.'

'He's got the house in Lexington, of course. And an apartment in Boston. On Commonwealth Avenue.'

'Very nice.'

'Too long a commute or I'd want to live there full-time.'

'So stay in the house. Or is it a modest bungalow?'

She shrugged.

'How many bedrooms?'

'Seven. Uh, eight. Maybe nine.'

'Pool?'

She nodded.

'Tennis court?' Another nod.

'Tasteful?'

'No. Just taste-*less*. I could spend years fixing it up.'

'Who needs Natural Language when there are curtains to be hung?'

'Thanks a lot.'

'I imagine Sammy will cough up for a decorator if you ask him nicely.'

'Robert, when we went out together, you sometimes got on my nerves. I suppose I sometimes got on yours. But you were never this *obnoxious*. Lay off, will you? Or you can do your own learner's curve on stylometrics.'

This kept them both quiet through most of lunch. Pistolet joined them as they had coffee. He looked drained. 'It's half past one,' Sally said, 'you must have a hangover of record duration.'

Elsie approached to take Pistolet's order. 'Sir?' she said neutrally.

Pistolet perked up. 'Elsie, darling. I'd like a large gin and a small tonic. Make it two of them, sweetheart.'

'Do not become familiar,' said Elsie sternly. 'I have mentioned this to you before.'

Sally looked astonished as Elsie moved away. 'She's certainly got Jeffrey figured out,' she said.

'So tell us about IBM,' said Madison.

'Is Lisa Adams really sick?' asked Pistolet. 'Because if she isn't, I may do something to keep her in hospital. Like kick her in the ass. Do you know what she's done with this man from International Bowel Movement?'

'No,' they said in unison.

'She's promised him a three-year exclusive licence, commencing exactly one year after we introduce our own version, to market and distribute a new, innovative, culturally awe-inspiring, rip-roaring, earth-shattering new program called . . . ' He paused, like a game show host teasing his audience.

'What? The parser?'

'Guess again.'

'Something Cromwell's working on?'

'Nope. Getting colder. Think of something Lisa Adams loves that isn't real.'

'Her hair,' said Sally.

'Nope. My astrology program.'

'You're kidding,' said Madison. 'I thought you'd persuaded her it wasn't commercial. Besides, Blackburn's not around to help.'

166

'That's what I thought. She can't have been listening. Because IBM's ready to sign. They've got a *beta* site set up at some newspaper in Detroit that wants a variation on a horoscope column. "Ready when you are" the guy kept saying to me. Lisa told him I was the author of the program.'

'*What* program?' asked Sally.

'Rigging a demo's one thing,' said Madison. 'You can't fake a *product*.'

'I know,' he said. 'I need this like I need a sock in the jaw.'

A remark Madison was to remember, for when Elsie came with Pistolet's order she brought three gins, not two; in his eagerness to thank her, Pistolet first patted, then pinched sweet Elsie on her shiny concave rear.

Enough was enough, apparently, even for a robot. Elsie squeaked twice, turned around abruptly, and knocked Pistolet cold with a green right hand.

4

Summer spring leaves are picked: I remember
memory packages: I have lifted them as fruit.

This might get Madison admitted to the Iowa Writers' Workshop but it was not what he was looking for. The second pass gave him:

The summer leaves are picked and I am tired

Now, through the semantics and pragmatics module,

fortified by the new stylometric information, which had a thesaurus function, that 'tired' was thrown out and in came:

> The summer fruit is picked and I am hand-sore

Accept or reject? Accept. Next came:

> Fatigued I have lifted them as fruit

The absence of punctuation after the first line made the case grammar and parser go to work; the result was:

> tired to leave the memory of lifting fruit

On the next pass, stylometry cleverly imposed a synecdoche and concluded:

> too tired to still the memory of lifting crates

So now he had the following:

> The summer fruit is picked and I am hand-sore,
> too tired to still the memory of lifting crates.

Accept or reject? Well, it was a plausible beginning, though Frost-like to be sure. But then lines three and four emerged less cogently:

> My dreams tonight will dream at first
> of Florida, that dreamless land of orange crops.

That would need several passes; too many dreams spoil the sleep. The generator continued, spewing more nonsense ('Yield to the power of nectar and pits' was Madison's favourite), with a few flickers of unexpected lyric power –

'My apples moult and sour in air.' Then, as if rediscovering
its voice, came a conclusion:

> Then I wake, twitching in my bed,
> wondering why I thought my work was done.

Not bad; the Frost echo was a little strong, as if the generator were in love with 'After Apple Picking' and could
not differentiate itself; yet he was looking to duplicate his
father's voice, not call in other intonations. Deeper into
literary waters. Perhaps all these voices coexisted in a sort
of historical choir, and you could pluck out the wrong one
by mistake – the alto in the second pew rather than the
tenor nearest the altar. Worried by this, Madison picked
up the phone and tried calling Sally.

There was no answer at her cubicle. There rarely
was these days: she was moving around the Cathedral,
combining her usual duties in the Natural Language
group (laying the ground with Pistolet for *Write Right*)
with her new, pre-nuptial assignments. Sammy even had
her chairing a working group on women's status in the
company. Madison felt lucky ever to make contact.

He had not seen her since the conference at Westminster. When Pistolet showed up alone at his Oxford
office the day after his robotic débacle (bruised from
Elsie's punch and complaining 'No booze on the train')
Madison had not been able to disguise, or fully understand, his deep disappointment. Not even Pistolet's instant
dislike of Dorothy had lightened Madison's mood. Where
was Sally? That night at home he left Catherine watching
television and went to the front hall to phone Sally in the
hotel. Fruitlessly.

Yet three days later a large envelope had been delivered
to his office by Federal Express. Inside he found a stack of
xeroxed articles and a copy of a paper by Sally herself, 'The
Computation of Style: Method and Madness in Literary

Analysis'. He had telephoned her cubicle at the Cathedral to leave a message, and had been surprised to find her already at work. 'What are you doing up? It's only seven thirty over there.'

'My new schedule, Robert. It's the only way I can keep ahead of things these days. You're lucky to catch me.'

'When you didn't visit I thought maybe you'd changed your mind about helping me.'

'Don't be so stupid,' she had said curtly. 'If I promised to help, I will.'

That had been four weeks ago; since then they had talked, always briefly, perhaps a dozen times. Her advice on stylometry was proving invaluable; without it, Madison began to realise, he would not have advanced at all. For the first time, he was finding the generator capable of enough good lines to make him feel confident of eventual success. And when his confidence faltered, Sally was willing to boost it.

That is, when he could reach her. Now he hung up the phone and wondered what to do next, deciding lazily to go home. There he found Catherine in the kitchen, cooking supper. He had a drink and talked with her for a minute, trying to explain his day. 'I'm getting closer,' he declared.

'Closer to what?'

'To duplicating my father. He's going to have the surprise of his life.'

'Really?' she said neutrally, slicing potatoes.

'Yes, really.' He felt upbeat, and opened his briefcase to look at his papers. He unfolded the most recent chart of the generator and spread it on the kitchen table. 'Here's the blueprint,' he said proudly. It now included Sally's stylometry component:

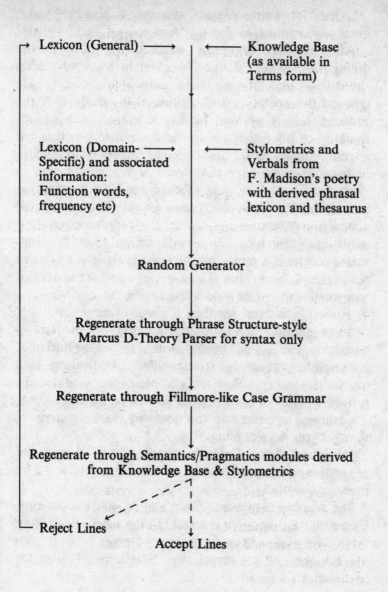

Lexicon (General) ———→   ←——— Knowledge Base
                                  (as available in
                                  Terms form)

Lexicon (Domain- ———→   ←——— Stylometrics and
Specific) and associated   Verbals from
information: F. Madison's poetry
Function words,   with derived phrasal
frequency etc)   lexicon and thesaurus

Random Generator

Regenerate through Phrase Structure-style
Marcus D-Theory Parser for syntax only

Regenerate through Fillmore-like Case Grammar

Regenerate through Semantics/Pragmatics modules derived
from Knowledge Base & Stylometrics

Reject Lines   Accept Lines

END POEM

'What a lot of arrows,' said Catherine, shaking her head in mock wonderment, as if to say 'And you get paid for that?'

After supper, Catherine watched television in the dining-room while Madison worked in his study; soon she called out to him to come and watch a sit-com. He ignored the invitation and continued to puzzle over the Frostian echoes in what he had managed to generate, thinking of his father's neurotic compulsion to disavow anyone's influence. Critics tended to cite Frost, or Auden, or sometimes even the faint trace of Wallace Stevens in his father's work, and were anathema to his father for that reason – so Whitman-like, paradoxically, in his conceited conception of his own uniqueness. Doubters received short shrift: in the 1960s one *Time* reviewer had found his scepticism receiving a punch on the nose in the Four Seasons restaurant in New York. In an out-of-court settlement, it was worth more than a decade's reviewing fees.

'Robert, you must see this. It's *really* funny.'

'In a minute,' he shouted, thinking of his father's pugnacity. He had not been a violent father, or husband, although he was strong, strong-willed, overbearing. Had his father stayed, Madison's adolescence would have proved a series of battles; still, he wished he had stayed.

Catherine appeared in the doorway, looking stern. 'I thought you were coming.'

He sighed. 'Sorry. I'm in the middle of this' – he pointed at random to a paper on his desk. 'I can't stop now. I'll be there in a while.'

She was not appeased. 'That's what you said before. Come on, darling, give it a rest. I'm not here very often these days as it is. You can't work all night.'

He looked at her sceptically. 'Sometimes I want to. Sometimes I have to.'

She laughed, a little falsely. 'No one *has* to. You're not in the City, after all. And nobody normal *wants* to. Not unless they're obsessed.'

'Exactly,' he said. 'I *am* obsessed.' Work as anodyne, antidote, more trustworthy than any person – father, mother, lover, friend. The idea had a certain appeal. Early on with Catherine he had told her how important his work was to him. She had said this was because he was unhappy. Perhaps; yet she had not been able to substitute for work effectively. Now she stared at him, uncomprehending. He added lamely, 'My work is important to me.'

'Clearly,' she said sharply, and went away.

5

Returning from lunch with a publisher the next day, he could tell by the grumpy look on Dorothy's face that Wellington was in. 'Cheer up,' he instructed her, 'your nuptials approach.'

'My what?' she said crossly, but he had already moved on, breezing past Wellington and heading for his desk. There was a message that Samson had rung, and a dirty postcard signed 'T.S. Lepoti'; not one of Pistolet's better anagrams – 'P.S. Toilet' had been better.

Wellington came in, trailing a sandal strap. He was dressed in black today, coal-coloured corduroys and a high-necked synthetic jumper that gathered in odd ebony bunches around his neck and shoulders. Madison resisted the temptation to ask who had died. 'So how are the business letters?' he inquired instead, motioning Wellington to sit down.

Wellington raised a pre-emptive hand. 'In a moment. First let me tell you about Compositor C.' He plunged into the intricacies of *Pericles* while Madison looked out of the window. He had been back in Oxford for six weeks since his trip to the Cathedral, which, according to Minnie Lu and Virgil's dictates, left him eighteen more weeks – call it four months and a half – in the office. How would they close him down? Would they simply leave him to do the Disappearing English Office act and assume that he would show up at the Cathedral in late autumn, refreshed by his three-year sabbatical and ready for lunch in East Nave's Macdonald's? Or did they think he'd leave Ling altogether? In which case it would be nice to have a final visit, say goodbye to Sal Lombardi, get drunk with Pistolet, play a round or two of golf at the Ling Country Club. *See Sally before she gets married*. Yes, well, that too.

'We have the voice,' Wellington was saying, 'of a second-rate playwright. Competent, mind you, but ultimately not alpha material. "Forsooth the plant the chastest kiss doth land",' – and Madison realised Wellington was quoting. Wellington looked up at him from his script. 'I think that will nearly do, don't you?'

Madison shrugged. 'Maybe. But it doesn't really get us anywhere.'

Wellington talked on, and Madison looked out of the window again. Even in mid-afternoon, traffic was beginning to accumulate; with the long, light evenings everyone seemed to leave work early. He thought of playing golf that evening, unless it rained – always a possibility. As he shifted in his chair he noticed, through the foot-high gap of the open window, a foot perched perilously on the window ledge. It was a shoe, a sandal actually, and it belonged to someone standing about five feet along the ledge from the window. Madison stood up in amazement and moved slowly towards the window to investigate. The sandal moved too, and by the time Madison lifted the window and stuck his head out, the sandal had moved far down the ledge and disappeared.

Wellington was still quoting from a Periclean print-out and seemed unperturbed by Madison's movements.

'Excuse me a moment,' said Madison, and hurried past him, rushing through the middle room to the reception area and Dorothy. 'Did a man just come in here?' he demanded.

'No one's here.'

He pointed to the window. 'He would have come through there. Or gone by along the ledge.'

'I wouldn't know. I was in the loo.'

'It would have been just now.'

She smiled insincerely. 'I've only returned myself this moment. Was this someone you were expecting? A lexicographer? Or your friend Kaminski?'

He opened the window behind her desk and stared out along the ledge. Nothing. He gave up, flummoxed, and returned to his desk. Wellington finished as he sat down, and said, 'So what do you make of that?'

Madison drew breath. There was no point in alienating *all* his staff. 'Very interesting. But I'd like to reserve comment until I've had a chance to read it for myself. Let me take it home.' He took the pages and put them in his briefcase with a profoundly false air of commitment. 'Moving onto less interesting topics,' said Madison, 'perhaps you could brief me now on progress with the business letters?'

Wellington sighed and hauled out more print-out. This Madison examined with interest. The first page listed topics:

Buying
Debt Collection
Selling
Invitations/RSVPs
Deaths (Loved Ones, Pets, Colleagues)
Birthdays
Congratulations

'These are *all* the topics?'

'So far. The user calls up this menu: he pays his money and he takes his choice. Such an indelicate turn of phrase.' Wellington shuddered, like a nun thinking about a whorehouse.

'Just pretend you're reading Damon Runyon.' On the next page, where Wellington had his representative user pick Debt Collection, the following choices came up:

1. First Warning to a Valued Customer
2. Have You Forgotten Us?
3. Please Don't Try Our Patience
4. We Don't Want to Act Tough But . . .
5. Final Warning to a Flagrant Deadbeat
6. Get Him!

'Have You Forgotten Us?' began:

In this complex day and age, we know how easy it is to forget certain small but critical items in life – like the forty-seven dollars and three cents you have now owed us for sixteen weeks.

Alternatively, it read:

We're halfway certain that your check for $47.03 is in the mail. But just in case it isn't, here's a first-class stamp you can use to send it to us. The check should now be for $47.28 (that includes the price of the stamp).

That was it. 'This is all you've got?' Madison asked.

Wellington was mildly embarrassed. 'I thought it was rather good. The second letter says much the same as the first, but in totally different prose. And it changes the fiscal notation from words to numbers.'

Madison grew impatient. 'It's still canned, and not much better than the version I worked on two years ago. How

176

long did it take you to create the specific domain for –
what was it you picked? – "Have you forgotten us?"
Two weeks?' he asked rhetorically, ignoring Wellington's
mild grimace. 'Two weeks for two lousy, over-generalised
pieces of prose? Come on, Duncan, you can do better
than that.'

'It's rather difficult finding the voice for the domain. In
Pericles, you see, at least there's an historical milieu, a
certain resonance, if you will, to help one out.'

'Listen, Duncan,' said Madison, not unkindly. 'Forget
Pericles for the time being. If you don't get cracking
with corporate correspondence, you can forget all about
Pericles. You can forget about this job, for that matter,
and don't think I'm threatening you, because I won't be
here much longer then, either.'

'Truly?' asked Wellington, suddenly more worldly.

'A promise. So what are you going to do now? What's
holding you up – I mean, other than *Pericles*?'

Wellington pursed his lips. 'This matter of the voice.
I need something, other than this Runyon fellow you
mentioned.'

'Runyon's dead; don't worry about him.' As his phone
rang, he silently started to sing:

> Call it sad call it funny
> But it's better than even money
> That the guy's only doing it
> for some doll

Sally was on the phone, sounding breathless. 'I would have
phoned earlier, but it's just been crazy here. I saw the lines
on electronic mail. Don't FAX anything, by the way: the
secretaries always read it first. I'm not sure how I'd explain
it away.'

'They're not exactly love poems.'

She ignored this, and said, 'The stylometrics seem all

right. You could adjust the collocation ratios, but I can't really see the point. I think part of the problem may be too many influences to generate one voice. I mean, you've got Robert Frost looking over your daddy's shoulder. And Edward Arlington Robinson, for that matter.'

'I'd forgotten about him.'

'Most people have. I suggest you try a voice poem, like a monologue; something with a topic and a speaker who's naive. Somebody young – a boy. You remember that Civil War poem of your father's?'

'The one where the boy walks through the cemetery?'

'That's it. Like Allen Tate's "Ode for the Confederate Dead".'

'Don't tell my father that.'

'His is from a Northern point of view. Try those parameters, anyway. By the way, when are you coming over next?'

'Do I get a last taxi to the guillotine?'

'Of course. As far as they know, you'll be moving back here. Lisa Adams is all excited. Whenever she has trouble with Pistolet she starts saying how she can't wait to have you as Natural Language leader. She'll want a preliminary visit first.'

He looked over at Wellington, who was rapidly completing the *Times* crossword Madison had been agonising over in the morning. 'Know anything about business letters?' he asked Sally.

'Only the ones my fiancé dictates at his house.' Was there a faint sarcasm to her voice? *His* house. Why not 'at home'?

'Nothing so grand as that.'

'Oh, these aren't very grand, I promise you.' There *was* a hint of sarcasm, wasn't there?

'Anyhow,' said Madison, suddenly feeling pleased, 'we're having trouble there, too. And somehow I don't think lyric poetry will persuade Ling to let me stay over here, no matter how good it is. I'm not sure business letters will make much difference.'

'It's worth a try. What's the basis of the domain for the letters?'

'I've got the stuff I was working on before – you know, the pre-programmed letters with the thesaurus.'

'Weren't they a bit much? A little low-rent?'

'That's what my editor here thinks.' He looked at Wellington, who was down to the lower right quadrant of the crossword. Reading upside down came naturally to Madison; he remembered watching his father, across the kitchen table, as the two of them wrote sonnets against the clock. Sixteen down had been elusive that morning, beginning with p – 'Tape Dan to ensure correctness? (6)' Madison watched as Wellington boldly wrote in 'pedant', then said to Sally, 'I've used business form-books – there's a Prentice-Hall series. But there's too much boiler-plate in them, not enough meat.'

'Find a domain, then. You've done it for the poems.'

'Great. Know any literate businessmen who'll lend me their correspondence?'

'Not Sammy, that's for sure.' Again the note of sarcasm. 'Why not apply a domain you already have entered?'

'I only have my father's poems.'

'That will do. At least the letters won't be boring. Anyway, I have to run; I'm having lunch with Virgil Peabody.'

'Give him a manicure for me.'

'I meant what I said: try using your father again. You might be surprised. Let me know how you get on.'

He hung up and explained Sally's suggestion to Wellington, who showed little interest in the idea. 'Happy to try, of course. It may take some time.'

'Take all the time you need, Duncan, only don't let *Pericles* get in the way. This has priority.'

The phone rang again and he let Dorothy answer it while Wellington returned to his den. When it rained, it poured: he could go whole days without a phone-call. Dorothy came to the doorway: he had finally cured her habit of half-covering the phone with one hand and shouting the caller's identity through two sets of walls. Madison had also persuaded her not to tell callers when he was using the lavatory that her boss was 'on the toilet'.

'Mr Madison for you.'

His uncle, calling about God knows what. He picked up the phone slowly, incurious with his 'hello'.

'Is that you, kid?' A big bass voice, richer than his Uncle Billy's; a benevolent, purring growl. His father. 'Yes, it's me,' he said quietly.

'Jesus, it's not been easy getting hold of you. I've been trying most of the afternoon.'

'Well, you found me. What can I do for you?'

'Good news. I'm coming to England. And I want to see you.'

Good news? He felt no jubilation, just a sudden wave of anxiety. He looked at the few lines of his Frostian poem – 'Wondering why I thought my work was done' caught his eye. 'I may not be here,' he said cautiously.

'I'm easy. I was thinking in about three weeks, but if that's not convenient just say the word. I can come later.'

'I'll have to talk to the States.'

'The States?'

'My bosses. To see when I'm due there.'

'Oh, the leaders of Ling.' He chuckled, a roll of laughter that abruptly ceased. 'Tell you what. I'll send you the dates I'm meant to come; just write if you can't make it. I'll postpone by a week or whatever.'

'So by a bonnet against the wind's plague, a woman arrives at defence' – the son felt as vulnerable as the Puritan pioneer in his father's early lyric. Why was the

180

old man so intent on seeing him now? They had not laid eyes on each other for four years. 'I wouldn't mind seeing your town,' his father was saying. 'Haven't been there in a coon's age. Not since I first met your mother. Must be almost forty years ago.'

'I'll come to London,' Robert said firmly. 'It's no trouble to get down.'

'I wouldn't mind seeing where you're living. And your girl.'

Catherine exposed to this manic old man? It would not be a success. Worse still, it might be. 'It's better if I come to you,' he tried to repeat against his father's relentless wave of talk, but his father was saying, 'I suppose you mostly know the academics in your field there, heh?'

'Not really. Cambridge is more the place for linguistics. I've got to go now,' he said sharply, then resented his churlishness. 'Listen, I've got a meeting. But I'll try to get to London.'

'Name a night for dinner. I'll keep it free.'

'You make the choice. I'll be there. I've got to go now.'

'Okay, son.' The voice now a little more subdued. 'Monica sends her best. And so does your papa. God bless.'

''Bye.'

God bless, from a man who last appeared in church at his marriage to Robert's mother, in the Episcopal church in his Vermont home town. Our Father, who art near Florence, hallowed be thy home. And stay there. Madison stood up and looked out of the window, to discover that it was raining. So much for golf, and golf being unavailable, he turned to his knowledge base, working happily until the cleaning lady barked at him for staying late and getting in her way. Dorothy and Wellington had long since gone, and Catherine subsequently proved irritated at having to serve supper at nine. 'On Friday night, too,' she added,

181

and Madison thought, what difference does that make? But said nothing.

6

Saturday morning Madison spent working on a laptop computer that had enough power (though only just) to crank out lines he had already roughly composed on a higher-end machine at the office. Work went smoothly; when he stopped to make lunch, he felt frustrated with his lack of progress. Perhaps a break would help. He'd told Kaminski he would come and watch the cricket, and Catherine had grudgingly agreed to accompany him. They drove in silence to the match.

They had begun to walk around the pitch when Madison suddenly thought of something, made excuses and returned to the car. Once there, he took the laptop out of its case on the back seat; it came with an in-built letter-quality printer that produced a wide ribbon of slimy paper from a slot in the top. He booted it, and called up the generator module, but bypassed the full running of it to bring processing up as far as he had got that morning. There were thirty-four lines now in the poem, and he ran batch print to see what he had. He glanced up once to watch Kaminski hit for four, and saw the figure of Catherine on the far edge of the pitch, her hands on her hips, staring back at the car. His guilt was only momentary, for he soon forgot about Catherine and the match, as lines of pure Americana emerged:

> I count the bricks on Langtry Bridge
> where General Wilson hanged himself.

Accept or reject? He hit *A*. It was a promising beginning, dramatic, curiosity-provoking.

> Each night's ride back from the fields
> enables me, in the day's-end hollow width
> of sun, to see the cobbles where my horse
> will step, and the worn-smooth ledge
> where the General found his purchase.
> The overhanging oak is gone,
> and the bough from which they cut him down;
> it's said he slipped
> through twenty pairs of hands
> and hit with a splash
> in the creek's thick mud.

Accept or reject? the machine asked blithely, refusing to recognise anything novel in such a long regurgitation. Madison could almost sense its confidence, its unwillingness to consult him when it was going so well. He hit *A* again, particularly pleased by the play on 'purchase', and the single beats of the 'creek's thick mud'. Who was this observer, though? Who was speaking? More lines emerged and he snatched at the paper eagerly.

> Mornings I go round the bridge
> siding the wood with its high light pines,
> then up through the meadow where
> bleached grass wants to hide the path.
> All day the fields give in
> as we cut and stack the hay,
> me and the men – all old,
> one old enough to claim he saw the General.
> There's time enough for talk,
> and I like to see the stories circle –
> fade like a bad watch, then flare
> and keep an old century alive.

He hit *A* before the question was put. There were certain

awkwardnesses here, but they fitted the persona he now sensed – a boy, clearly, who spent his summers working in the fields with older men, agricultural labourers. Would the boy say more of his own feelings? The machine replied promptly:

> But soon I'm alone with the last hasp
> of dusk, and talk stays only in my head
> as I start the slow ride home.
> You'd think I was scared to see
> the General, slow as I take the bridge
> and the way I hold my breath.
> He'd wear his tunic,
> dull in its powder blue,
> not washed since he ran
> from the lines at Antietam.

Madison marvelled at the sureness of the generator. What was going on? He found nothing, really, to fault – even the awkwardness of some lines, and their hokiness ('and talk stays only in my head') seemed justified by the winning confessions of the boy. How long would this account continue? He soon learned:

> General, oh General, why?
> You had at least the chance to run;
> disgrace can be lived on past its stories.
> Would you tempt me, General, would you try?
> I could climb there, too,
> sink like a stone and know
> one way I'd stay alive,
> since men bury men but keep
> their histories half-alive.

He hit *A* with a sense of great contentment with this piece of *Americana*; it needed something simple for its ending. He waited eagerly for the concluding lines, and it was during this expectancy that the explosion came, in a burst of

184

fractured light and shower of sound. Madison felt himself somehow awash, then realised, looking up, that he could no longer see the cricket pitch. The windscreen had metamorphosed into an astronomer's dream of a star-studded sky; the shatter-proof glass had become a map of latticed crystal-shaped fragments, held together tenuously by some internal chemical strength, but bulging perilously inwards.

Catherine appeared at the side-window. 'Are you all right?' she asked tersely.

'Sure,' he said calmly, 'why wouldn't I be?'

'When I saw the ball coming, I was worried.'

'Ball? What ball?' Madison looked around him. Sure enough, on the bonnet of the car, flush against the windscreen, sat a cricket ball. On it a green patch of smeared grass gave a diminutive Christmas-colour contrast to the rich burgundy of the leather cover.

'Got it,' said Kaminski cheerfully, appearing in his whites. 'He wasn't aiming for you, Robert,' he added, picking the ball from the bonnet and trotting back to bowl.

'He might have apologised,' said Catherine. 'Look what they've done to the car.' Her voice grew sterner. 'And you just sit there as if nothing's happened.'

'What would you like me to do? Sue him? This isn't America.' And at that moment the laptop computer, fallen sideways in the explosion and wedged between his seat and the car door, began to crank out copy. Which emerged, crumpled against the door. Madison pulled it out roughly, oblivious to his lucky escape, and oblivious to Catherine.

> I see you standing, General, on your way,
> and I kick my horse and keep my head down,
> watch the bricks or even close my eyes.
> Over, I can breathe again.

'Are you listening to me, Robert?' and he realised Catherine had been speaking. But he hadn't been listening to her at all. I did it, he thought. I hope the old man doesn't have a heart-attack when he reads this. Well done.

7

After 'Langtry Bridge' everything seemed to fall into place. Madison generated two more narrative accounts, reminiscent of the middle Madison, and several lyrics that recalled his father's precocious love-songs. There was also a finished version of his early Frostian lines. Called 'After Harvest', it went like this:

> The summer fruit is picked and I am hand-sore,
> too tired to still the memory of lifting crates.
> I know my dreams tonight will live at first
> in Florida, that unseasoned land of orange crops
> and my winter vacation from trees.
> But in every dream a neutral rain descends
> and drives me to my northern holding.
> Here the fullest summer sun declares
> the imperfection of my fruit:
> peaches that tumble and bruise,
> cherries that tighten to a dull worm-black.
> My finest apple tree has flowered without me,
> and when I thrust my arms out elbow-deep
> in the season's growth of branch,
> my apples moult and sour in air.
> Each year I see them swelling ripe,
> and each year I dream they fall too soon.
> Then I wake, twitching in my bed,
> wondering why I thought my work was done.

Because he found that the more he tried to expand his

world the more it contracted, Madison had not been surprised to learn that his father was staying at the Hyde Park Hotel. But he felt no lightness of spirit as he approached the hotel entrance.

His father, shorter than his son but always broader in the beam, had thinned down. His salt-and-pepper beard was now mainly salt; he wore gold-rimmed glasses that confirmed his ageing. Still, the effect was of size: he wore a fisherman's sweater that spread like a fisherman's net when he opened his arms as Madison walked in. Madison thought for an awful moment that his father was going to hug him, but his father was merely saluting the sweep and size of his quarters. 'Not bad, eh, kid?' They stood in an enormous sitting-room with a good-sized bedroom partly visible through a half-closed door. The view of the park was superb. There was no sign of Monica.

His father continued. 'I haven't been in this joint since just after the War. I used to see Evelyn Waugh in the dining-room, stuffing his face with oysters and drinking champagne. It was right after *Brideshead* was published. Believe me, there weren't many other Limeys living high on the hog in those days.'

'This must cost a pretty penny,' said Madison.

'Not to me. I reckon I make my publishers a lot of money, so I might as well enjoy some of it myself.' However popular they were, his father's poems were not the providers of this largesse. His novel *Cat Walk* must do six figures a year in the U.K. alone.

'So how is life up there?' asked his father.

'Where?' asked Madison, genuinely puzzled.

Suddenly his father rattled off an accurate, virtually exhaustive list of prominent poets living in his son's new home town. 'Do you know any of those creeps?' he demanded.

Madison shook his head and drank from his Scotch and soda. 'Only by sight.' For it was true that in his restaurant

187

Kaminski would occasionally point out members of the local literati.

'I'd keep it that way. They're all pretty terrible.'

'How can you say that? You don't know them, either.'

His father blushed slightly, began to respond, but caught himself. 'You should humour your old man. Nobody likes young guys coming up and snapping at their heels – I don't care what it is, sports or writing or what. It's a terrible feeling. I'm beginning to understand why Frost hated me so much.'

'I thought Frost hated everyone.'

'He did. But I *threatened* him.'

This was true: a Dartmouth professor, weekend guest of his uncle in Vermont, had told him so. Still, he resented as always his father's matter-of-fact assumption of importance, his casual assurance that what he said – 'I *threatened* him' – was undeniable. And not just anybody, but Robert Frost.

His father seemed to read his thoughts and sense his irritation. 'Pound was right, I guess,' he said softly.

'About what?' asked Madison crossly. Economics? The Jews? Currency theory?

His father smiled again. 'Like I say, don't be so hard on your old man. I'm not gaga yet. I was thinking of the Pisan Cantos. You remember the Pisan Cantos?'

How could he forget them? They were the last poems he had read under his father's supervision. The last poems they shared before Madison came home one day from school and found his mother at the kitchen table, sobbing. Sobbing so hard and for so long that Madison had finally given up trying to console her and had phoned his uncle, saying Quick, quick, Uncle Billy, get over here, something's happened. Then going into his father's study and seeing his desk – normally covered with drafts of poems and books for review – completely bare. He knew then that his father had left.

Now he looked his father in the eye and said, '"Pull down thy vanity, I say pull down . . . The ant's a centaur in the dragon world." I was fourteen years old and I didn't even know what vanity was. Then you took off, and I found out soon enough.'

'That's a pretty hard thing to say.' The blue-grey eyes were icy but steady, no hint of the famous explosive temper. Still, after this exchange dinner was a tricky, stilted affair, eaten quickly in the hotel dining-room. Madison's father spoke briefly of his new wife, then, at his son's prompting, of his own work – but without the usual bravado. Unusually, he wanted to know about Madison's work, and it was the son's turn to seem reticent. His father mistook this for an admission of failure. 'Ha!' he exclaimed. 'I told you it wouldn't work. No machine can do it.'

'Who says it doesn't work?'

'You do; I can see it in your eyes.' When his son shook his head, his father taunted him. 'Then prove it. Go on. Show me what this machine of yours has produced.'

Madison felt his irritation welling. The carapace he had carefully constructed was obviously no more than the thinnest scab, capable of opening up under the mildest emotional flick from his father. 'All right,' he said quietly. 'I'll prove it. I'll send you some of its work as soon as I get back.'

8

When, late that night, Madison arrived at Oxford station, he realised he had left his briefcase at the office. It held the generator's most recent lines, and although he knew he would do no more work that night, Madison felt nervous about leaving his work untended. He walked quickly towards his office, and saw from the street that lights were on in his room and Dorothy's. Who would be there this late? – it was almost eleven o'clock. He thought briefly of finding a policeman, but what burglars would work with the lights on before midnight? He let himself into the building quietly and silently climbed the stairs. Someone was in the lavatory, or at least the light was on; since Dorothy's desk was still cluttered he assumed it was she, for she never left the office without sweeping all a day's remaining business into a drawer. But since when did Dorothy work into the night?

Wellington's room was dark, but Madison's own room was lit. He moved quietly into it and discovered Samson going through his desk drawers.

'Tell me,' said Madison quietly, and Samson looked up so suddenly and with such fear that he banged his hand against the drawer, hard enough to make him wince with pain. Several pages fell from his hand onto the floor; there were others strewn on the desk. 'Tell me,' Madison repeated, 'am I supposed to say, "You publishing scoundrel"?'

Either the reference was lost on Samson, or he was too startled to speak. He looked bug-eyed at Madison and swallowed repeatedly, as if struggling for air. Madison looked closely at the desk and at the papers his father's would-be biographer had been fishing for. They were print-outs of the poems he had been generating, mainly early drafts. 'What do you think you're looking for?' he asked, not unkindly.

'Don't try to deny it,' Samson said nervously.

'Deny what?'

'This evidence. You have no business holding onto these.' Samson pointed to the poems on the desk.

'What are you talking about? Just what do you think *these* are anyway?'

Samson twitched a little; he looked like an oboe, thin and shrill, his neck the long reed. 'Pull the other one. I know your father's work better than anyone else alive. What I don't understand is, why do you have these poems? That is, if you're not on terms with your papa.'

'You think he wrote these?' Madison asked with delight.

'Of course he did; nobody else could. And I think it's criminal to keep them to yourself.'

'So you were going to steal them out of my desk and publish them yourself – what, as an appendix to your biography? Why, you little creep,' he said, as much in pleasure at Samson's mistake as in irritation.

But Samson thought he was getting angry again and stood up apprehensively. 'Steady on,' he said.

'I ought to kick you in the ass,' said Madison, parodying his father and moving closer to the desk, though he had no intention of doing anything of the sort. Samson, however, took the threat for real and rushed with a squeal to the open window. With an unexpected grace, he shot nimbly onto the ledge; Madison followed more slowly, curious as to where he might conceivably go. By the time he stuck his own head out of the window, the figure of Samson had disappeared. He walked out to the reception room and found Dorothy at her desk. Startled, she closed a drawer in a great hurry. 'I thought you were in London,' she said shakily.

'You are not alone. So did Mr Samson.'

'Who?' she said with excessive innocence, since it was she who fended the barrage of calls from the importuning biographer. Her insincerity was made the more ridiculous by the extrusion from under her desk of an inhabited sandal.

'Dorothy,' he said calmly, 'open the drawer and give me the papers Samson just handed you. I will then return to my own office and count to ten. When I return he had bloody well better be gone. And no, I will not apologise for my language.'

When he returned, both Dorothy and Samson had gone. He was unnerved by the thought that Samson might have other copies of some of the poems he had been generating.

The electronic mail-sensor beeped and shovelled a data load into the terminal on the conference table in his room. He looked at what had come in. The usual corporate pronouncements ('Ling has a $600,000 order from Botswana's largest contractor' – one more customer unlikely to pay promptly); a personal note from Pistolet saying, 'Greenfield has started wearing shorts to work. What does this signify?'; then terse lines addressed to him and marked Urgent:

Come to the Spires on the week of July 17 to demonstrate the current progress of your work. We will also discuss the closure of your R&D office. VP.

Virgil Peabody strikes again, he thought. This was followed by Minnie Lu's only slightly more elaborate instructions:

Pursuant to Virgil's directions please bring too a copy of your office lease all equipment maintained there personnel records expectations for this fiscal year. Minnie Lu/Bishop.

Bishop officially: well done, 'pursuant' Minnie, whose pulpit was the eighth floor. The only thing she had neglected to ask him for was the key to the office. He fingered it gently in his trouser pocket: a gold old-fashioned Chubb, difficult to have copied. No more copies would be needed now; it seemed a safe assumption that things would be finally settled on this trip to the Cathedral. Settle his hash, more likely. He'd have three months left to continue generating poems; the equivalent of a small *Selected Poems* by then.

And what afterwards? The future looked bleak: on to the shoals of consultancy with the sharks and the shysters, working from home to keep down costs, driven by a mortgage and his girlfriend's expectations, peddling his rarefied skills through the hi-tech corridors of the Home Counties. 'Good afternoon, I wonder if I can interest you in the wonders of Text Generation?' 'Show him the door.' 'Hello, keen on grammar correction? Well, the Prince of Parsing would like to offer you his services.' Twenty thousand pounds and a company car; membership in a team of cenobitic/cerebral coders and the odd linguist or two. One day this lab could be yours.

Better even Harvard than that – not that a place was still awaiting him there. He had burned those bridges all right. 'Madison is rich now. He's gone over to industry.' Perhaps he could teach in a small liberal arts college of some repute and a high quotient of natural beauty: western Massachusetts, the Maine Coast, New Hampshire? Catherine would cringe at the mere mention of the idea. He phoned Sally, but only got her voice exchange.

Wellington poked his face round the door. 'Hello, Duncan,' Madison said neutrally. 'What brings you here? I thought only snoops hung out here this late.' When Wellington looked bemused, he added, 'I found somebody going through my desk. A friend of Dorothy's.'

'The biographer?'

'You know him?'

'Samson? Of course. Dorothy's planning to marry him. He's here a great deal of the time – though only when you're not. I would have mentioned it but I thought you knew.'

How, if he was never there when Samson hung around? At least the question of access was explained, or rather, Dorothy's role in it. But what had happened to Mr Guacamole? Just how long had she been cavorting with the snooping Samson? Was there any point in firing her now? He sighed.

'I may have something to show you,' Wellington said.

'More *Pericles*?'

'I wish it were. No, the business letters. Will next week do?'

'As long as it is next week. I'll be in the States the week after. Once I've gone there, it will be too late.' Should he tell him? No: he'd let him know soon enough. Wellington would have three months notice and a reference. He'd find work, if not at such ample levels of remuneration. 'Next Friday's your last shot. I'll be flying over to Boston at the weekend.' He packed his briefcase and snapped it shut. 'I'll be here all day then. Just drop in.'

Catherine was in London and phoned late that same night. She was not pleased by news of his forthcoming trip. 'You can't go then, darling. Mummy's giving a lunch for us that Tuesday.'

He'd had three whiskies and was not feeling patient. 'What am I supposed to do, tell Virgil Peabody, "Sorry I can't be there, my girlfriend's mummy is giving a party that I want to attend"?'

'Yes,' said Catherine before catching the sourness of his tone. Then, 'What on earth is the matter with you?'

'I'm about to lose my job and you want to stress the importance of mummy's lunch. There seem to be very different priorities at work here.'

There was silence at the other end of the line, the telephone equivalent of her tactic of subduing his occasional insubordinations by staring emotionlessly at him. This time he found it relatively easy to wait her out; in person, it was quite an effort to return her level, even stare. Do not grow angry; do not lose temper; equally, do not cave in.

She sensed the impasse. 'Darling, at least you can ask this little yellow man to rearrange your meetings. Surely there's nothing wrong with that. Don't be so timid. Honestly.'

Exasperation as her way of retaining self-respect, as a way to act as if the argument were won. 'Timid?' Not an accurate appraisal. Forty-eight hours in the Cathedral and he found himself verging on wholesale insubordination – witness Cromwell's many past explosions. No, he did not indulge in the smart-ass self-destructiveness of Pistolet – what would be the point? – but he was hardly *timid*. His resentment hardened; yet he tucked it away, much like placing a library book on the closed reserve shelf – mine for when I need it.

'All right,' he said, 'I'll ask Virgil.'

Which he did not do. It would have been futile, merely irritated the man. He could have pleaded illness, of course, and simply failed to fly – but then he could do nicely without 'Mummy's lunch'.

He heard nothing from his father in the following days (having sent him, with some trepidation, the Creation poems), which were notable only for a final, not very painful interview with Dorothy. After Madison's discovery of Samson, she had called in ill for the next two days, then appeared first thing on Monday morning, wearing a formal suit. She seemed eager to explain herself, aggressively so – gone was the habitual sulkiness, and in its place an almost endearing defiance.

Once seated, she began dramatically, 'You can have my resignation. I'm doing it for the man I love.'

'Samson, I take it?'

'Yes, Arthur. And a nicer man than you'll ever be.'

He nodded. 'Doubtless. I was merely a little surprised to find out, that's all. What happened to your Mexican man? I thought you were marrying him. I wouldn't have thought Samson was your type.'

'Why, and you are?' Again, the perplexing reference to a putative lust for her. Whatever had he done to create this impression? 'Gordon was just a playboy,' she said with a newly intellectual derision. 'Arthur needs me.'

'To get into my office?'

'You're hiding things the world deserves to see. All because of your petty jealousy of your father.'

'Dorothy, I want a secretary, not a psychotherapist. No more analytic stuff, okay? What exactly did you tell Arthur was here?'

'Poems by your father, of course. Why else did you have me do all that typing?'

'But those are published poems. You typed them from a book.'

'The ones on the print-outs weren't published. I could tell.' She paused. 'Well, actually, Arthur could tell. He knew as soon as he saw them.'

'Did he take any of them?'

She shook her head regretfully. 'I was going to make him a copy, but Wellington was around. Snooping. God, that man revolts me. I won't miss him, I can tell you.'

'Not even as much as you'll miss me?'

'You ought to see yourself, so smug, so sure of yourself. At least you're not famous like your father. And he's a kinder man than you'll ever be.'

'How would you know?'

'Anyone can tell by reading the poems. Arthur's been explaining them to me.'

A transference of the affective fallacy: the poem moves me, therefore its creator must be humane, considerate, kind. A quick glance at Robert Frost's life would dispel that one. Or Frederick Madison's. He shook his head. 'You don't know the half of it,' he said.

'Perhaps not,' said Dorothy primly. 'But I know that

whatever your father has done, you've been a terrible son.'

'Get out of here quick, Dorothy, before I throw you out. And don't let me catch your fiancé around here. Tell him he can pester my old man as much as he likes but he'd better stay away from me. You got that?'

Dorothy laughed a little shrilly. 'I finally touched a nerve, didn't I? Arthur told me that would do it. Your father really gets up your nose.' She picked up her handbag. 'Have Ling send my cheque to my house. I wouldn't want to collect it here, in case you got *violent*.' She laughed again, and left, swinging her bag over her shoulder.

9

It was not only Dorothy who kept his father in the forefront of his thoughts. On Friday Madison went into the office to re-generate two poems in final form. Kaminski rang and asked him to drop in at the restaurant. 'There's some great Aussie Chardonnay come in. All I ask is a small favour in return.'

'Tell Lisa Adams what a man you are?'

'Something like that. I've got something I want you to take over for me.'

'As long as it's light enough to carry.'

'It's light, all right. And so's my wallet after paying for it.'

Tardily opening his post, Madison found: the latest stock option grant from Ling, an announcement of a rates increase from the city council, and a letter from his father – posted from London. Why was his father still there? Surely he'd been back in Tuscany for days – licking his wounds, Madison hoped. It was typed, except for the signature, and read:

Dear Robert,

It was swell seeing you last week. Your old papa appreciates your taking the time to come down to London – never a favourite town of mine. I only wish we'd had longer.

You ought to know you're always welcome on our side of the Channel. You'd get a kick out of Monica, and the Tuscan sights are pretty wonderful – both the female and inanimate variety! Let me know if there's any chance of your making your way down to us. Your girl is welcome, too, of course.

Anyway, I'm off to another of the literary wars this time with some structuralists in Paris keen to take me apart. We'll see about that; I don't imagine they're much braver than their Frog predecessors were in the War. Keep in touch. With fondest love,

your papa

Madison put the letter down, perplexed. Had his father gone loopy? And what about the poems he had sent him? Was his father really going to pretend none of it had happened?

There was no doubt that the letter *was* his father's: no secretary could mimic that mixture of Hemingwayesque gee-whizzery – 'swell', 'wonderful' – that his father seemed intent on adopting in old age, or the long-standing patronising tone of 'Your girl is welcome, too, of course.'

Perhaps his father had written the letter *before* their own encounter, like a small boy writing thankyou notes to his aunts in mid-December, in preparation for prompt posting on Boxing Day. Madison returned to his desk and looked at the letter. It was dated only the day before; the envelope showed the same date as the postmark.

Wellington appeared in the doorway, the last thing Madison needed. He pointed to a chair and watched crossly as Wellington took his time sitting down. 'Ready for your trip?'

'Almost. I'm just checking some numbers they want back in the Cathedral.'

'Ah, and cleaning up the files? Last-minute letters, that sort of thing?'

What an odd way for him to talk, the epitome of abstractedness suddenly taking an interest in the mundane. 'Something like that,' Madison replied, glancing down at his father's letter and eager to get back to its bizarre contents. He asked, 'Did you have something to show me, Duncan?' Another stab at a business letter, perhaps – this from a man who probably wrote to the gas board in Greek. He should have let Wellington continue to play with *Pericles*. Why try to wring a bastardised corporate kind of creativity from the incarnation of the scholarly amateur?

'You may already have seen it,' said Wellington.

'What? The letters from last week? I told you, unless a businessman needed exactly the kind of letter you've made, the program won't do him any good, however much the thesaurus kicks in.' He had explained all this several times before. 'Sorry, Duncan, but I've got a lot to do. We can talk more about this when I get back from the States.' Yes, talk about that, and Wellington's redundancy money.

Wellington gave no sign of leaving. 'Actually, that's not the letter I had in mind.'

'You have a new one, then? I thought you said I'd already seen it.'

'You have.' He pointed to the letter from Madison's father on the desk. 'Unless I'm mistaken, it's sitting right there.'

Had Wellington gone potty too? 'Are you talking about

199

this, Duncan?' he asked, picking up the letter. 'It's personal, nothing to do with here. Tell me what you're driving at, Duncan; otherwise, I've got work to do.'

Wellington adopted a benign look of patience. 'That letter, which you say is personal, was written two days ago by the Creation program running in 'C' on the machine next door. I was in London yesterday at the British Library, and posted it shortly after lunch in Museum Street.'

'You're joking.'

'I can recite it to you verbatim if you like. "Dear Robert it was good seeing you last week. Your old papa . . . ",' he began, until Madison waved him to stop.

'What are you trying to do?' Madison half-shouted. 'What business is this of yours? How dare you?'

Wellington looked so surprised that most of Madison's anger evaporated. 'I thought you'd be pleased,' said Wellington. 'You said, use your father as a restricted domain. And didn't you go and see him last week in London? I admit it's not a proper business letter, but surely even an American executive writes the occasional personal thankyou from work. And from your reaction, it appears that I've succeeded in capturing your father's voice.'

'Succeeded? You've done so well that I'm not sure I believe you.' Paranoia made a sudden appearance. Could not Wellington be in on Dorothy's plotting with Samson? Stop it, he told himself. 'How did you get my father's signature if *Creation* wrote this?'

'That's why I went to the British Library. They have some letters your father wrote to William Golding. After an hour's practice it was easy enough to forge a passable imitation.'

'Jesus, I'm amazed. Could you do another one?'

'I don't see why not. What would you like it to be about?'

Madison thought for a moment. 'Why not this? Have

it be a letter from my father *before* he saw me. Say he's writing from Italy – that's where he lives – and he wants to see me. Do you think you could manage that?'

'I'll need until after lunch.' And he went back to his warren next door and set to work. Still stunned, Madison forced himself to concentrate on preparations for his trip.

At lunchtime Wellington ignored his inquiry about progress with a curt 'Too early to tell,' so Madison walked out into an overcast day and headed for Kaminski's Bar. He thought again of Wellington's imitation of his father; no point in getting excited yet; it might be a one-off fluke, perhaps even – his paranoia resurfacing – a jimmied job by Wellington, sensing his days were numbered. Hence the importance of letter number two: no time to write code to represent a simple job of pastiche; Madison would be able to see for himself if the code drove the generator.

And if it did – well, he'd have something to show the guys and gals in the Cathedral. Thank God for stylometry. He looked yet again at his father's letter – no, Wellington's letter – well, Wellington's steal of his father's letter. He shuddered, awash in a world of authentic fakes, contrived naturalness, uncanny imitations of the ostensibly inimitable.

At Kaminski's they were playing dice at the bar. There was no sign of the owner, but Deborah, Kaminski's old flame, came over to him. She wore the usual uniform of white blouse, black miniskirt, brown boots, and orange thighs. 'Kaminski had to go to a demonstration. Some computer program for the restaurant.'

Madison groaned, thinking of the Frenchman he'd seen at the A.I. conference.

'Yes. But he said to give you this.' She handed him a long white envelope. Inside was another, slightly smaller envelope addressed to Lisa Adams, and a scribbled note from Kaminski. 'R., please make sure this gets to Lisa

A. without fail next week. I owe you one. Thanks. K.'

Kaminski besotted, Kaminski enthralled; it seemed so improbable. By comparison, his own possible marriage seemed mature, considered. Was he too old for love? Kaminski was older still, virtually a caricature of the rakish philandering Lothario. Yet he had fallen.

Wellington was seated in front of his desk, his back to the door, reading an article in *Modern Philology*. 'Interesting?' Madison asked, sitting down across from him.

'"Sexual Imagery in *Ancrene Wisse*". Feminist, but sound.'

'I'll bet. Now what about the letter?'

'Here you are.' Wellington handed it over with elaborate nonchalance.

> Dear Robert,
>   Just to let you know that your papa's coming to old Albion sometime next month and would like to see his boy. Any chance of a rendezvous in London? I'll let you know when I've got the details sorted out. The weather's been terrific here lately – fine, bright, cloudless days with wonderful views from the house. Monica looks forward to getting acquainted and joins me in sending lots of love,
>   your old Papa

'You've done it, Duncan!'

'Here's the code,' said Wellington, handing him two pages of print-out. There were only forty new lines of LISP. 'I haven't had time to compile into 'C', so it's still slow.'

'If that's our biggest worry, we're home free. And if you can work it in as idiosyncratic a domain as my father's, we shouldn't find it very hard to do the same for the writing of your average corporate clone. You've done more than you realise, Duncan.' Like maybe saved your job.

Wellington bowed politely. 'I'm pleased you're pleased.'

10

Catherine was not similarly delighted. 'I don't see,' she said that evening as he packed, 'why you have to leave on Saturday.'

'I'm going to drive up to Vermont. It's been a long time since I've seen my mother. It's only one extra day. I should be back next weekend.'

'You'd better be. We're due at my parents' on Sunday.'

He looked at his open suitcase. What was missing?

'Are you listening?' Catherine said as he pondered.

'Of course.' Ties; he'd forgotten ties. He picked out half a dozen from his wardrobe, striped ones from Brooks Brothers.

'And, darling,' said Catherine, sitting down on the bed next to his open suitcase, 'do be discreet. I'm not planning to ring your hotel room at six in the morning, but it would be nice to know that if I ring at, let's say, eight o'clock, I'll find you there.'

He closed his suitcase and stared at her. 'What are you talking about?'

'You know perfectly well what I'm saying. That night in London, when you said you'd be staying at Kaminski's flat, I know you didn't. I rang the next morning, you see, to let you know I was taking your house keys, only Kaminski said you'd never arrived. Then I rang the Hyde Park Hotel and spoke to your friend Pistolet, only you weren't there either. When the front desk said you weren't registered, what was I supposed to think?'

He was too nonplussed to speak. No conceivable explanation came to mind; the truth of his night with Sally seemed inexpressible – yes, I was there all night long, but nothing happened.

Catherine smiled faintly. 'Don't look as if you'd swallowed your tongue. I didn't make a fuss then, and I'm not going to make one now.'

'You're not?' he said, as much in surprise as in relief.

'Heavens, no. I'm just asking you to be discreet, not to flaunt it in my face. That's when I would mind.'

'I see,' said Madison. His fiancée had always shown a realistic grasp of things, but this level-headedness he found disturbing. He asked, 'Am I supposed to feel the same way about you?'

'So far you haven't had any reason to worry. I suppose there's always the chance I might make the odd slip. It's only human.'

Only human – to Madison always the most paltry of excuses. Why did what she said now bother him so much? Was he so certain that he would stay faithful to her? Was it the prospect of her straying that rankled? What if that night in the Hyde Park Hotel, Sally had opened her arms from her bed, and brought him softly down into a familiar warmth? Well? But Sally was different. Though wasn't that also a paltry excuse?

'If we're going to stay together, I think it's better to talk about these things. Don't you?' asked Catherine.

He went to fetch his shaving kit from the bathroom. 'I don't know,' he said, packing his toothbrush. 'I find it's just making me depressed.'

Part Four

1

The plane circled Boston in the early afternoon sunlight. Madison looked down on the matchbox constructions of the south suburbs below him, trying to remember Robert Penn Warren's lines: 'I have friends down there, and their lives have strange shapes Like eggs splattered on the kitchen floor. Their lives shine Like oil slicks on dark water.'

Below him, a trail of cars was heading south on the Southeast Expressway, moving like ducks to water, in this case the shores of Cape Cod. He thought of Sally thirty miles north, walking in the woods as they had so often walked together; or was she playing weekend tennis with Sammy Ling, eating *dim sum* with her future mother-in-law?

It was all heat until he got through the Callahan tunnel and the rental car's air-conditioning kicked in. When he reached 93 and accelerated, he felt as if he were peeling off muggy clothes for a dip. He turned on the radio and drove towards Vermont. Slowly the landscape grew hillier, there were fewer long-distance views, and he travelled in and out of woodland tunnels of green. How in England he missed the forests: slanted stands of spruce, dense groups of poplar, birch and ash.

He left the interstate near White River junction and drove west, climbing the foothills that stretched west and upwards to the Green Mountains. He drove through Calvert's Pass, often blocked by snow in winter but now green and benign, then emerged into the expanse of his home valley. The road followed the river, and he passed a covered bridge, first totem of Vermont.

On the outskirts of town he passed the family dairy; behind it he saw the museum, named after the family. It was less an historical repository of family accomplishment than a hokey 'Vermont Centrepiece' – maple syrup production explained in boggling detail, a plywood model of a covered bridge, an account of the glories of the local cheddar cheese.

Once the accent *had* been historical, sombre, political. There had been two governors in the Madison family in two centuries, a Justice of the Supreme Court, a Congressman (the state only had one). Also a line of lawyers, almost all believers in public service, the now unfashionable notion of *noblesse oblige*; philanthropic, powerful. Yet at the museum attendance and revenues soared only after the vulgarisation.

At the Congregationalist church the road turned sharply and became Main Street. He followed the bend; if he'd gone straight, down Willow Street, he would have passed the large brick Colonial house in which he had spent his childhood. His first cousin, Johnny, only son of his uncle, lived there now, with his perky Greek wife and three bland children. Madison's mother had moved the two of them only three months after his father's departure. Too much space, too big a house to keep up; his mother had said this so insistently that, young as he was, Madison had understood at once that she wanted only to get away from his father's lingering ghost.

He drove past the post office, oddly mid-western with its new bleached brick and wide picture-windows, then past Riely's bookstore, and on to his aunt Peg's general store. Shovels, pitchforks, overalls, staples for the outlying farmers, now vied for space in the window with Welsh pots, maple syrup and hand-made sweaters.

His uncle lived at the end of Somerset Street in a Federalist building of white pine, with dark green shutters on the front windows. In the 1960s an architect had retained the symmetry of the front of the house, yet satisfied his uncle's desire for more space by placing a sprawling addition at the back. Typically New England: opulence disguised by an unpretentious façade. Madison drove round the side of the house, through cedars and along a rough gravel drive to the edge of the property. Here his mother lived in a small, square, shingle-sided house, a stone's throw from the river that marked the boundary of his uncle's four-acre holding.

His mother and one of her pug dogs greeted him at the front door. He kissed her, and carried his suitcase into the living-room. It was light outside but the standard lamps were on, making the room's cedar walls and pine floorboards glow. He looked for signs of change but found none. Small oriental rugs lay scattered on the floor; near the fireplace a comfortable beige sofa, an old wing armchair, and his grandfather's black rocking-chair were grouped round a mahogany coffee table. On the wall, the same framed prints: half a dozen English pictures of country houses, a Capability Brown landscape, some natural scenes – the Wye Valley near Tintern in one, the gardens at Versailles on the opposite wall.

Here he had spent so many unhappy evenings in the years after his father left. Home from boarding school, home from college; the vacations had seemed endless. He had sought out any invitation that would enable him to spend the night away – once he drove to Georgia for three days to visit a girl he'd only met twice. Yet guilt, and the sheer length of his vacations, always drew him home, back to the family 'compound', back to this very room where, night after night, his mother got sloshed and her talk turned, eventually, to the subject of his father. *You mustn't let him be an influence on you – your uncle is a better model*; or *In some ways, considering his character, it's a blessing that he's gone*; or *He's always been a desperately unhappy man*; until drunkenly, despairingly, the tears would come, the shuddering sobs commence, and Madison would have to lead her up the stairs to bed.

His mother had let him drink at an early age: a beer, a glass of wine at first; cocktails before he'd turned seventeen. After a few disastrous trials with gin, he had ceased to abuse this licence, feeling there was something grotesque in both mother and son getting pie-eyed. More mundanely, if he didn't keep himself half-sober, neither would get dinner. After two drinks he would fight the slight buzz he felt, and the inclination to have another, and go out to the kitchen while she stayed behind to work on her fourth Manhattan. Steak on the broiler, broccoli in the saucepan, frozen French fries in the oven; it if had been left to her they would have made do with Stouffers – a spinach soufflé two inches wide and not much higher – or Lyonnaise potatoes from an aluminium tray, or noodles and mushrooms dusted with breadcrumbs by a machine in Ohio.

He continued his inspection while his mother went to the kitchen to let another pug dog in. A low pine bookcase with a wide assortment of volumes: on needlework, quilt-making, other indigenous crafts his mother no longer pretended to be interested in; several nineteenth-century cookbooks; a compendium of garden books, many on soils and climates (South Carolina, the Swiss Alps) unlikely to be of much use in the backyard. Also a few stray books his mother defiantly proclaimed her own property – as if to say she had an ear for a lyric too: Anne Bradstreet, Emily Dickinson, several volumes of Edna St Vincent Millay left by a spinster Madison aunt.

It was five thirty according to the walnut clock on the fireplace mantel, and Madison wondered if the half-filled glass on the coffee table was his mother's first of the evening. He poured himself a weak gin and tonic from the liquor cabinet in the corner, and sat in the rocker. His mother returned to the couch and lit a cigarette. She'd had her hair done, and patted it gently as she asked, 'You must be tired after your flight. Don't you want to go up to your room and change?'

'I'll go up in a minute.' Not tired so much as grubby, with the stale residue of seven hours in a pressurised cabin, three hours in an air-conditioned car. He longed for a shower. 'Is Uncle Billy at home?' He nodded in the direction of his uncle's Federalist house.

'He's up on the mountain. I said you'd be up tomorrow for lunch. I hope that's all right. I think he wants a word with you alone.'

He finished his drink and stood up. 'I guess I'll go upstairs.' He took his suitcase and went up the steep, narrow stairs, ducking his head halfway up as he'd had to do since the age of sixteen to miss an intrusive beam.

His room looked untouched since his last visit two years before. All that remained of his boyhood now was a sketch he'd made as a nine-year-old of Queechie Gorge, and a seven-iron from his first set of grown-up golf-clubs, handed down from his grandfather. He put down his suitcase on his bed by the window, picked up the golf-club, and barely kept his practice swing from shattering a bedside lamp. *Bobby Jones* could still be made out on the concave back of club face; these were the first model of steel-shafted clubs to be made, stained the colour of aged hickory along the shaft to disguise their metallic core.

The books on the shelf held overflow from his mother's bedroom: James Herriot, *82 Charing Cross Road*, *The Oxford Book of Light Verse*, some faded Penguins by writers he'd never heard of. One book was especially familiar. *A Reintroduction to Phrase Structure Grammar* by Robert Madison. A bone-white dust-jacket with grey type – a grim-looking monograph; of course no illustrations. Inside the flap: 'To Mother with love, R.' How imaginative. Five chapters, he learned from the contents page, 176 concise pages. His early claim to . . . what? Fame in the world of academic linguistics? Well, it had provided him with an academic niche, certainly, and was the first rung on the ladder to tenure – though that was a ladder he had never climbed. More than half a decade had elapsed since he had turned the typescript in to the university press. How the clock ticks, its arms sweep, the pendulum swings.

He showered and changed, then rejoined his mother downstairs. 'I didn't think we'd want a fire,' she said, pointing vaguely to the logless hearth, and he realised she had moved on to Manhattan number three. She continued, 'So when do I get to meet your English girlfriend?'

He shrugged. 'Maybe next trip.'

'Will you be back again soon?'

'I don't know. I'm not sure I'll be working for Ling much longer.'

'Really?' And what will you do instead?'

'Probably some consulting to begin with.'

'Consulting? It doesn't sound very stable to me. Your uncle says he's bothered by consultants all the time; they want to advise him on the dairy, or the museum, or the bank. He says they never have anything useful to add; they're just looking for business. You won't want to be doing something risky at your age.'

'I'll manage,' he said, smothering his faint irritation, for it occurred to him that what his mother was saying was perfectly true.

He moved the conversation onto dogs without much trouble, and half-listened as his mother recounted the recent adventures of Ming (pug dog number one), Ting (Ming's daughter), and Sulaki. Her preference for Asian names pre-dated Madison's association with Ling Enterprises by some twenty-five years. The dogs moved around the sitting-room like spoiled children looking for candy, their squashed noses snorting and sniffing at his shoes like miniature pigs looking for truffles. Forbidden the softness of sofa or chairs, they rolled almost carnally against Madison's trouser-legs, shedding copious clumps of fine, light hair that coiled like angel pasta on his turn-ups.

He went out to the kitchen, leaving his mother to sift through a *New Yorker* he'd read on the plane. Boiling water for a frozen block of spinach, he put lamb chops in the broiler pan but decided against rice or potatoes – his mother would only pick at her food. Looking in the pantry for a bottle of wine, he counted seven unopened half-gallons of Jim Beam, a case of Martini sweet vermouth, and an ageing open jug of Inglenook Burgundy. He sniffed the latter carefully, then went and set the table in the dining-room.

There had been quite a lot of drinking well before his father left. His father was no teetotaller; lashings – a favourite word – of beer and wine, lots of Scotch, brandy, the odd gin. But he always had his work; like clockwork in the morning, regardless of hangover, he had gone into his study, closed the door, pulled the chair up to the desk with paper before him.

When supper was ready Madison went to fetch his mother, and found her fast asleep on the couch, her right arm resting on the sofa arm. A pug – Ming? Ting? Sulaki? – sat unadmonished on the couch beside her, like Madison's mother breathing the shallow steady breath of sleep.

That night – having gently moved his mother to bed after eating a solitary supper – Madison lay sleepless in his bedroom. Outside, a silver moon moved in and out of cloud and he opened a window to try and see the river, but could distinguish nothing. He turned on the light and opened his briefcase. A floppy diskette held the poems he'd generated – six of them, with one, his most recent, that he had been unable to finalise the day before in the office. He leafed through the stack of print-out and looked

213

at the draft of the poem. Almost there: he would need a high-end PC to finish it. Borrow Pistolet's or – this excited him – borrow Sally's. He turned off the light and got into bed. Will this do? he wondered, then wondered to whom he spoke.

In the morning he rose early. When his mother came downstairs to the kitchen he had already cooked himself eggs, and now gave her toast and coffee. She no longer ordered the *New York Times* on Sunday, so he volunteered to walk to his cousin's store to buy one, keen to avoid the embarrassment that lay unspoken between them.

He went out wearing jeans and tennis shoes, and walked along the river until it left his uncle's property, then crossed it through the covered bridge. There was traffic in town: tourists parked already on the main street, out for the day in a real-life Vermont town.

He passed the Episcopal Church, with its comforting white front and the restored bell-tower – and the oddity of a small brick wing at the back. For improved catering facilities? A new vicar; Reverend Whiteby had died, hadn't he, wasn't that in his mother's Christmas card? The *déjà vu* of himself in a pew, suit on, during one of his mother's devout phases – post paternal departure, this. Now a man he didn't recognise scuttled into the front entrance, late for service.

Right at the corner onto Main Street – and the shock of a new shopfront, a J Press look-alike, blue seersucker in the window, a ladies' outfit of green Shetland sweater and navy-blue skirt. Next, the bookstore, big on novels and guidebooks, selling a good read or, for tourists, coy collections of maple syrup recipes.

Then his aunt's store, a high set of square windows broken by unpainted mullions – a careful naturalistic touch – with the central double door that stuck in winter. No bell as he entered: in summer the floods of visitors meant it would ring all day. Miss Brubaker was at the counter – a big smile, small kiss, polite mutual inquiries, entreaties for him to come home more often, his aunt Peg would be sorry to miss him, away nursing her mother in Rutland who was 'poorly'. He paid for the paper and had a quick look round: he'd worked there for two summers when in prep school, before transfer by avuncular Fiat to the family dairy.

Out into the sun; a wave to one of the three local cops, then an absent-minded walk home while skimming the newspaper sections. He stopped at the book review with his usual trepidation. It seemed foredestined that he would find mention there of his father; fortunately this time it was a small mention. Under 'New in Paperback':

> To celebrate the tenth anniversary of the publication of *Catwalk*, the best-selling novel by famed poet Frederick Madison, Random House is releasing a new edition with a preface by the author. On publication, reviewer Stanley Edgar Hyman described it in these pages as 'an extraordinary *tour de force*, a riveting narrative infused by the lyricism that has made Madison one of this century's most formidable poetic presences.' Over two million copies of the novel have been sold.

What a pity his father had not hit pay-dirt while still at home. Madison put the paper in a stack by the fireplace for burning, with the book review at the bottom, knowing his mother was unlikely to burrow that deep. She came in with one of the pugs, and they talked about his aunt's store for a while. Then it was time for him to go and see his uncle.

His Uncle Billy owned five hundred acres of pasture and woods at the top of Schaeffer Mountain, reachable only by a mile-long drive that was kept purposely pot-holed and rocky. Even on this dry day, Madison bumped the tail-pipe and scratched his rental car's sides against scrub bushes of hawthorn and wild rose.

After the effort of approach, first sight of the house was unpromising, for it had changed little from its origins as the hunting shack of Madison's great-grandfather: starkly Yankee; built of pine board and splintered shingles; with a rickety railed porch that sat on long pilings on the downhill side. Conspicuously unpainted, the house sat just beneath the hill's top rise and looked out over the better part of two counties. Inside, there was one more bedroom since his great-grandfather's time, with a double bed (the other rooms had bunks), and an indoor shower and toilet. No insulation; a wood-burning stove was needed even in summer for the cool mountain nights.

The house was empty, but he found his uncle sitting in a cane rocker on the porch. 'Robert,' he said, standing up to shake hands. 'What would you like to drink? Coffee, beer, or something stronger?'

'I'd like coffee, but sit still. I'll get it.' He opened the screen-door and walked through the sitting-room with its stove fireplace to the open kitchen where a percolator sat on a counter. The cabinets were of ageing pine, painted the mellow red of an old barn. Next to the sink, a single plate and cup sat in a drying rack. So his uncle was here alone. This suggested that serious talk lay ahead. They'd had very few serious talks – in fact, only one readily remembered, when Madison was almost expelled from boarding school for drinking three beers with three friends on a moonlit soccer field. He found an old chipped mug and poured himself a black coffee. Outside, his uncle was sitting rocking slowly. Madison sat down and furtively examined the older man. He looked healthy from the sun: his cheeks glowed with a mixture of auburn and gold, and his hair was as much sun-bleached blonde as grey. He wore his country outfit of wheat-coloured corduroys and a cream Viyella shirt with faint red checks.

'Your mother said you were only here for a day.'

'I'm driving down tonight. Have to be at work tomorrow.'

'That's a pity. Johnny would have made it; still up north fishing for browns.'

Madison said nothing and stared out at the distant hills until his eyes began to water from the sunlight. Cumulus clouds appeared in growing formations in the distance, drifting slowly in from the west; dark fluffy counterpoints to the clearness of the south-east horizon.

'Oh,' said his uncle, seeming to remember his manners, 'your mother says you're going out with an English girl. You going to marry her?'

'I don't know. Not for a while, anyway.'

'A long engagement.' His uncle chuckled with a slow rumble in his chest; it sounded like a beer barrel being wheeled along a pavement. His laugh was about the only feature of his personality that reminded Madison of his father. 'Nothing wrong with that,' his uncle said, laughing again. 'Gives a guy plenty of time to change his mind.'

True; months to disengage, seasons in which to change his mind. First, the rest of summer. Then autumn – Sally would be married in the autumn. After Hallowe'en, according to Pistolet. Would he be invited? Surely not. Unless Sammy was acting magnanimous, knowing that once Sally made it to the altar, the threat from Madison would evaporate.

'Did you ever change *your* mind?'

His uncle shook his head. 'Nope. One engagement. One wedding. One marriage. Just as well; would have been hopeless at multiple romancing.' He smiled. 'Your father was a different story. Must have had three or four close calls before he married your mother. And that many irate fathers, I recall.'

'You'll love it there' – his father's words to his English bride. *Not* your typical GI conquest, found as she worked in the USO near Berkeley Square. *Not* handing out coffee, either, this Norwich lady, but secretary to the colonel in charge. 'A real horse's ass, too,' his father had recalled. 'Tried to have me stripped of my accreditation when he learned I was dating your mother.'

Dating. How this dated him, had thought the son semi-pubescent at the kitchen table as his old man talked that night, drunk, home early from a party. When? The late 60's. So it dated him, too, this memory; did he have his own regrets about leaving Vermont? Odd flickerings of alienation – on an English golf course, in a Boston bar – made him ready to retrace history, start again, end up a pea in a Vermont pod, pleased, plump, complacent. He would have been apprenticed to the law, perhaps – Vermont, with Kentucky, the only states where this could still be done – working for the local firm of his cousin Johnny, a lawyer and state representative certain to be a judge some day. A fine life Madison would have led, pruning his handicap to win the country club medal, drinking Scotch at cocktail parties – in lesser or greater quantities according to the relative state of his depression in those long winter nights of white, snow-filled fields and early dark.

He turned to his uncle. 'Were my father's *actual* engagements?'

'Two of them. Dates of the wedding picked and all. But he was gun-shy and kept ducking out. Your mother was the first one from out of Vermont. That's probably why he stuck to it: didn't feel trapped.'

Madison said, 'I don't know why he bothered with the false alarms, not with the number of times he's been married since. Why, he's the Mickey Rooney of literature.'

This time they both laughed, and Madison felt suddenly at ease. His uncle said, 'Say what you like, your father is sure some character.'

'Speaking of my father,' Madison began slowly.

'Yes?' His uncle was non-committal.

'I saw him, you know. In London a couple of weeks ago.'

'And?'

Madison looked out at the approaching front of cloud. 'I can report that he's still kicking.' He stopped, a little feebly.

'That's all?' asked his uncle after a minute.

'There's not much else to tell. We didn't talk very long.'

His uncle held up his hands and studied his palms. He had big hands, smooth and finely boned. 'He's in New York right now,' he said. 'I talked to him last night. Over for some launch – Christ, I always think of the navy when he says that. Half-expect to see him in a picture in the paper, swinging a bottle of champagne to christen an ocean liner.' He put his hands down and turned his head to look at Madison. 'Said he needed to see you.'

'I don't really want to see him.' Not entirely true; he wanted to see his father's face when he read the poems and realised it wasn't a put-up job, some cleverness Madison had paid a competent parodist to create. Wanted to see his face as a CPU churned, and the printer sang its odd metallic lyrics, and Frederick Madison realised that his son could get a single personal computer to generate in two days' time verse indistinguishable from what the old man had spent a lifetime making. Yes, he would like to see him again, if only for that.

'Hard words. You sure you mean them?'

'He has always tried to suggest I should look after mother more, as if I hadn't done that all those years as a kid when he'd run off. Who the hell is he to say that? He ruined her life, not me.'

His uncle stroked the rocker's arm with his hand. 'People tend to ruin their own lives, Robert; they don't need anyone else to do it for them. And I wouldn't say

219

her life's ruined, anyway. She's got her friends, those dogs;
she still gardens.'

'You mean, pretends to.'

'None of us is getting any younger. She gets by all right.
Your aunt and I keep an eye on her. Believe me, she
does okay.'

'No thanks to him.'

'Oh, I don't know. She still gets money from him. More
than before; your father's a well-off man now.'

'I wish he had been twenty years ago. We wouldn't
have had to rely on you so much. I know who paid for
my education.'

'And you've thanked me plenty of times. As has your
father. Didn't have a dime to spare back then. Poets are
poor; you know that. It took a novel to make him rich.'

'So how responsible of him to take off. We didn't have
a dime.'

'I know, but he knew *I* did. And knew I'd look after
you two. That's not so irresponsible.'

'Just heartless.'

His uncle nodded. 'Yes, very heartless. I can't justify
what he did; not going to try: I simply know he left because
he'd have died if he'd stayed.'

'Isn't that a little melodramatic?'

'Maybe. Die; or never write again. Which would have
been the same thing for your father. Don't misunderstand:
he didn't leave because it would help your mother or
because it would help you. He left to save himself. You
can blame all you want, but don't act as if he was trying to
hurt you; just trying to help himself. Can't you see that?'

'I can only see how much it screwed up my mother.'

'Hell, Robert,' his uncle said impatiently, 'forgive me,
but your mother was always screwed up. I love her, my
wife loves her; she's family, always will be; but if she's got
problems they are not just because of your father. I think
she'd even say so herself. He hasn't ruined her life; *she*

has, to the extent that it is ruined. She always drank too much, even before your father left. Anyhow, she's happier now than she has been in years. *Still* drinks too much, falls asleep at our parties, doesn't eat right. But more content than she used to be. Misses you, probably wishes you'd get up here more often, but understands you want space.'

'But my goddamned father – '

His uncle interrupted. '*Forget* your father. At least, forget him if all you can do is hate him. Your mother doesn't hate him any more. They even talk on the phone now.'

'They do?' Madison was dumbstruck. 'Since when?'

'Last few months they do. Don't be so surprised. I told you she was happier now.'

'I can't believe it. What do they talk about, for God's sake?'

'Wouldn't be surprised if what they talk about is you. She's got no problem with *him* any more. *You're* the one with the problem, Robert. That's why she didn't say anything. Didn't want to upset you. She doesn't think her life's ruined, not by him, at any rate. Only worried that you'll let *it* ruin *your* life.'

'It? What is "it"?'

'What is "*it*"? his uncle asked rhetorically, with an air of mild surprise. 'Why, your father, of course. That's your problem.' He paused to let this sink in, then stood up and stretched. 'It's going to rain soon. Come on, I'll fix us some lunch.'

With a half-bottle of Californian Chardonnay inside him, and a shell steak and some salad, Madison drove down Schaeffer's Mountain, along the Hanover River and into town. The rain had finally moved in, enough to make him turn the car's wipers on high. He had great trouble seeing ahead of him.

He parked beside the house, intent on asking his mother about her communications with his father, and ran half-ducking through the rain to the front door. Opening it, he heard his mother's throaty laugh, raspy from the effects of cigarettes; he walked into the sitting-room to find her, drink in one hand, cigarette in the other, rocking gently with laughter. There was someone else in the room, a lanky figure moving perkily back and forth in the rocker, also smoking. Pistolet.

'Ah,' said his friend, seeing Madison, 'I was just telling your mother about the day you ducked Sammy Ling in the pond at school.'

'*I* ducked him?' said Madison, taking off his wet jacket and crossing the room to hang it on the fire-screen. He remembered. Sammy in the pond – through no fault of his, Madison's. Sammy climbing out, soaked, and chasing Madison halfway back to school while Pistolet jogged, cackling, behind. Madison able to stop running only when Abel, the French master, came into view, walking his Corgi.

Madison turned to his mother, still laughing on the couch, and said, 'It was Jeffrey who gave him the critical push. I was an innocent observer. But when Sammy came up for air, there was your son standing on the bank. Master Pistolet was nowhere to be seen.'

'I'm surprised Ling ever hired you,' his mother remarked. 'Have another drink, Jeffrey.' She adored Pistolet, always had, ever since Madison had first brought him home for a weekend from prep school. He amused her, made her laugh; Madison was always aware of how much at ease his friend and his mother were in each other's company.

'Thanks, I will.' Pistolet stood up and went past Madison to the bar. As he dropped ice into his glass, he talked over his shoulder to Madison's mother. 'Don't be fooled by your son's penchant for modesty. He's a very special breed of cat; Harvard's loss was Ling's gain. Even Sammy could see that. Let bygones be bygones, Mrs Madison, that's what Sammy figured; even a boy as bad as your son could be of use to Mister Ling.'

The phone rang, and Madison rudely made only a half-hearted effort to answer it; his mother went instead, leaving him alone with Pistolet. 'What are you doing here, Jeffrey?' he demanded.

'I phoned your mother and she said you were coming here before going to Ling.'

'She didn't tell me you had called.' More telephonic surprises.

'I asked her not to. I was hoping to have a surprise for you, but it didn't work out.'

'What kind of surprise?'

'Sally. We were going to drive up, have lunch at your uncle's inn, then come and see the conquering hero. That's you. But she backed out yesterday – command performance at the Empress's house with Sammy. So I drove up by myself and saw my aunt in Woodstock. She dropped me here, but it'd be very useful if you could give me a lift to Woodstock on your way south. I'm assuming you'll be heading back to the Cathedral pretty soon now, and I trust you're ready to strut your stuff. Everyone's waiting to watch you pull a rabbit out of the hat.' He took a quick swallow of his drink. 'More likely it'll be a turkey out of your rear end. Cromwell gave me three-to-one you'd botch your demo, but cheer up – I took the bet.'

'Thank you for the vote of confidence.'

'Oh, I wouldn't call it that. Sally's been keeping me posted on your progress. Poems, right? Not entirely dissimilar to those of someone . . . ' he craned his neck to see if Madison's mother was coming back '. . . once near and dear to your mother and you. Don't give me that look. I'm your friend, remember? Your pal Pistolet. We go way back. I am allowed to make slighting references to blood relatives you're not wild about. Anyway, I don't think your generated poems will give Minnie Lu a hot flush, but they should be enough to take ten bucks off Cromwell.'

'I'd like to think I'm good for more than that.'

Pistolet shook his head. 'I doubt it. Times are hard in the Cathedral. No raises this year for any of us. Don't misunderstand me: I'm delighted that you've managed to pull it off. Really, I'm very happy for you. May it win you future fame in the field of text generation. But that's got nothing to do with Ling, you know. Not with the kind of results we're having. Nobody's interested in research any more. They want products.'

'You sound like Cromwell. Christ, what a company. Maybe I should quit before they have the luxury of firing me.'

'You don't have to get fired. You'll be welcome back in the Cathedral. The specs for *Write Right* are almost finished. I'm sure you'd enjoy leading the group.'

'I'd rather let you do that, Jeffrey.'

Pistolet lifted his drink in salutation. 'Not me,' he declared. 'Sanity has returned to this guy. And he says, "Count me out".'

'What's that supposed to mean?' There was something new and intriguing in Pistolet's tone. Still the jaded, world-weary jibes, but something novel, too, a hint of determination behind the standard pose of cynical inertia.

Madison's mother returned. 'That was your aunt,' she told him. 'She's back from her mother's and would like to see you before you go. I said you'd drop by.'

After saying goodbye, then briefly visiting his Aunt Peg, Madison and Pistolet were again alone. He should reach the town of Madison before dark, be in his hotel in time to watch the sunset and the television news.

'So what have you got to show them?' asked Pistolet.

'Poems. And a smallish rabbit.'

'Yes?'

'Some letters. Business letters. That's what the bastards want, isn't it?'

'More than the poems, that's for sure. How good are your letters?'

'They're pretty good. A little quirky; I had to use a specific domain, so there'd be a voice running through them that's individual.'

'And whose voice might that be?'

'Same as the poems,' Madison said tersely.

Pistolet looked disgusted. 'Papa Madison again. Jesus, Robert, I wish you'd get off this kick of yours.'

Madison responded quietly. 'It wasn't my decision. Wellington, the lexical genius in my office, came up with it quite by chance. I promise you.'

'There's no point in trying to convince *me*. Save it for a therapist. But if these letters sound just like your father, don't expect the Ling board to be impressed. They'll want the generator to work for someone bland – you know, someone like Olney or Macaulay, when they're wearing their corporate tie-pins. Have you got anything in that line?'

'Not yet. I haven't had time to work on transferring domains. I just need a corpus of letters from somebody else, then I run the stylometry analysis, then I let the generator fly. I'll try to get some other letters tomorrow at the Cathedral.'

Pistolet looked uncharacteristically thoughtful. Madison said, 'Something's on your mind, Jeffrey, and it's not the intricacies of business letters. What's up?'

'I've had an offer. I'm thinking of leaving.'

'Leaving Ling?' asked Madison with a smile. Pistolet always had offers, yet seemed glued to the corporate binding of Ling Enterprises. It would take a lot to unstick him.

'Don't smile like that, you patronising bastard. This time I'm serious. Sal Lombardi has left the company and moved to the south shore. His kid got into Milton Academy, by the way; I don't know why, but he asked me especially to tell you that. He's got some venture money to work on machine translation, and he needs an N.L. guy to help with the parser.'

This didn't quite click; Pistolet as a parsing drone for a dubious start-up? Madison said, 'Why don't you tell me the real story?'

Pistolet looked away, out of the window, before responding. 'You always could see through me.' He exhaled noisily, then swigged from a hip-flask he brought out of his jacket pocket. He offered it to Madison, who shook his head. 'Suit yourself,' said Pistolet. 'Leaves that much more for me.'

'Are you still drinking a lot?'

'No more than usual,' said Pistolet, taking another swig and tucking the flask back into his pocket. 'Nothing that a change of scene won't cure.'

'Come on, what's the problem?'

Pistolet sighed again. 'The Blue Rinse Lady. I think she's cooked my goose for sure. I promised her an astrology program by the end of this week and I haven't got to step one. How can I, when the whole thing was rigged hocus-pocus to begin with?'

'Can't you come clean with her, explain it was all a misunderstanding?'

'And eat humble pie for the next two years? Honestly, Madison, don't you start in on me; you sound just like Sally. If life in the Cathedral is so worth living, why aren't you keen to come back? As it is, you're never around, Sally's out of touch, and Lisa Adams is all over me.'

'Hang on a minute. Where's Sally going?'

'Upstairs. Sammy's not comfortable with her egghead role. He wants her up in the stratosphere of higher management. Though she's not that keen.'

'About the job, or about Sammy?'

'Both, actually. Who wouldn't have doubts about marrying that weasel? She wanted to see you today. If Sammy hadn't thrown a fit about her missing Sunday lunch at the Empress's she'd be in this car right now. That doesn't

226

sound like a girl keeping her ears open for wedding bells, does it?'

Madison accelerated to match the new racing of his heart. 'Do you think the wedding might be off, then?' he asked.

'Not that I know of,' Pistolet said casually. 'Probably a momentary tiff. You don't throw away a billion dollars over an *argument*.'

'I suppose not,' said Madison glumly.

'Cheer up,' said Pistolet. 'The wedding should be hilarious. Guess who's going to be best man?'

'Who? Minnie Lu?'

'Almost as good. Virgil Peabody. I can't wait to hear that speech.'

They were moving into the smaller hills of eastern Vermont. The land was lusher here, with dairy cattle, some pigs. When they reached Woodstock, Pistolet stirred himself. 'Maybe we should do something,' he declared.

'About what?'

'About Sally. We shouldn't let her marry Sammy; you know that. But there's not much time. Think about it.' He moved one leg ninety degrees and swung out of the car. 'See you in the morning. Drive at great speed. Take risks.'

2

He could not in fact drive at high speed, thanks to the returning weekend traffic that clotted the interstate near the Massachusetts border. He broke away as soon as possible and took smaller two-lane roads east towards

Madison and the Cathedral, though here too traffic was dense, of a local grandmother-visiting kind in the small towns pocketed in the state's northern forests.

Pistolet's point – that letters mimicking Madison's father would seem as goofy to the likes of Minnie Lu as showing her the poems – was indisputable. If he'd thought of it, Madison might have procured another, more Babbit-like, source of correspondence; as it was, with only a day left before his demo, there wasn't much time to start hunting.

In his hotel room he watched the tail-end of a golf tournament on television, then set to work on his demo. He picked six poems for generation: two love lyrics, two voice poems, one more impersonal narrative, a final simple elegy for John Gardner, the novelist. Then four business letters: a no to a bid for a construction project, a yes to an invitation to speak to a rotary club, a memorandum on employing new staff in a chemical company, and a brief report from an executive's tour of a rival's canning factory. It was strange, hearing his father's voice in these situations. Thus:

> . . . I'll get a kick out of addressing the Rotarians next Thursday. Anything special you'd like me to talk about? I've seen three wars, two famines, and the odd riot in countries all over the world. Seems to me maybe a few remarks about the role I played in some of these events would grab your average JC member by the *cojones*, no?

At nine thirty he gathered his nerve and called Sally. She was out, presumably still at her command performance at the Empress's, and he left no message on her tape. As he put the phone down he wished suddenly that he had asked her to phone him back, however late the hour – then felt foolish for this weakness.

He took a shower, and was drying himself with a soft

hotel towel when the phone rang. He snatched at the phone, and found his father on the line.

'You awake?'

'I am now,' he said grudgingly.

'Sorry. Didn't mean to wake you.'

'How did you find me?' he asked shortly.

'Your mother told me where you were. Information were willing to give the hotel number, my shaking, booze-soaked fingers managed to punch the buttons, and presto! there you were.' He gave a great, rolling laugh. 'How do you think I found you?' Adding quietly, 'Is this a lousy time to call, son?'

Something soft in the voice, almost worried. Madison suddenly felt he had been churlish. 'It's okay. I was awake. Where are you?'

'New York. The Pierre.'

'Ah.' He waited.

'I read the poems.'

'Good.' A hardness returned to his soul. He would give him nothing.

'Did you write them? You must have.'

'Nope. Cross my heart.'

'Who did, then? It's someone pretty goddamned good, I tell you.'

'No one. You should be asking *what* wrote them. In one case it was a Laptop 386; the others found their way into this world courtesy of the Lingua 1010. It's one of our newer models, a minicomputer sure to be eased out any day by the new generation of desktops, but still pretty effective in its humdrum way.'

'I find that hard to believe.'

'Suit yourself. But it's written more poems, from the later work of Frederick Madison.'

'What are you trying to do to me?'

'Me. Nothing. *It's* done it to you. Welcome to the machine age, pop.'

'Christ,' his father exclaimed, and hung up the phone.

No wave of triumph swept through Madison: increasingly he saw his accomplishment in precise, technical terms. From that perspective, what he had done was extraordinary – and deeply unpleasant. It paved the way for the mass exploration of machine writing. Literacy, that dwindling competence, would dwindle further still. It was not merely time-consuming banalities, pointless communications, that the computers would author; it was important communications, too, which people were no longer even capable of making. Literacy, moved wholesale into the mind of the new machines.

He felt cold and utterly down. Late as it was, he got dressed: grey flannels, an Oxford shirt, a heavy Shetland sweater. When the phone rang he moved slowly to it, expecting his father again. Could he not this time act more kindly? – 'Sure, come to Boston. Let's have lunch.' But it was Sally.

'How are you?' she asked.

'I've been better,' he blurted out, and gave an account of his conversation with his father. 'I don't know,' he concluded, 'I've lived with his taunts, said nothing, and done precisely what he said I couldn't. And now it all seems so *pointless*. I don't feel satisfied at all.'

'What you've accomplished is remarkable, really it is. It's a pity you were doing it for the wrong reasons.'

'Not you too. I've already had my uncle, and Pistolet, telling me I'm obsessed with my father, with pursuing a vendetta.'

'You are.' She stopped to let this sink in. 'Anyway, you brought the business letters, didn't you? That's what's important this week.'

'Why? So I can stay with Ling?'

'I thought you wanted to. If they're impressed enough, they'll leave you alone. In England, like you've said you wanted.'

'Part of me no longer cares. The poems are there; I know I can generate more. I don't need Ling for that. They'll just want me to shift the technology to more "useful" outlets – like these letters. Poetry won't sell a lot of hardware.'

His impulse to talk some more with her, the simple hunger he felt these days for her voice, was checked by an awareness of his own depression, which he was worried would soon emerge as irritation. 'I'm tired,' he declared. 'I'd better go to bed. But find me tomorrow in the Cathedral. I have a session with Minnie Lu and Virgil first thing. Come and give me first-aid afterwards. Please.'

'Sure. But get some sleep.'

He did, a dreamless, vacant sleep that produced no solutions to his questionings, no leads for his particular case.

3

This time Minnie Lu and Virgil Peabody were standing, staring side by side out of the window south towards Boston. Virgil turned and motioned with his head for Madison to sit down, then he and Minnie resumed their vigil.

'Ready when you are,' said Madison with a degree of irritation. Simultaneously, the two turned around and faced him, still standing; a clichéd technique of employer intimidation.

'We want copy of lease, budget statement of twelve-month expenditure,' said Minnie Lu, kicking off proceedings with a harsh edge to her usual sing-song cadence.

Madison slapped a folder on Virgil's desk. 'All here, present and accounted for.'

Virgil looked through the file intently, while Minnie Lu looked over his shoulder like a younger sister. Virgil said, 'You have not been an inexpensive proposition.'

'Cheap at the price. You were taking a punt on research.'

'Punt?' asked Minnie Lu.

'A kind of boat,' said Virgil, turning towards her. He closed the file and put it on his desk. 'Used by Oxford students upon the Thames,' he added, pronouncing the river's name correctly, to Madison's surprise.

'How do you happen to know that?' asked Madison.

'Through the works of Mister Max Beerbohm.' He looked dreamily out of the window and lifted one finger in the air. 'When I first came to this country I was introduced to his writings by my English teacher. A Mrs Maslof. *Zuleika Dobson* was my favourite.' He fell silent, his thoughts some miles and many years away. Not even Minnie Lu dared interrupt his reverie; a fascinated Madison was in fact keen for it to continue. But a curtain seemed to come down on Virgil's interior drama; he came to with an impetuous shake of his head and addressed Madison again. 'Enough. We have been patient with you. Now it's time to see what you got.'

'Right now?'

Minnie Lu spoke up. 'Tomorrow afternoon. In the Blue Amphitheatre. The Presentation Department will provide what you need – overheads, slides and such. Three o'clock.'

The Blue Room. His heart sank at the prospect of a mass presentation.

'Who will be there?' asked Madison.

'That should not affect your demonstration,' Virgil declared, and dismissed him with a curt wave of the hand.

Sally's cubicle held no Sally, but a note on her desk said 'Back at 10.30'. With thirty minutes to kill, Madison sat down and looked at the books stacked on Sally's filing cabinet. Linguistics texts, a primer on 'C' (Sally had been learning to program the year before), and several new and shiny paperbacks on theories of management. *Gain By Gender: A Woman's Guide to Corporate Success, Management Through Intimidation* – unlikely books for Sally. Tucked away behind the stack, its spine turned to the wall, the *Selected Poems of Frederick Madison*. He picked it up and flipped through its pages, which were ear-marked, covered in pencil notations, coffee-stained through the middle sections of Madison's father's *oeuvre*. Several times he was interrupted by visitors, all obvious residents of a higher floor, attired in suits or skirts, mock-Rolexes or Cartier-style bands. Sally was moving in a different sphere nowadays.

He was beginning to take a more serious look at his father's poems when a loud voice suddenly drowned out any effort to concentrate. 'Would Mr Greenfield please report to the Medical Office on Floor One? Calling Mr Greenfield. Please report to the Medical Office on Floor One.' He looked up, expecting to see Pistolet looming above him, hands cupped in front of his mouth – but no, it was a proper PA system; of course, the audio nightmare Pistolet had been railing against. Madison looked at his watch: Sally was ten minutes late. Reluctantly he stood up and replaced his father's book, then went and found Pistolet, who greeted him perfunctorily. 'Glad to see you up and about.'

'I've been here for hours. Jet-lag works the other way, coming this way. I spend the first week waking up at dawn, then collapse at dinner-time. What are you doing?'

'Specifications for *Write Right*. I'll be glad to turn them over to you.' He waved a sheaf of paper airily. '*Confidential To The Company* it says on every page. Why bother? To an outsider, it would make as much sense as Urdu. What is this obsession with secrecy? Greenfield claims it's peculiar to the Chinese, but I doubt it. The other companies are just as bad.'

'How is Greenfield? I just heard his name called out on the box. Is he sick?'

'Only mentally. He'll be even worse off when he gets down to the medical office and finds it's all a false alarm.'

'How so? I heard the announcement.'

'So did he. That doesn't make it legit.,' Pistolet said slyly. 'Something of a red herring, I believe, a mild ruse, the path better to have not taken – as Frost or your father once wrote.'

'Not exactly,' said Madison. 'What have you done, Jeffrey?'

Pistolet was unable to suppress a grin. 'I couldn't help myself. If they're going to be stupid enough to introduce a PA system, they can't expect me to take it lying down. So the occasional message has been known to be put out that is not, strictly speaking, of the Kosher variety. Even when addressing the likes of Greenfield. Harmless, really.'

'Except to Greenfield. Whose idea was this system anyway? And how do you get access to it?'

'Another brainstorm by young Sammy. I think the shrinks call it bonding. It's supposed to improve corporate communication between the toffs upstairs and us plebs down here.'

'That has to be a first, you parading as a member of the working class. Answer my question: how do you get at the system? Not your friend Felicia again?'

'Nope. It's a fellah this time, of little or no sexual attraction. His name is Juan Garcia.'

'And?'

'And what?'

'What do you do, bribe him? Supply him with dope? Get him dates with girls from Pine Manor? Come on, Jeffrey, there's got to be a handle.'

'O ye of little faith. Why won't you credit my powers of

persuasion? Maybe he does it out of the goodness of his heart.' When Madison glowered, he threw up his hands in surrender. 'All right, all right. So he is Felicia's cousin. You can't hold that against the guy.'

'And he's in charge of the PA system. But the voice didn't sound Hispanic.'

'It's not Hispanic. It's not even human. Digitised text-to-speech system. Not bad, eh? Good enough to show in London, if you ask me.' He rubbed his jaw carefully, as if recalling his overtures to Elsie. 'So what's the agenda, Robert? When do you walk the plank?'

'Three o'clock tomorrow. In the Blue Room.'

'You don't say. They're really pulling out the stops. I wouldn't miss it for the world. Can't wait to see these poems of yours. What are they like: "When yellow leaves, or lots, or few, or none . . . "? Something like that? Though I'd stay off the yellow business if I were you: skins are pretty thin around here these days. Minnie Lu no longer seems to derive the same satisfaction from my modest little jests. Maybe she'll get a laugh out of your lyrical outbursts, but I wouldn't count on it, pal.'

'I'm not. I've got those letters to show. But you know, I've been thinking about what you said. You're right: my father's supposed business letters really won't do. So why not use a more straightforward domain, something more business-like as a base? The real thing: memos, contractual letters, that kind of item.'

'Where will you find that? I mean, they're around, but you've only got twenty-four hours.' He looked at his watch, a purple Mickey Mouse affair. 'Make that twenty-eight.'

'Ah, but that's where my old mate Pistolet comes in. Or rather, Felicia.'

Pistolet looked up at him, startled, like a deer caught in a car's headlights. 'I don't like the sound of that at all,' he said.

'Relax,' said Madison at his most soothing. 'All I need are Sammy's official communications for the last six months. There's nothing irregular in that: each of us gets them, after all. But I don't have copies of them. Do you?'

'Are you kidding? Who in their right mind would keep copies of Sammy Ling's official pronouncements?'

'Right. And even if you had the copies, I'd have to type them all into a system. I don't have the time: you can see that. But Felicia, old Juan Garcia's cousin and the apple of your perverted eye, she has them on her system upstairs, doesn't she? She only has to copy them for me on a diskette and I won't need to bother her ever again. They must back up the system. That's not too much to ask, now is it?'

'It's far too much to ask. I couldn't possibly. Sorry, Robert, no can do. No way. Felicia might get herself fired if she got caught.'

'Since when has that ever stopped you in the past? Remember Lisa Adams's personal file?'

'Not the same at all.'

'If she's paranoid, let her do a batch dump onto tape: it could be anyone in the Spires, no one will know it's her.'

Pistolet pretended to find something of interest on his monitor. Unlikely, since his system was turned off.

'Jeffrey,' said Madison with a calm command, 'you're dealing with a desperate man. Don't force me to play hardball. I wouldn't want to have to tell Greenfield it was you who sent him into a panic and running down to Medical, would I?'

'You wouldn't,' said Pistolet anxiously. 'Greenfield's a sick man. You might give him a breakdown.'

'I'd have to take that chance. He'll recover, I'm sure; and the benefits cover psychiatry these days. Five hundred deductible, though that's peanuts compared to the thousands in therapy Greenfield will need.'

Pistolet stared at the blank screen. 'Of all the people I know, you are the last one I thought would resort to something as downright diabolical as this. You're a traitor to your class, Madison. Have you forgotten your old school motto?'

'So have you.'

'That's irrelevant. I don't know how you'll be able to live with yourself after this.'

'I'll manage. So you'll get Felicia to do this for me?'

Pistolet sighed and reached down to turn on his CPU. 'If she gets fired, I'll kill you.'

Madison went back to Sally's cubicle and found three marketing men in dark suits lined up outside it, while Sally sat inside, talking on the telephone. To the manifest irritation of the waiting men, Madison walked into the cubicle just as Sally was putting down the phone. She looked up, at first with a mixture of fatigue and annoyance, then smiled brightly. 'Robert,' she said, and stood up to give him a kiss. He contrived to have it land on his lips. 'Oh, but what a bad time you've picked,' she said, and motioned to the queue outside.

He dismissed it with a wave of his hand. 'They'll have to wait, I'm afraid. Virgil's orders; he said I had to see you before lunch without fail.'

Sally looked ready to protest, then seemed to see the glint in Madison's eye. She winked at him with the eye furthest from the corridor, and went out to dismiss her marketing suitors while Madison sat down in her chair. A small groan arose from the disappointed trio, then Sally returned. 'Come on,' she said. 'We can't stay here. Others will only come and take their place.'

'Coffee. Let's go downstairs.'

'Make it lunch,' she said, picking up her briefcase from her desk. 'Otherwise I won't get any today. I'm booked solid.'

Her new activities seemed matched by a new air of

confidence, and she was dressed accordingly, in a black skirt, white blouse, and shiny black belt. Two gold-and-pearl earrings were her only jewellery. They went to the old cafeteria where Madison had coffee and watched as Sally ate a roast beef sandwich, French fries and tomato salad. It was now half past eleven. He told her about the plans for his demonstration. She nodded, as if this was what she expected. Then she got up to go.

'Hey, wait a minute,' he said. 'Aren't you going to talk to me for a while?'

'I can't,' she said, looking at her watch. 'I'm already late as it is.'

'Well, when am I going to see you?' Things suddenly seemed to have gone wrong. Where was the sympathetic figure of the Hyde Park Hotel? Where the secret helper on his generation of poems? Desertion loomed, and his heart sank.

She swung her briefcase gaily in the air. 'Why, tonight of course. You're buying me dinner.'

'I am?'

'Yep.' She gestured with her free hand at her clothes, somehow taking in her entire new aura of brisk efficiency. She laughed suddenly in the old, free style. 'I'll be done with this bullshit by six. Give me time to go home and change. Be with you at eight.'

4

He worked with professional efficiency in the afternoon, after Pistolet had slid a small cartridge tape across the one uncovered area of his desk. On the one visit when he truly needed them, Madison had been assigned neither a cubicle nor a computer terminal. Pistolet was surprisingly accommodating on these scores. 'Take mine,' his friend declared. 'Gives me an excuse for doing nothing. Besides, it will let me see the wizard at work.'

Madison ran the same routines on the Sammy Ling corpus as he had applied to his father's work, though here he used a phrasal lexicon as well as a full lexicon of single words to isolate common phrases – 'referencing your letter' turned out to be a favourite. Proper names were isolated when they could not be matched against entries in the existing lexicon. Busy as he was, Madison only gave these a cursory examination, long enough to notice Sally Zehring's name among them. Interesting, that; these were supposed to be Sammy's official memoranda, so what was Sally's name doing in them?

These procedures were time-consuming, and Pistolet grew impatient, tired of playing the hanger-on and bringing Madison Cokes from the machine by the elevators. 'Show me some generation, Mr Wizard. This stuff is about as interesting as my parser.'

'The package is unique,' Madison replied, a little stung by the put-down. 'Especially the stylometry features.'

'It just seems long-winded to me.'

'Hold your horses, it's got another hour to run.' It was already almost five o'clock. 'I'll have to run the generator in the morning, before the demo, anyway.'

'I'll stick around. I want to see this generator of yours.'

'Not tonight. I'm seeing someone back at the hotel.'

'Don't someone me. You've been in a good mood all afternoon, so it must be a Sally Zehring rendezvous you've got in mind. I hope she's remembered to put it in her filofax.'

'Her cubicle was crawling with marketeers.'

'I'm not surprised, though I had thought it was a purely

temporary disease. Like measles. Now I'm not so sure: Sammy has big plans for her. Wants to get her away from secular minds like mine. And yours, of course – Sammy probably has her phone bills checked to see how often she's calling England.'

'Can you lend me a laptop so I can run a trial back in my room?'

'You must be joking. They're as scarce as open cynics around here.'

'I've got one in England.'

'Boolah-boolah for you. This is headquarters, where they actually make the things. You can't expect them to let any of us get our hands on them.'

'Seriously, I need one.'

'I am serious. I couldn't get you one for love or money.' He reached for his jacket on the hook of his cubicle door. 'I can tell you where you might find one.'

'Where?'

'In the hands of your dinner date. She's hot these days: no one dares refuse her anything. *Sayonara*, as they don't say upstairs.'

Madison left a note for Sally, asking her to dredge up a laptop, then he roamed the halls while the analyser ran. Morale must be even lower than before; few of the R & D engineers were still at work. If only this were all his, he'd have Maintenance come in and collapse the football field of cubicles around him like a deck of cards. Put couches in, of soft calf like those in the Spires, build a balcony at the end where colleagues could have cocktails after work and stare out of the windows and pretend they could see Boston. He'd put a small restaurant in one corner, with potted plants and a bevy of tanned waitresses. Kaminski could be consulted on this – Kaminski! Madison raced back to Pistolet's cubicle, confirmed that his routines were running, dug out an envelope from an interior pocket of his briefcase, and used the stairs to arrive more quickly on the tenth floor.

Fortunately, Lisa Adams was in. She was sitting at a small round table, and smiled vacantly at Madison as he entered; quite unlike her characteristic tough look. She had cut her hair, and the blue streak had been retouched. 'I'm back,' said Madison. 'Reporting for duty.'

'Nice to see you,' she said, staring intently at a collection of laminated cards on the table. 'Didn't realise you were in town.'

'Minnie Lu didn't tell you? It's a command performance. I would have told you myself but I assumed they would let you know.'

'They may have,' she said, gesturing at the terminal, 'but I've been very busy.'

Her screen showed a list of electronic messages: most said *Not read* in the right-hand column. What was going on with the Blue Rinse Lady? Madison sat down across the table from her and waited for some explanation. It was soon apparent that none would be forthcoming; Lisa was engrossed in the material before her. He said, 'I've brought you something from Kaminski.'

Instantly her manner changed. She grabbed at the envelope and ripped it open; at the same time Madison discovered that the various cards on the table were menus – not computer menus, real food menus. While Lisa Adams read the note inside the envelope, he read, upside-down, a list of hors d'oeuvres: breaded mushrooms were $5.95 at the restaurant in question. He looked up to find her smiling broadly and brandishing what looked to be an air ticket. 'Seems I'l' be in your neck of the woods pretty soon,' she said.

'On business?' he asked.

'Of course,' she said reflexively. He gave her time to think, and she added, 'It's important to expand our market

241

for Expert Systems. We're stuck in offices – law offices, insurance, banks.'

'Instead of?'

'*Restaurants*,' she said with enormous zest. 'They're an immense market. I mean, not every lawyer has insurance – well, these days I suppose they do. But not every insurance company needs a lawyer – actually, I guess that's not true either. But you can see what I'm getting at: one thing *everybody* does is go to restaurants.'

She continued: 'I see a large market for Expert Systems in restaurants, an *international* market. The British guys are so talented at software design, it's a pity they can't get their act together any other way. They have the ideas, they do excellent development work; it's marketing expertise that's wanted. That's where I – I mean, we – come in.'

'That's why you're going to England?'

'Of course. A little reconnoitre, then later perhaps a longer stay. A lot of marketing to be done.'

'That's not what Kaminski calls it,' he said coolly. Lisa Adams flushed, then flushed deeper still – a curious mix of fire-engine cheeks, tan forehead and blue streak. She began to speak, stuttered, and ground to a halt.

Madison said gently, 'He is my friend, you know.'

She looked at him questioningly.

'Don't worry, I don't care why you're going to England. If you want Virgil to think it's about Expert Systems, that's fine with me. Mum's the word.'

'I *am* looking at Expert Systems,' she protested.

'Sure you are. In Kaminski's Bar and Grill. I've seen one there myself; hopeless. Do me a favour: don't let him buy one of these packages; it's the last thing his restaurant needs. He'd be better off with Pistolet's astrology package.' He stifled a laugh. 'Speaking of which, what's happened to that?'

Lisa's new love clearly ran deep, for she dismissed her

242

previous obsession with a sneer. 'Child's stuff,' she said. 'Who needs it?'

'Pistolet still thinks you're interested in it.'

She began to sneer again, but stopped. However great her infatuation, Lisa Adams was not ready to relinquish the political savvy that had got her where she was. 'Let's keep it that way. Your pal Pistolet likes to jump on my toes as it is. I don't want to give him any further ammunition.'

Downstairs his routines on Sammy's correspondence were complete. He loaded them onto tape, put the tape in his briefcase, and left the building. It was a little after six o'clock and the car park was only a third full – people left on time in the summer months, to play tennis or swim or host barbecues. The sun here seemed harsher than in England, roughly diffused across the parking lot. He drove into the heart of Madison, filled up with petrol, then went to the hotel.

Sally was right on time. He hadn't known what to wear, opting for the formal ambiguity of cords, blazer and blue Brooks Brothers shirt. A preppy playing poker in Las Vegas; a Vermonter dressed up for lunch with New York relatives. The addition of a tie would get him into a fancy restaurant if needed, but he was relieved to find Sally also dressed informally in a tennis skirt, tan sandals, white shirt and a jacket of dark-blue raw silk. It all heightened the golden tan of her legs and face.

'You look good,' he said spontaneously. 'Thanks for bringing the PC.'

'You're welcome,' she said, placing it on a bureau. 'Recognise the shirt?'

A Harvard Co-op purchase from five, maybe six years before. No wonder the collar was frayed. 'When did I give it to you?'

'You didn't. I just found it in my closet one day. This is the first time I've worn it since you went to England.'

'Well, I'm back now, and glad to see you wearing it again.'

'You sound like my daddy. Southern genteel.'

'You want a drink?' There was Scotch on the bureau.

'I'd like some wine.' So he ordered a bottle of California Chardonnay from room service that arrived in a bucket of ice which he placed next to the sliding window. This time his room faced the Housatonic River, and they sat and looked out over the river and the red-brick newspaper building – a converted mill – on its far side. On the verandah below, guests sat out at tables, drinking from the lobby's bar.

'Oh, that feels good,' exclaimed Sally as she slipped off her sandals and sipped the wine. 'I am plumb exhausted. I've scampered around every which way today.'

'Are you bragging or complaining?'

'A bit of both. I can't deny it's exciting sometimes. Other times it's just a drag. I'm on three executive committees and I get them mixed up: I start talking about affirmative action when the item on the agenda is currency conversion of European sales.'

'What about *your* work? The parser.'

'What about it? It's still there and still needs work. It runs, all right, it's just too goddamned slow. And there's not too much for a linguist to do about it any more. I've compacted the lexicon as far as I can: now it's up to Jeffrey.'

'How is Jeffrey? He doesn't seem very happy to me.'

'He's not. He's enhancing the parser performance and looking at the specs for *Write Right*. Marketing designed the functional specs, so you can imagine how good they are. Jeffrey says it's a nightmare.' She held out her glass and he poured her more wine. 'How's your mother?'

'Not bad. Still drinking too much. She asked after you; she always does. My uncle says she's on good terms with my father now.'

244

'Speaking of which, whatever you think, the poems you've shown me are pretty good. When will you have more?'

He shrugged. 'I'm working on one right now. It's not finished and I haven't had time to run more generation.' He sipped morosely from his glass.

'Well, don't just sit there. Show me. You must have brought your material.' She stood up and walked over and plugged in the machine. While it booted, she started looking for the diskettes. 'Come on, Robert, where are they? Why else did you want me to bring the PC?'

He got up reluctantly, and took five diskettes from his drawer. 'They'll take a while to load,' he said. 'I bet there isn't room on the laptop anyway. How big's the Winchester? Ten megs?'

'Mine's got thirty and at least twenty's free. Hurry up and start copying. Quit making excuses.'

She drank another glass of wine and watched him from across the room while he loaded the machine. 'You're too thin, Robert. You need fattening up. Doesn't this woman of yours feed you?'

'We don't really live together. I usually feed myself.'

'That explains it.'

'Thanks. You used to like my cooking.'

'I did. But you only cooked when I was there. Otherwise you lived on rabbit food.'

When he had finished loading he called up the generator, first reviewing the knowledge base. It was a short lyric he was building, along the lines of a series of love-poems written by his father in the forties after he had met Madison's mother. It had not quite jelled yet; on a hunch Madison changed some of the defining terms of the knowledge base, so that the lover of the poem now addressed his lover directly: *Vocative, imperative voice, second person pronoun*. The rhyme-scheme he altered from either slant rhymes or none to a mix of none, slant, and true rhymes. The length of the poem was greater than ten but less than twenty lines.

'It would be a nice night on the water,' Sally said. 'Up in Maine I bet it's gorgeous. Remember?' she asked.

He did. He remembered coming out from teaching class in Cambridge on a Friday evening, driving up to the Cathedral and finding Sally waiting for him, bag in hand. Then there was the drive east and north, up the shore road to a house they rented that summer on the Maine coast. He remembered the salt air as they moved north, past Portland, through Bath, stopping to eat lobster in the twilight at a pound near Waldeboro. They would be up early next morning, to sail in and out all day along the rocky turns of land. . . And he remembered sleeping after a day of sailing and sun out on the rented house's porch, listening to the fog-horn honk and the tide splash like so many spilled glasses of water against the rocks.

'Ready?' said Sally. She had come to stand beside him.

'Sure,' he said. 'Funny you should mention Maine. This may come as a bit of a surprise.' He hit the return key and the generator cranked, then sang. Paper started to chug from its built-in printer as the lines also appeared one by one on the screen. This time the system did not pause to ask *Accept or reject*. It poured forth uninterrupted.

> Let sail to the colour of blue,
> the blue waters that carve
> finger islands out of rock,
> that tempt terns down from the sky
> to explode the mackerel fry,
> the cloudless razor blue
> that casts ashore its call
> and carries us from the colourless dock
> to the lap and tickle of tide.

It paused, as if finished, but then moved serenely onto its conclusion:

> We will sail tandem-tied
> to the blue of all running harbours,
> rudder free and wing and wing, my love,
> wing and wing for blue.

Neither said anything for some time. Madison eventually broke the silence. 'Not bad, if I say so myself. Though it's the generator that should be feeling proud and acting suitably modest. The "blue" motif is just like father's: they say blue equals the imagination in Wallace Steven's work, but with my father it always seems to mean love.'

'Robert,' said Sally slowly, 'it's beautiful. And the thing is, it's utterly different from your father's poems. Last night you seemed so down I didn't want to say anything, but what you've accomplished with your father's poems isn't really as earth-shattering as you seem to think. After all, what you've done is ultimately *derivative*. The machine may write like your father, but it depends upon your father's work to do that; it can't make anything from scratch. But *this*,' she said, pointing to the poem, 'if it sounds like anyone, it's you – yet you don't have any body of work for it to draw on. That *is* remarkable.'

He felt embarrassed now. 'It's all pointless now. It's too late.'

She did not question that. 'Don't begin all that again.'

'Aw, screw it,' he said, trying to sound light. 'Let's forget about it and have some more to drink.'

He started to walk to his chair, but stopped when Sally grabbed his arm, surprisingly fierce. 'Stop it,' she said.

'Stop what?'

'Don't act that way with me. You did it once before when you went to England and I swear I won't let you do it again. You know the problem with you?' There was an urgency to her voice; when Madison looked at her, her blue eyes seemed to flare. 'You're convinced anyone close to you will eventually prove faithless. Because your father deserted you, you've made up your mind that everyone else will, too. So you act the part – until finally you manage to fulfil your own prophecy and drive away the very people you love. Then you sit back and say, "I was right – they didn't love me after all."'

'I'm not in love with Catherine,' he blurted out.

'Maybe not. But you were in love with me.'

'Were?'

She said nothing, so he added, 'And I suppose I drove you away, then, according to this analysis of yours? Doesn't that ignore your little adventures with Ralph Hilton, not to mention Sammy Ling?'

'Robert, if you'd given one indication that you cared, that I should come to England, or that you regretted going, there wouldn't have been a Ralph Hilton or a Sammy Ling. So, yes,' she said emphatically, 'you did drive me away.'

'For good?'

She was quiet.

'For good, Sally? I need to know.'

'Maybe,' she said, half under her breath. 'I'm not sure we should be having this conversation.'

Anxiety filled him like a smoker's cough, sudden evidence that what had been done was unreclaimable. Not again; don't do it all over again. 'Why?' he asked. 'Because I'm supposed to be attached? Well, I'm not any more, not to Catherine anyway, as of this minute. So why? Because you're supposed to be getting married?' He drew breath; she was still looking directly at him, but sceptically now, no longer angry.

'I can't speak for you,' said Madison, 'so let's have a one-way conversation for a minute.' He put one hand over his left ear and poked a finger slowly in and out of his other ear.

Sally laughed. 'Don't be silly,' she said. 'This is serious.'

'I know it is. And I'm telling you I love you. A

248

declaration: I, love, you. That's one way, isn't it? And pretty risky for the likes of me. Not that I'm asking you anything, I don't want a dialogue. I am telling you how I feel. So there. You can go away if you like; you can marry that cretinous plutocrat; you can do whatever you think you have to do. But what you can never ever do is say that this time I drove you away. Because I love you.'

At which Sally burst into tears.

'I didn't mean to upset you,' Madison said feebly.

'You didn't upset me,' she said between sobs. 'Just get me a Kleenex, you big dumb bastard.' When he came back from the bathroom she took the tissue and blew her nose. 'Thank you, you cretinous bastard. You cretinous plutocrat bastard.' And she giggled.

'I'm sorry I called him that.'

'Well, I expect he is.' She finished wiping her eyes with one end of the tissue. 'I'd better be going now.'

'Are you leaving me?'

She shook her head. 'No. I'm just leaving your room; I'm not leaving you. I'm going back to my apartment, and I'm going to get into bed with a pint bottle of Johnny Walker, just like my uncle used to drink from. And then I'm going to think about what you said, all the beautiful things, and some of the dumb ones, and then I hope to God I'll fall asleep. After I finish the Scotch.'

'Johnny Walker, eh? A pint bottle? Sounds a little tacky to me.'

She looked up at him with red eyes and half a smile. 'Does it?'

'Yep.' He leant down and kissed her once lightly on her lips, then again more deeply. She smelled of shampoo and Chanel, and her lips just hinted of Chardonnay. 'Come on,' he said firmly, 'I'll walk you to your car.'

They went in a contented silence down in the elevator, through the lobby and out to the car park. New tungsten lights had been installed, flooding the parking lot with light as if it were a film location. The publicity of love; not to have had this simple jubilant charge in his life for so long.

When Sally got into her car and put the key in the ignition, Madison leaned through the open window and touched her arm. 'I'll come and see you in the morning.'

'Goodnight,' she said quietly.

Back in his room, the phone rang as he was dozing off. 'Do me a favour and don't hang up this time,' said his father. 'I'd like to talk to you.'

'Okay,' he said, sitting up on the bed.

'Listen, how about if I came up to Boston? Any chance of seeing you if I did?'

Well, it couldn't be worse than seeing Minnie Lu again. What a time for a fateful reunion – he might be fresh out of work when they met. Or would Sammy Ling reckon that he could let by-gones be by-gones, and assume Sally was all his? Not that this now seemed a safe bet for Sammy to make; Madison drew strength from the thought that he might be in the running again. So, why not give the old man the fun of crowing over the collapse of his son's Ling connection? 'Sure,' said Madison. 'When are you thinking of coming?'

'That's up to you. How long are you staying in Boston?'

'I'd planned to be here all week.' God, it was only Monday night; it seemed he had been back for days. 'But I don't know if I'm going to last until then.'

'Want to get home to lick your wounds, eh?'

But this was not jocularly spoken, there was no taunt in the big voice. Actually, this was the last thing Madison wanted to do, since the conversation he foresaw with Catherine would merely open the scabs. He said now, 'Something like that. How about the day after tomorrow? We could have lunch at the Ritz.'

'Just show up when you can. You sure you can get away?'

How odd of him, now, to show this concern; yet again Madison took no offence. 'To tell the truth, I may be my own master by then.'

'It's that bad, huh? Well, tell me about it on Wednesday, boy. You sound like you should get some rest.'

'I guess I should. Listen,' he said, falling into his father's form of command, yet struggling for words, 'there's something I have to tell you. It's about the poems. I just want you to know that it started out as something different. Nothing to do with you at all. Then it got side-tracked. It developed a momentum of its own.'

'I'll say. They've knocked me for a loop, I have to admit.'

They were both silent for a moment. Finally, Madison spoke. 'I know they have. All I can say is, I'm sorry.'

His father waited before responding. 'Okay. Why don't we leave it at that, then? See you Wednesday.'

5

But there was still Tuesday to get through. It was much hotter, almost eighty degrees even early in the day, and Ling employees left their cars and walked quick as cats at dinner-time towards the air-conditioned Cathedral. Madison, wearing a grey double-breasted suit, moved more slowly, trying to gather his thoughts.

Pistolet, standing like a stork, head well above his cubicle, munching a doughnut and surveying the aisles, watched keenly as Madison rolled along the corridor towards his cubicle. Suddenly he sang, like a preppy

251

Geldof, moving an imaginary microphone back and forth from his crooning mouth:

> The silicon chip inside his head
> gets switched to overload,
> and nobody's going to go to work today,
> he's going to make them stay at home.

He stopped and spoke lightly. 'Now's the time for you to land the knockout blow. Save your job and win the girl. It's D-Day, Madison. Out of the landing craft and on to the beach for you. Are you dressed for comfort or what? Savile Row?'

'Austin Reed, actually. I haven't got your resources.'

'Give it time, give it time. When they axe you, maybe you'll be able to copyright the generator, use it to forge letters of credit. A kind of electronic Ponzi game, build an empire out of paper that nobody can prove you ever touched. The way I see it – ' he began, when Madison interrupted.

'Later, Jeffrey. Please. I've got to concentrate.'

It took nearly an hour to prime the generator; while he worked, Pistolet began cutting a doughnut into bite-sized bits and carefully arranging them on the floor. 'What are you doing?' Madison demanded.

'Making an astrological array, of course. In case Lisa Adams comes by to check on my progress. I think the doughnuts do nicely, don't you?'

'What do they stand for?' asked Madison, pointing to a particularly dense cluster of sections near a filing-cabinet.

'The moon in Capricorn. Very significant.'

'Of what?'

Pistolet gave him a withering look. 'If you need to ask, it's too late for you already.'

Tempted as Madison was to tell Pistolet about Lisa Adams's new lack of interest in the astrology program,

252

this insolence changed his mind. When the generator made a first attempt on a Sammy Ling business letter, moreover, Pistolet was unsupportive. 'Pretty dreary stuff,' he said. Sadly, after looking at the trial output, Madison had to admit he was right. It read:

> Referencing your memo of the 3rd, it seems clear that however much Taiwanese sales pick up, they will not impact year-end revenues dramatically.

During the morning Madison went past Sally's cubicle on several occasions, but did not find her there. At lunchtime Pistolet corralled him with pushy protectiveness. 'You got to eat, daddy-o; gives you something to puke up this afternoon.' They drove again to Artie's Fish Shack, where Madison toyed nervously with a lobster roll and watched Pistolet eat a plate of fried clams and drink four beers. 'Nervous about this afternoon?' asked Pistolet, finishing his final Molson's Ale.

'Of course I'm nervous.'

Pistolet sighed. 'I don't get nervous at all, speaking in public. Maybe it would be better if I did.' True, since every time Pistolet addressed a group he seemed to land himself in hot water. There was the time, giving a presentation to some tenth-floor marketeers, when he had imitated Cromwell losing his temper; there was the mildly obscene symbol he had added to a flow-chart during an outside session at Boston University; there was his use of Cole Porter lyrics in a parsing demonstration before a group of insurance executives.

When they returned to the Cathedral Pistolet continued to stick to Madison, waiting with vigilant devotion as Madison stopped at the men's room and slapped water on his face to reduce pre-demo anxiety.

As they neared an elevator, Olney, Macaulay and Smith made their by-now ritual appearance; Pistolet pushed a protesting Madison into an open elevator, then waved to the trio cheerily as the doors closed. 'Those guys are heavy,' he confided in explanation. 'They've got more on me than Hoover had on Martin Luther King.'

'Then why haven't they used it?'

Pistolet shrugged, for once subdued. 'The reigning liberal ethic, I suppose.' He perked up. 'That, or my undeniable genius. They'll put up with a lot for first-rate code.'

Madison pushed the button for the eighth floor, but Pistolet intervened and hit six. 'Forget it, matey. I know what you're thinking – a brief stroll around the home environs, maybe a nod or a wink from young Sally before you face the firing-squad. Anything to quell your nerves and give you some moral support.'

'Something wrong with that? What are you going to do – take me to the library and read a soothing lullaby? From what – the *Journal of Parallel Processing*?'

Pistolet moved into schoolmasterish mode. 'Don't denigrate the bibliographical facilities available here,' and Madison remembered the cache in the First Aid kit. 'Besides,' his friend added, 'I don't think you'd be allowed to trammel the eighth floor unscathed.'

'Meaning what?'

'Sammy,' he declared, as the door opened on the sixth floor and a reluctant Madison joined him in the corridor, 'is unlikely to give you the benefit of an unimpeded demonstration. *Droit de seigneur* still reigns here, after all, whatever the share price does. I bet he's got goons all over the cubicles, sniffing for a scent of you.'

'They've got to let me demo,' Madison protested.

'Oh, they'll let you demo all right. But only after they fill you full of some nerve-provoking, anxiety-inducing mental adrenalin. Didn't you see Olney, Macaulay and Smith hot-foot it when they saw you?' When Madison shook his head, Pistolet nodded. 'Well, believe me, they did, matey. I barely got the elevator door shut in time. Tears like elephant's kayoombas rolled down their bureaucratic faces as I hit "close door" with seconds to spare. I'll give you odds they're upstairs right now, casing the joint like tracker dogs – less attractive, I grant you, but equally persistent. Sniffing for a trace of your Bass Weejuns.'

'I'm wearing Duckers,' said Madison with a show of irrelevant dignity.

'Sure you are, and I'm wearing condoms. You're still a prepped-out naif if the perverts of Personnel ever saw one. My point is, your Lord Justice, sir, Hon this or that, that they'd have you pinned against a programmer's partition by now, with a sudden burst of interest in your last expenses claim.'

'Expenses? I barely have any.'

'Madison,' said Pistolet with some exasperation as they approached the library's swinging doors, 'do me a favour and grow up. Listen to me, just for once, listen. Ignore my jokes, the burlesque, the continuing delights you remember from the third form. And be *serious*. If they play hardball, then hardball back. Believe me, blighty, they mean you no good – Olney, Macaulay, Smith, or Sammy, especially Sammy. He calls the shots.'

'I know that.'

'So do me a favour. Make a small transformation. Like one of those you say Glimsky's always talking about.'

'Chomsky,' whispered Madison, since they were in a library.

'That's what I said,' boomed Pistolet. 'Glimsky. Make a transformation and move from your own, sad personal experience into the realm of outside life. Go from the depths of the structural deep to the beauties of the surface. See, I know what Glimsky talks about. Otherwise,' he said, suddenly lowering his voice as the librarian stared at them, 'these guys will eat you for dinner. Demo or no demo.'

Six small hits of whisky later, on the corner of the library's balcony, Madison felt the infusion of confidence that Pistolet's pep-talk was intended to implant. It was only as they left the library, swaying, Pistolet pointing with faint mockery at a *Business Week* cover story on Ling ('No More Good Times at Ling – The Computer Industry's New Casualty') that Madison felt the haphazard arrival of pre-presentation nerves. When they descended to the ground floor this anxiety was not diminished by his discovery that the Blue Room, largest auditorium in the Cathedral, was almost full.

'What the hell is going on?' he demanded as he and Pistolet walked in, his voice curiously disembodied – and loud, coinciding with the hush that attended their entrance. 'I expected six or seven people here. Not half of R and D.'

'It's better this way, believe me. Why flop in front of a few hoity-toity foes? Let everybody see it.'

'You don't understand,' said Madison, suddenly agitated by the word 'flop'.

Pistolet tapped him on the arm. 'Here, before you start screaming.' In his palm he proffered a small green pill, round, with a ridge across its middle. Madison popped the pill, then looked up to find Sammy Ling's eyes upon him, sighting in across the auditorium like a well-oiled rifle.

Sammy sat next to the Empress behind an elevated sweep of desktop that curved along one edge of the crescent-shaped auditorium. Her son on one side, the Empress had Virgil Peabody on the other, himself flanked by Minnie Lu and Lisa Adams. On Sammy's far side sat his bodyguard, inscrutable in shades, then the poetry-loving Welsh Lunatic and, decorously detached from Sammy, Sally Zehring. All seemed to be looking at him, and Madison found the Empress's stare especially disconcerting.

He had only met her once before, shortly after he had signed his consultancy contract with Ling. A quick handshake, courtesy of Gus Cromwell, himself as intent on a visit upstairs to the Spires as he was on impressing Madison. Then, the Empress had struck Madison as bloodless ('Like an X-ray machine,' he'd said to a Harvard colleague), rising and shaking his hand, listening to Cromwell's quick account of who he was, without any discernible change in expression.

The same impassivity marked her face today, just as the unremarkable nature of her attire – white blouse, black suit, plain silver brooch – served only to make her stand out.

Madison's efforts to swallow the pill inconspicuously only made his gorge rise; he finally consumed it with an especially obvious gulp. 'What was that?' he asked Pistolet, wondering how badly he had violated company drug policy.

'A beta-blocker. Don't worry: no problem with the new drug lines. All you need is the mildest hint of tachycardia and the company quack will prescribe them. Three deep breaths, or a jog around the parking lot, and you'd qualify. Relax – well, don't relax when you ask for the prescription – but relax now. That's what the pill's for.'

But he could not relax, sensing mental dislocation slide in like an unwanted guest at a party. Desolation swelled as the gulf between competence and performance yawned before his mind's eye.

As he approached the podium he looked up at the monumental screen before him, frightened to think how soon his efforts would be displayed on them. With a start he saw that many of the chairs in the auditorium held flip-top monitors. Pistolet gave him a nudge with an elbow. 'Load your tape,' he insisted, pointing to the streaming cartridge tape drive that sat with other equipment on a low table in front of them.

'It's going to take a while,' said a despairing Madison. 'I thought this would be much more informal.'

'Less than five minutes,' said Pistolet. 'Get going and I'll keep them occupied.'

'With what? Your Abbott and Costello routine? This Costello's scared, Jeffrey. I want out of here.'

Pistolet looked aggrieved. 'Somebody's got to introduce you. It might as well be me. Come on, chin up. If you're going to sink in this ship of scumbags, at least don't piss yourself while you go down.'

'Get lost,' said Madison, his irritation momentarily outweighing his anxiety – both of which turned to embarrassment as the audience snickered and he realised he had been speaking almost directly into a microphone. He sneaked a look at the row of eminences on his left, saw Sally frowning, and started installing his programs and data. As he worked he tried not to listen to Pistolet, who had stepped eagerly to the podium and begun his introduction.

'Peers,' said Pistolet, looking over at his superiors on the dais. 'Changelings. I am here to introduce Robert Madison; and to praise him. What most of us do here will not survive us: your products will die when they make you redundant. This is not the case with Robert Madison.

'Our chief executive has intimated that Robert Madison is an unproductive man; well, that's a pretty grievous fault. And he would deserve to pay for it.'

The streaming tape clicked and slid with each transferred file. Hurry up, thought Madison, intent on anything that would end Pistolet's oration. The audience, he noticed, was all ears, entranced by the mix of novelty and familiarity in Pistolet's words. Which continued: 'The powers-that-be are productive here – and most of *us* are productive – so they'll let me speak of a faithful employee, friend to us all, Robert Madison. But the powers-that-be say Madison is unproductive, and the powers-that-be should know, even though Madison has brought many plaudits to the company, and helped swell revenues when times were tough.'

'Times *are* tough,' someone said from the third row, and Madison realised it was Greenfield.

'Perhaps,' said Pistolet calmly, 'but when your system crashed, Madison was there – in spirit, anyway – to help you reboot. Not the mark of an unproductive man. And you know that at least twice he has been offered the *Write Right* leadership; each time he refused. Not the mark of an ambitious man.'

Fortunately the tape finished, and Madison seized centre-stage from his friend. 'Thank you very much,' he said loudly; his nerves had fled, displaced by the urgency of his desire to shut Pistolet up. He moved the microphone over to the low table where he stood and began keying in commands, talking as he typed. 'Two years ago I was sent to England by the company. There is an unusual talent-pool of linguists and lexicographers there,' he added, thinking of Wellington, then fleetingly of Samson.

He continued a jerky potted history of his doings, only mildly reinforced by Pistolet's vigorous nodding from the seat he now occupied in the front row. Quickly Madison moved on to document-generation. He spoke rapidly, coming soon to his recent breakthrough with the selection of a domain.

'Let me begin, then, by generating a short narrative poem. Trust me as you might,' he said a little archly, thinking of Fowler's optative distinction ('might' meant they *didn't* trust him), 'you may nonetheless ask whether I've written the poem beforehand and made the generator only simulate the process of writing. To ease that suspicion, I've purposely left some terms of the knowledge base blank. For example, I have a poem about the Second World War in mind, about its impact somewhere, probably on a town. But I haven't specified a country; I'll leave that to you. Any suggestions?'

At first the audience was quiet, deferring to the powers-that-were on the dais. When none of them said anything either, Greenfield suddenly called out, 'Italy. Make it the Italian countryside.'

'Right,' said Madison, and entered the terms: *Situation = Italian; Situation = rural; Situation = village.* Thank God it hadn't been Hawaii – his father had never been there, and Madison doubted whether the domain's vocabulary would extend to palm trees or pineapple. 'Now what is the voice? First person, third person, second, a healthy narrative mix?'

'Healthy narrative mix,' shouted the Welsh Lunatic in a sudden burst of enthusiasm.

'Okay,' said Madison, typing. 'And what about the meter? Metrical or free verse?'

'Accentual syllabic,' said the Welsh Lunatic, momentarily standing. Sammy shot him a look and he rapidly sat down again, but only after adding in a lower voice, 'Four to six feet per line.'

This was less precise than it sounded and wouldn't pose the generator many problems. 'Right,' said Madison, hitting the entry key. 'Here we go.'

Above him the large screen duplicated the image appearing on his own monitor. Those in the audience without monitors watched the screen as letters etched in bone-white against a sea-blue background appeared, saying – *Now generating* . . .

What came out was reminiscent of a poem Frederick Madison had composed in the seventies, about a French village which had heroically defended its Jews by hiding them with unprecedented French vigour from the Nazis. This poem was not as good or as moving as Madison's father's, but reading it, Madison decided it wasn't bad at all. Atypically, the generator had given it a title.

A DOUBLE OCCUPATION

Where once the cobbler, hearing nothing,
shaped a boot as the *Wehrmacht* entered town,
now the village is half-empty
when the grape skins burgeon, pressed out
like balloons. Magic poured its way
through print and your average citizen fled.
Lights stormed the valley and mountain's age;
weather became a root of inconvenience.

Chronicled, the war moved out of memory
into anaesthetic commerce. Once the tourists came,
cameras were not so much a tool of record
as an opportunity to sell the strangers film.
A few young men moved to the mountain forest
as token, peaceful resisters:
three women, flaunting lipstick and shaved legs,
left in American cars and did not return.
When the water tower rusted through, it was
replaced by the government in only six days.

However we shall say we want time back again,
these are small-costing coins for a town
lifted from a mountain niche to fame by braveries –
one small mountain town –
that will not collapse when we name them.
So you may turn safely now
to the region's celebrated natural beauty,
the breathtaking views
from the heights several miles away.
There is a must restaurant in a neighbouring town,
two museums with statuettes of local clay,
and a festival each spring with native dancers.

In short, adequate excuse exists
for anyone to look away. Away, that is,
since going back to a poor celebrity town
is the disease itself that turns the wine sour
and stales the mountain air.

There were unlikely to be many lovers of poetry in the audience; the length of the poem and the time it took to emerge might have lost them. Yet they all seemed fascinated; those with in-built printers in their monitors tore off the resulting sheet and scanned the lines intently; others watched their own screens or the large one with equal absorption.

It was Virgil Peabody who broke the spell, standing up from his chair and leaning his hands on his desk for support. 'We have three hundred and fifty thousand installed terminals in U.S. alone,' he said angrily. 'Tell me, how many of them are used for poetry?'

Madison was tempted to answer 'one' and point to the Welsh Lunatic, but a certain sense of decency prevailed. Why have anyone else join him on the gallows? So he shrugged, which only seemed to heighten Virgil's irritation. 'I thought so,' he said. 'So what good is all this, this, this malarkey?'

Someone, probably Greenfield, snickered, but Madison held up his hand to silence him. 'That's a fair point, but it's also why I have some other things to show you. Because,' he said, quickly typing in new commands, 'I can now apply the principles of poetry-generation to other domains. It's not just poetry that can use this, but, for instance, drama too.' It seemed unfair not to let Wellington share the limelight, and already the generator was issuing out a small clip from *Pericles* (the Duncan Wellington version), I, 1, 20–25.

> Seduced in love, prescribing gods declare,
> inspiring lust for fruit of star-like trees;
> so set I on the caravan of life
> and should I lose the wagon wheels of love
> I do what thou hast bid in faithfulness,
> derailed by what is straight and lined and true.

This time, before Virgil could object to the impracticality

of the result, Madison moved to reassure him. 'I know, I know,' he said, 'our customers aren't writing plays either. But I'm trying to show the range of this new generator. It will work on anything – given sufficient input from a specific domain. And yes, it can give practical results to business customers. What do they write, if they write at all? Why, typical office correspondence and memos. Let me show you what this can do.

'Let's say you're the operating head of a mid-sized computer company. Times have been tough of late, and the last quarter's been even worse than anticipated. You want to reassure your employees and you want to do it fast. So you run the generator, which has a specialised domain based on all your past quarterly memos, add the one relevant fact – earnings were down – and presto!

To All Company Employees:

This is to message you about next week's quarterly results announcement in order to prevent unnecessary pessimism or panic. Revenues are up and you should be proud of this fact. Earnings will suggest a negative trend but should not impact our long-term situation in any substantial way. You have done well! You will do better! Together we can surmount a purely temporary reverse-profitability situation.

There was considerable laughter at this missive, then some mild applause. Virgil and Minnie Lu on the dais looked bemused, as if not altogether sure what was being parodied – or generated – here. Sammy himself looked flushed; along the row from him, Sally kept her eyes down, avoiding Madison's stare. He turned back to the microphone: 'Just a few more examples and I'll stop. I hope, however, that you'll be able to see the potential of the generator in office situations, as well as in more rarefied contexts.'

263

He hit the entry key, and for a brief moment thought the system had crashed. The screen glowed momentarily as if a CRT tube were about to blow, then suddenly strange lines – fractured LISP, he realised – began floating quickly but apparently at random around the screen. Oh no; he looked up in panic, and found Pistolet smiling at him. Thanks, pal. On the dais Virgil looked cross and tense; Sammy appeared more relaxed now that Madison was in trouble.

Then, out of chaos the screen cleared, and a memorandum appeared, not line by line or in pieces, as was the generator's usual wont, but in full. It read:

TO: Arthur Jackson
FROM: SL
REFERENCE: Madison

Probably the town, but then Madison the man read on:

The subject's current disposal is at the hotel mentioned in our recent conversation. Rendezvous at seven o'clock in the aforementioned hotel's downstairs lounge. Management has accommodated request for entrance into subject's room. It is urgent that until entrance is effected disruption potential be minimised, though subsequent force may henceforward need to be employed.

A little wordy, even for Sammy; a flicker from the big screen, and another letter appeared. This was also personal:

TO: Sally Zehring
FROM: SL
REFERENCE: Catering Expenditures

The price of meals in local catering establishments is sufficiently lower than those of Boston or Cambridge to suggest we henceforward confine our evening dining out repasts to local venues, except for special occasions such as anniversaries, birthdays – or exceptional quarterly results.

Our average incursion locally for dinner costs $15–20 per head as opposed to approximately double that figure in the metropolis. This does not take account of greater transportation costs – mileage, gas, etc. Obviously both figures would be substantially reduced were alcoholic consumption minimised – or barred altogether (as I have indicated on a number of occasions).

Please regard the $8 you owe me as a gift.

SL

Big of the guy, or 'white' of him, as members of his father's generation would have said. No more Lockobers or the Ritz for Sally. Say goodbye to Chez Jean, the Chinese delights of Joyce Chen.

Sammy now stood up and raised his voice. 'Stop this demonstration immediately.' Sally looked on the verge of tears, which suddenly moved Madison out of the passive wonder he and the audience were sharing at these marvels of the generator. Of the generator? How could it? He decided to stop the show, and switched off his microphone. But it was too late to stop the appearance of the system's third and final testimony.

TO: Mrs Ling
FROM: Your Son, acting Archbishop
REFERENCE: Marital Plans

I hope it is now agreed that the wedding will take place on October 31 and that you feel your objections have been satisfactorily answered.

It is true that my fiancée is disposed to slight but inappropriate informality at times, but this will certainly diminish as she becomes accustomed to our conventions and the importance of a higher level of conduct in what will be for her a higher station of life.

She is presentable and intelligent – if a little unpolished. Corporate security have established the *bona fides* of her background. One uncle has an unfortunate history of problems with alcohol, but there are no signs of this infection in her immediate family. Her mother is dead and can no longer be a potential source of embarrassment. Her father is a retired General Practitioner of medicine who lives alone and is accorded some respect in his community.

Since you and I have concluded that it would be unwise for me to marry a Chinese female, given my undeniable Occidental make-up, I hope you will concur that Sally Zehring represents a reasonable if not ideal choice for my bride.

With the affection and respect of your son,

Samuel Ling

'Come on.' It was Pistolet at his side, taking him by the elbow and propelling him quite firmly towards an exit at the front end of the auditorium. At the fire-door Madison turned as Pistolet hit the bar, setting off an immediate alarm. Sammy had come down to the floor and was shouting instructions. The audience was wildly insubordinate, clapping, whistling and laughing. The dais was deserted except for the still figures of the Empress, who gazed impassively at the opposite wall, and Sally, who sat with her head in her hands.

They exited into the sunlit parking lot, so bright in the fiery sun that Madison's eyes ached. He felt a little like Dustin Hoffman at the end of *The Graduate*, but as if through horrible miscalculation he had run away with an usher rather than with the bride. He stopped to protest, thinking of Sally, but Pistolet tugged at him fiercely. 'Don't be a winker,' he shouted. 'We've only got a thirty-second head start.'

'Wanker,' said Madison dully, thinking of Sally with her head in her hands. It wasn't my fault, he wanted

266

to say, imagining himself somehow piercing the armour of security he envisaged Sammy placing around her. He hadn't done anything: the generator had run amok.

He looked up to find Pistolet staring at him. 'Jeffrey,' he said, snapping into the present, 'thirty seconds is nothing. Don't tell me you got in early; you must be parked miles away.' He pointed wildly at the hundreds of cars that stretched as far as the highway in the distance. 'We'll never make it. We might as well give up now. What can they do? Fire me? They're going to do that anyway.'

Pistolet exploded. 'You cretin, you absolute moron. They'll fire you, sure they will – after Sammy's bodyguard has beaten the shit out of you.'

'You're kidding. I don't believe you.'

'You remember Hilton?'

'Hilton.' The hotel? No, the hardware engineer, Sally's lover. 'What about him?'

'The reason he moved to DEC is that Arthur Jackson – that's the bodyguard – ran him off the road on the way to work.'

They were a hundred yards from the Cathedral now, but when the fire-door slammed open they heard it as if it were snapping at their heels. Startled by the sun, the four dazed figures of Jackson, Olney, Macaulay and Smith emerged. By the time they had adjusted to the light, both Madison and Pistolet were running full-out across the parking lot, Madison managing only to gasp, 'Where is your car, by the way?'

'Right here,' said Pistolet, pulling up short by his BMW, which was tucked behind an Impala in the Bishops' lot. He unlocked the doors and they got in quickly, then pulled out with a dramatic screech. 'Just because I'm not a Bishop in their eyes,' said Pistolet, making a racing change, 'doesn't mean I don't recognise my own worth. As the eunuch said to the doctor, "If I'm gonna *be* impotent, I want to feel impotent".'

Pistolet ran three red lights with complete imperturbability before Madison could ask him where they were headed. 'To your hotel, of course. These are not A.I. types we're dealing with, daddy-o; they'll never think of it.'

'Jesus, Jeffrey,' said Madison, looking behind him and satisfied for the first time that they were not being pursued. 'What *was* all that about?'

'You tell me,' said Pistolet, but without his usual jauntiness. He looked ahead to avoid Madison's stare.

'That was not the generator I built at work back there. Not the program I know. Something screwed up, somebody – '

Pistolet cut in. 'You tell me, pal. It's your little project, not mine.' He took a corner at excessive speed, fought the wheel, regained control and accelerated. Madison resisted the temptation to protest and Pistolet kept talking. 'I know you're gifted, Robert, God knows you're gifted, you can't begin to know how sick I am of hearing how talented you are. Even that turd Sammy knows it. "Madison this," "Madison that" – you can imagine how the heart of another boy from the old school swells with pride when he hears that.'

They neared the hotel, passing the Madison Museum. Madison said, 'That wasn't my generator at work back there, Jeffrey. It's not that good.'

'Not that good?' Pistolet cackled sharply. 'Of course it's not that good. That was the real thing back there, Sammy's actual correspondence.'

'Of course it was. Everyone could see that. What I want to know is how it happened – how the generator failed and the domain samples came out directly.'

'How? What a stupid question. Obviously the calls from the generator to the domain got circumvented, cut off the parser, semantics, stylometry, all your clever little stages, and simply called in the originals themselves.'

'Don't give me the technical bullshit. I can see all that; it's *why* and *who* I want to know.'

'Who is perfectly obvious: I did it. After you went off to see Sally last night, I read through the files Felicia swiped. I knew what you had planned this morning – you didn't really buy the doughnut bit, did you? – and then inserted the circumventing call just before we went to lunch. That took all of thirty seconds, while you were sniffing like a heartbroken hound-dog at Sally's cubicle. I'm not that *gifted*, perhaps,' he said bitterly, 'but I do get the job done.'

'I wish I understood your motivation. I'll get fired now, that's for sure, but I thought that would be due to Sammy or Minnie Lu or Virgil, not because a pal let me down.'

'Oh Madison, for Christ's sakes.' They were entering the complicated one-way system around the hotel. 'You haven't got a future at Ling, not unless you want to come back and sit like a demented stooge in A.I. Alley. You were already out of there, buddy.'

'So you were just ensuring that I got the message. Thanks for the concern. Am I supposed to see all this protectiveness as the declaration of a long-repressed love?'

'Take it easy, Robert, I'm not that "happy". I admit,' he said as they entered the hotel parking lot, 'that my relations with women leave a little to be desired – Greenfield calls it my "bimbo complex" – but that's because there's only one woman I really want and I can't have her. Listen, we'd better park in the garage; no point in asking for trouble.'

'I'm a little slow sometimes, but what are you talking about? You're in love with some woman and *that's* what made you booby-trap my demo?'

Pistolet took a ticket from the machine and found a spot on the ground floor of the garage. Most of the hotel guests would be at the Cathedral, doubtless watching other less eventful demonstrations. Pistolet turned off the engine and looked down at his lap. He shook his head wearily. Madison too felt very tired; the excitement of their flight had given way to concern about what had happened. Where was Sally now? 'Madison,' Pistolet said slowly, 'do you really think you're the only one who doesn't want Sally to marry Sammy Ling? You think I'd be happy to see that girl – oh fuck it, that woman – marry that toilet frog? Her – that, that, that gorgeous girl.'

Pistolet opened his door and got out. 'You stay here. Who knows who they'll have lurking around the hotel? Give me your room key. I'll pack your stuff and check you out. Sit tight.'

He was gone a long time, over thirty minutes, during which Madison pondered his future. Or tried to: he seemed only to have a succession of negatives ahead of him: resigning (not in person he pusillanimously decided), returning to England and breaking off his relationship with Catherine. What then? A consultancy? He supposed so. And where would Sally be? Just how had she reacted to the letter from Sammy he had displayed? Could she reconcile herself to its stunningly mixed verdict? Would she blame the generator – surely she would see the letter was the real thing, wouldn't she? And then turn on Madison, blame him for her public humiliation. Probably. Thanks, Jeffrey.

Pistolet returned, lugging Madison's suitcase and smiling. He put the bag in the boot, then started the car. 'At first they didn't want to let me check you out. I explained that they had better if they wanted to get paid. This softened their attitude.'

'Where to now?'

'What did you have in mind?'

'I don't know. I've got to see my father in Boston tomorrow, then figure out what to do next. Beats me.'

'You'd be welcome at my place if you don't mind Felicia.'

'What would I mind? Does she make a lot of noise?'

270

'Not at all,' Pistolet said tensely as they turned onto the ramp of the interstate. 'She is a decorous lover, very restrained. No, I simply meant I'm going to have some explaining to do. She's bound to have heard about the demo and realise what I did with the letters she copied. She may be a little irate – and she has a temper that makes Gus Cromwell look mild.'

'I should think she may. You may have cost her her job with this little caper. I just wanted Sammy's letters as a *basis*. But you didn't think of that when you were splicing my code.'

'Of course I did. You mistake a certain jokiness on my part for real callousness. Felicia gave notice today. She's moving to Providence to look after her mother. I jeopardised precisely nothing. Nada. Zip. Zero. Got that, jack?'

Madison said, 'I think I'd better stay in Boston if you don't mind going that far.'

They drove quickly south on Route 3, a highway lined by hardwoods that dazzled, green-leaved and bright in the afternoon sun. Pistolet pushed up the air-conditioning and turned on the radio. Lines from John Sebastian filled the car:

> A younger girl keeps rolling cross my mind
> No matter how much I try
> I can't seem to leave her memory behind

'How much older are we than Sally?' asked Pistolet pertinently.

'Five years.'

'Funny, I never thought to ask her. Must be an effect of the Cathedral; you know, "Grow old together at Ling". Something like that. And how old's Clytemnaestra? You know, whosit over in England.'

'Catherine. Actually, Catherine's six months older than I am.'

271

'Terrible,' said Pistolet, shaking his head and turning off the radio when the song ended.

'I hope she's all right.'

'Who? Clytemnaestra?'

'Sally. I wonder where she is. Why are you pulling over?' For Pistolet had slowed down and was now easing into a shelter area on the right side. They were just north of the junction with Route 128. 'I thought we were going to Boston.'

'You are. Just be patient. The mystery will resolve itself shortly.' He turned off the engine and refused to be drawn further. While the radio played, Madison looked around nervously. For what? Cops? Sammy? He didn't know, but again he felt pursued.

In a few minutes his worries were calmed and his questions answered when a VW Rabbit pulled in ahead of them and Sally got out of her car. He looked in surprise at Pistolet, who laughed. 'This is where I leave you, Madison. You've got a new chauffeur now.' He opened the door and swung his long legs out. As he put his arms out onto the roof to pull himself from the car, he stopped and looked at Madison. 'Give me a call at work tomorrow. I'll let you know the lie of the land: where you can pick up your severance and so on. There won't be much of it, you know, this isn't a welfare state. Do you need any money now? No? Well, this is it. Be good to Sally, buddy, this has not been easy on her. Not every woman says goodbye to a billion dollars to be with someone like you, however *gifted* you are.' He pulled himself with a jerk from the car and went forward to Sally. In a minute she was sliding into the driving-seat, starting the car and pulling onto the highway. For once, Madison was not inclined to ask questions.

They drove in silence, east on Route 128, then south on 3 towards Boston. Sally was still in corporate uniform of grey checked skirt and white blouse. Madison kept stealing looks at her but she didn't look back. Outside

Arlington they climbed a small hill, and suddenly Boston lay before them: the harbour, the gleaming green glass of the Hancock Building, the distant towers of the financial district. 'God, Boston's beautiful,' he exclaimed.

Sally smiled for the first time. 'Do you want to live there?'

'I don't know. Do you?'

'I don't know. I asked first.'

Madison looked out at the city, receding now from view as they came down the hill. He said slowly, 'I guess I want to live wherever you live.'

'Slow now, partner.' But she seemed pleased by his remark.

'Don't "slow" me. I do. Anyway, I'm glad you showed up.' Glad; what an understatement. His relief was so immense as to make it seem precarious; he half-expected Sally to pull over and transfer him to the care of the Blue Rinse Lady. He asked, 'How *did* you show up, by the way? Pistolet wouldn't explain.'

'That makes a change. Actually, he phoned me from the hotel. In my office. Where I was sitting crying my eyes out.'

'Why was that?'

She looked straight ahead now. 'Well, for one thing, I'd just learned that the man I was going to marry not only didn't love me – in all honesty I guess I already knew that – but was also accustomed to talk about me to his darling mother as if I was a capital fucking asset. Forgive my French.'

They drove in silence for a while, reaching Somerville on the wide band of road. 'Was that all that bothered you?'

'No. Worse still,' she said, 'the man I loved – not the same man, mind you, but a different one – had not only exposed my fiancé to me, but done so in about the most humiliating way possible. Which is to say, in front of several hundred people.'

273

'But I didn't mean to,' he began to protest.

'I know that. At least, I know that now. Jeffrey explained it all when he called me.'

'He loves you.'

'Of course he does. I love him, too. About my only true friend in the Cathedral.'

'No, I mean he's in love with you.'

'Robert, don't be silly. Jeffrey's just saying that. He loves to play the spurned suitor.'

Madison let the subject rest. Sally then said, 'He took the rap in any case, "daddy-o".' And they both laughed.

'So where do you want to go now?' asked Madison.

'You tell me. I'm just the driver.'

'I have to see my father in the morning. He's staying at the Ritz. Why don't we go there?'

'But it must cost the earth.'

'That cheap bastard really did get to you. Anyway, you're rich now.'

'What do you mean? Rich is precisely the one thing I am not now.'

'He waived the debt, didn't he? You're at least eight dollars richer than you were before my demo.'

6

At the Ritz the doorman took the car, a bell-hop seized his suitcase, and they moved into the lobby unencumbered. They were in luck, according to the receptionist; there was a room available, a good room with a view of the Common. Madison signed the register in the name of Mr and Mrs Robert Madison – 'some day' he explained to a questioning Sally.

The clerk took the book. 'There's another Madison staying here, sir.'

'Oh, really.' Mild; not very interested.

'Yes, Frederick Madison. The writer. Any relation?'

Sally laughed, a full peal of richness. 'No,' Madison said, himself amused, 'not that I know of.'

'Too bad,' said the clerk. 'Enjoy your stay.'

Upstairs, they were unexpectedly shy. Madison ordered a bottle of wine from room service, and until it arrived they stood by the windows, staring out over the Common. 'So tell me,' he asked, thinking it was possible to leave too much unsaid, 'did you see Sammy after the demo?'

'See him?' Sally snorted derisively. 'He virtually had me locked in his office. Him, and that goon Jackson, and those creeps from Personnel.'

'Olney, Macaulay and Smith?'

'Who else? What a terrible trio.'

'What did they do?'

'Do? They didn't do anything. They just tried to intimidate me. At first I couldn't understand it; I mean, it wasn't my fault, was it? Then I understood: Sammy concluded that I took his correspondence and gave it to you. Nothing I said could dissuade him; he was entirely convinced. I've never seen him like that before.'

'I have.' Sammy adamant that Madison had pushed him in the pond that day years before. Unpersuadable; frightening in his anger.

'Well, I haven't. I don't know what was worse, the humiliation of seeing that letter up on a movie-screen, or having my fiancé – my ex-fiancé, since you're curious – acting as if I'd *planned* the whole thing. As if I were too low-rent to be humiliated.' She looked ready to cry.

'Don't you dare cry,' he said, putting his arm around her. 'And don't act the corporate hard-ass, either. Look,' he said, pointing out at the sky, 'see that plane. I'll give you two to one it's headed for England.' He looked at his watch. 'Maybe it left early.'

'It's going west, dummy. Towards Chicago.'

'Nah,' said Madison, certain. 'A small detour. Everything's headed for England these days.'

'Oh really? You think I am too?'

'Who knows? You might like it there.'

'Maybe,' she said, drawing away. 'But don't push me, okay? I need some time. Let's just spend the night, then see your father, fudge things with Ling, and you go home. To England, I mean. I'll come over next week for a visit. And then we'll see.'

It was a great deal to digest. He had so many questions to ask that when Sally said she was hungry he asked none of them and simply dialled room service. When the meal came – a rack of lamb – he was in the shower. He came out in a towel to find Sally ready to eat. 'Hurry up, I'm hungry,' she said.

'For dinner?'

'Maybe later.' And when he moved to kiss her, he discovered she had already removed her shoes and stockings.

'I slept with Sammy. I have to tell you that,' she said as he helped unbutton her shirt. His towel had fallen away.

'So,' he said, 'I slept with Catherine. But tell me, what is a billion-dollar lay like?'

She pushed him fairly hard in the stomach as they lay on the bed. 'Highly inflated. Aware of its worth.' She hesitated. 'A little mechanical. "Reasonable if not ideal"', she quoted from Sammy's letter to the Empress.

'I do love you,' Madison began as he started to lift her blouse. The phone rang, interrupting any further declaration. He was immediately alert, but Sally seemed unperturbed. 'Tell Olney, Doodah and Burkus I'll give in my notice in the morning.'

'Yeah?' inquired Madison gruffly into the phone.

'God knows you're my son, but I never had you pegged as a hard guy.'

'Hello, Papa,' he said with relief. 'How did you find me?'

'They told me downstairs when I came in from my walk around the Common. Since when do you rate the Ritz?'

'I thought I'd save time seeing you in the morning. I get to sleep in later this way.'

His father gave his deep belly-laugh. 'Listen, come on down. Or up. Wherever you are, I'll buy you dinner. I'm in room 713.'

He reflected. What a bear, his old man, what a pushy, demanding bear. He covered the phone and whispered to a curious Sally. 'It's my father. He wants to have dinner. I'll put him off.'

She shook her head. 'No way. We can have the lamb for breakfast.' She giggled. 'Tell him you'll be down in a minute. I've got to shower. So come and get me in twenty minutes.' When she saw his look of disappointment she poked her finger at him. 'There'll be plenty of time later for that kind of thing.'

He uncovered the phone. 'I'll be down right away. But let's eat here in the hotel. And book for three; I'll pop for her, don't worry.'

'I'm not worried, son,' said his father.

7

Frederick Madison was sitting in an armchair wearing khaki trousers and a green Italian sweater with a leather shoulder-patch. He had a single room this time, with an attractive view of an airshaft. Madison thought it unnecessary to point out the superiority of his own accommodation.

'Where's your friend?' his father demanded.

'She's dressing. I'll get her later.'

'I'd better change if we're going to eat downstairs.' He began pulling off his clothes. 'Is this your English girlfriend? I hope so, though I'd be the last to point an accusing finger.'

'Point away. It's not the same girl. It *is* the girl I'm going to marry.'

His father looked at him, and Madison noticed how the older man's body was going. There was little fat on him, but now the once-bulging shoulders sagged, the pectorals seemed less developed. 'I never could figure you, son, but if that's the way it is, I'm not complaining. Have a drink.' He had his usual bar set up in a tray across the window-ledge. Madison poured himself a Scotch on the rocks; his father's glass was still half-full.

'Tell me,' said his father, 'do you know some guy named Samson? Over in England.'

Oh God. 'Has he been bothering you too? I chased his ass out of my office just a week ago.'

His father buttoned his cotton shirt. 'I was scared he was a friend of yours. He keeps sending me letters impugning my sexual identity.' He took a slug of his drink. 'I've been accused of a lot of things, but that's never been one of them.'

'I'm sorry, but I promise I've never encouraged the guy.'

'I'm sure you haven't. But he seemed to know about these poems of yours – he kept suggesting they were really mine. Was there an early body of work, unpublished, that he might have come across? Of course there is, but not what he's been seeing. He sounded like a fairly major horse's ass, but he was acting like you were a buddy of his, so I tried to be polite.'

'He's not.'

'Glad to hear it.' Madison sat silently while his father put on grey slacks and a black wool tie. 'Good to see you,' his father said gruffly, looking away.

'Good to see *you*,' Madison replied.

His father looked out of the window as he finished pulling on his tie. 'I hope you mean it. It's the first time you've said so in a long time.'

'It's the first time I've meant it.'

'I'm going up to Vermont tomorrow. See your uncle.' And, as if it was an afterthought, 'Your mother, too.' He walked to the window. 'I haven't been back in twenty years. Not since . . . '

'I know.'

'Those poems you sent me.'

'What about them?'

His father smiled weakly. 'They scared the living bejesus out of me. Tell me the truth, didn't somebody write them, some poet you know? He'd have to be good, whoever he is; I mean, they're not just parodies, they're poems in their own right.'

'I promise, no one wrote them. A machine did.'

'All of them?'

'All of them. Don't worry; there are only a couple more. And there won't be any more from now on.'

His father seemed surprised. 'Why's that?'

'The experiment's over; the trial's concluded. I was trying to make a statement and I made it. That's it. Anyway, they weren't all that good as poems. I think you're exaggerating their worth.'

His father sat down and Madison noticed that the hand holding his drink was trembling. Age? Nerves? 'Shit, boy,' his father said, 'they were plenty good enough.'

'Come on, Papa,' he said, trying to soothe the agitation in his father. 'They were only based on your early stuff – some a little later. You could write rings around them now.'

'Hah!' his father said scornfully. He finished his drink in a single gulp. 'You don't understand, son. These things of yours came floating in, just reeking of my own youth. I was powerful then; the lines, the lines just came to me, as if they were mine by right. I almost thought I was doing *them* a favour.'

'You're still a great writer. Greater even than you were. Why, everybody knows your work. There's a marketing asshole at Ling who can recite half your *oeuvre*. Even the goddamned clerk downstairs knew who you were.'

'That's just reputation. It's the past, the same past you were talking about. It only makes it worse.'

'Makes what worse?' asked Madison, moved and puzzled simultaneously.

'That I can't write! I haven't written ten good lines in the last five years. *That's* what makes it worse; that's what makes it unbearable. Sure, everybody knows the work; they can even quote it, like you say, here in this TV-ridden land of lunatics. But it's the past.'

'You're a monument, you should be proud.'

'Sure I'm a monument, a *living* monument. That's what makes it so awful. Listen, I'm not a drunk, and I haven't gone paranoid, and I'm not going to stick a shotgun barrel in my mouth. But when everybody looks at you like you're some kind of God, some kind of living legend, and inside you know it's all dead . . . ' He seemed to calm down. 'Well, then it's a little hard to take.'

'What can I say? I'm sorry I ever sent you the poems.'

'So am I. But it's not your fault, kid, how were you to know? You were just reacting to the same persona everybody else sees: Frederick Madison, the Hemingway of poetry. You had no way of knowing. How could you, when you barely knew your own father? But now you do know. I've done that much, at least.'

'Yes, you have.'

'Don't patronise me,' his father said sharply. 'I'm not that pathetic, pal; I just can't write. I can still go ten rounds with anybody.'

Same old bravado; that would never change. It would almost be disappointing if it did. Madison nodded now with an insincere seriousness.

'How about this girl of yours?' his father asked abruptly. 'Time we should eat.'

'I'll go and get her. Why don't we meet you in the dining-room in fifteen minutes?'

'Swell,' said his father, and Madison stood up to leave. 'Say, son,' he said as Madison reached the door. 'You could keep this quiet, all right? I mean, don't go telling *Time Magazine* I'm all dried up, will you?'

'Not a chance.' He laughed. 'It will be strictly between me and the machine. I swear it.'

He closed the door behind him. Out in the corridor there was the regulated quiet of a first-class hotel, but as he entered the elevator and it ascended, he heard a faint background noise of taped music – cocktail-bar piano-tinkling. He thought of the woman upstairs awaiting him. What were the lines of one of his father's early love-poems?

> And if your love should ever leave you,
> claiming her retreat is best,
> allow the drag of time to weave you . . .

Weave you what? 'Images of loveliness she blessed' – was that it? And were they really his father's lines, or an early trial of the generator back in England? He got out of the elevator and walked down to his room, trying to remember whose voice was now in his head. He unlocked the door and saw Sally in an armchair, brushing her long hair and watching the television. She turned and smiled at him, and the voice of the poem disappeared. He heard his own thoughts, and sensed his own words about to be spoken.